Mario Mantese

IN THE LAND
OF SILENCE

Learning with My Master
in the Himalayas

Translated from the German by Mark Doyu Albin
Edited by Jane Lago
Coverdesign by Marion Musenbichler
© Coverpicture by Peter Reinhold/Werbung 2005 München
Typesetting by Martin Frischknecht

Original Title: **"Im Land der Stille"**
© 1996 Mario Mantese, first published
by Drei Eichen Verlag, D-97762 Hammelburg

Bibliographical Information of the German National Library
This publication is listed in the German National Bibliography of the
German National Library; detailed bibliographical
information can be accessed under http://dnb.d-nb.de
ISBN: 978-3-8423-9166-6

© 2012 by Mario Mantese
www.mariomantese.com

First Edition in English
Printing and Production by BoD – Books on Demand, Norderstedt

CONTENTS

PROLOGUE

Throughout time there have been people walking the planet Earth who have achieved an extraordinary level of spiritual cultivation. Many of them have opened themselves to the society around them. They assist those they meet to realize the true meaning of their lives and accompany them as they move to higher spiritual realms.

There are others who have the same spiritual capacities but remain unnoticed. They have withdrawn from the world and never wander far from their dwellings hidden among the great mountains of the Earth.

This book is the unusual account of a man whose fate it was to meet one of these remarkable reclusive masters in the Himalayas. The initial meetings between these two men reveal just how forcefully the hardened, rigidly structured intellect is challenged when it encounters such a universal human being.

As the student was confronted with this liberated master, a master who never allowed himself to be labeled or categorized, he fell into a deep crisis, a destabilizing of everything the man had thought and felt before. It was as if this journey had led him inside the crater of an active volcano.

The love, wisdom, and immense energy of the master, which the reader can directly experience from this book, open a pathway. Ultimately, this pathway leads to an end that is the liberation from all paths, a flowing back into never-ending Non-Being.

COMING AND BEING: NOT BECOMING

I was freezing as I went through the low wooden door and into the open air. A snow-covered chain of mountains rose up majestically on the far side of the valley, towering high into the deep blue sky, an awesome spectacle. The 6,000-meter peaks were covered with a layer of soft white clouds, which had drawn themselves to the huge rocks like floating shields of cotton, huddling around them as if trying to protect a secret.

An icy wind blew through the valley and struck brusquely against my cheeks. Spring had finally come. Without its arrival I could never have reached the small village. At such a high elevation, everything sits covered in deep layers of snow for much of the year. During those months the villages are cut off from the rest of the world.

I traveled by bus for many long hours along bumpy mountain roads to get to the village. At times I held my breath as the driver sped through narrow passages, one hand on the steering wheel, the other working the horn. I made my way by foot after that, walking for two more days, since there were no roads leading to the higher villages. Luckily, I found a trustworthy guide who knew the area well, for I would never have been able to find the way on my own.

The villagers were friendly and obliging. Soon after

arriving, I was invited to lodge with a family, which was a good and necessary thing, as there were no inns or hostels.

I stayed in the village for a week, preparing myself for the last stage of this journey upward. I would be joined by a merchant I had met in the village who wanted to trek in the same direction. I was informed that there was a very high pass to traverse, after which I would easily be able to reach my destination. That was what I wanted to believe because the strain from travel was wearing down my endurance. I noticed my fatigue increasing steadily each day, and my feet were covered with blisters, making walking almost unbearable.

I had come here as part of my work on a book that a publisher had contracted with me to write. I was to report on a spiritual master whose home was outside in nature, far away from civilization. For a long time I had been interested in Eastern philosophy, and I was always eager to track down accounts of unique people who stood apart, unconcerned and unaffected by their lack of things that most people considered necessities where I came from. My thoughts moved back and forth between fascination and suspicion. Were these people I read about living beings, or were they mere legends lacking authenticity? When the opportunity showed itself, I was determined to uncover the facts for myself.

I had investigated and researched for a long time before I came across something that seemed genuine. One day the office at the Ministry of Culture sent a memo I found intriguing. It reported the existence of someone who met the criteria that I was looking for. The description I received sent a bizarre sensation through me, as if

I had touched something from a source previously unknown to me.

I prepared myself exhaustively and then started out on my adventure to the Himalayas. I filled notepads with observations as I went along and made lengthy daily journal entries. I had no idea or notion of what lay ahead for me. I had no name for the man, nor the name of a specific place where I could find him. And I had no idea what kind of instruction this "wise man" would share with me. The one thing that guided me was a sketch of the region where he could be found. He would be there; someone had assured me of that. But the wild terrain and weather of the mountain did not invite a long stay. I was hoping to finish my business there as quickly as possible.

The day before my departure from the village felt heavy. I was up before the sun. It would be an hour before its rays would warm up the valley. My attention was drawn to the loud sounds of the wild rushing stream that flowed by the house and down into the valley below. My eyes could follow the flowing silver line as it descended, until it disappeared between two small houses. Next a row of hens appeared, followed by a colorful rooster, who amused me with his proud strut. He expanded and filled his neck with a bellowing crow, utilizing all the power in his throaty call to express his notice of me. He glared over as if to challenge me. Perhaps he assumed I was intending to test him for his harem. In the adjacent stall the goats had begun to grumble impatiently, waiting for someone to open the gate and let them roam freely.

The villagers had done their best to make use of the poor soil at their disposal, and they had managed to remain self-sufficient. In the valley basin below were small fields where the first crops were just beginning to sprout.

Slowly people started to move about inside the house. I listened as the grandmother spoke softly to the children as they opened their eyes. Soon, all eleven members of the family were awake. I went back into the house to greet them. Chiseled by the stark climate and lit brightly with smiling eyes, their faces had become very dear to me.

I was treated as a family member, as if I had always been there. At the same time I was the grand attraction at the house. My hosts thought it an honor and a pleasure to offer provisions and shelter to a foreigner. Each evening, relatives and friends would stop and visit, hoping to get a look at me and perhaps even have a conversation. At those times I was required to talk about the country I came from. Although I did not hesitate to mention the drawbacks of life in my homeland, they were convinced that I came straight out of paradise, where one could buy every object imaginable, where everything was possible.

The most exciting exhibition I could offer was to open my travel bag and display the different gadgets I was carrying. Again and again, I had to pull out the electric razor I had brought along, which operated on batteries. Each time I had to demonstrate how it worked, and each time they were completely dumbfounded. They had never seen anything so wonderfully strange and absurd in all their lives, none of them.

Soon we were having breakfast in the middle of the room, gathered around the large fireplace. Overcoming my instinctive disgust, I took small sips of the salty butter tea they offered. My taste buds and stomach were in rebellion, but I had been assured that beyond all doubt this drink was particularly good for my health. The intensity of my repugnance had withered to the point where I could swallow the tea down like a champ. But as I drank I always had inquisitive eyes fixed upon me, searching for an unusual grimace on my face, which would then become the topic of animated conversation among the guests.

Everyone knew that my departure was coming soon. The merchant had told me the day before that things were prepared from his end. There was nothing to prevent me from moving on. No new snow would fall on the pass, he assured me. Conditions for the journey couldn't be better.

Our destination was a small village that lay two days travel away, in a remote valley quite high up in the mountains. The merchant had promised to provide a mule for me as well. I was told more than once that the journey would not be easy. He wanted me to be clear about this.

While living in the first village, I had often gone to visit its oldest resident. Some said he was ninety-six years old, but no one really knew if that was right. His withered body consisted now of only skin and bones. The experiences of a long lifetime were etched into the form of his being. He spoke slowly and was constantly coughing, but his eyes were lively and his mind was clear. In the village, no decision could be made without consulting him. I had already had some very interesting encounters with this elder. But on this day I was going to say good-bye.

Soon after I entered his hut, a mischievous grin appeared across his lips. He asked me if I could do him a small favor. "Of course," I answered right away. But I had not the slightest idea what he wanted.

He hesitated awhile before finally speaking his wish, "Would you leave me your electric razor?" Now I was dumbfounded, and I had trouble not laughing out loud. This request was one I really hadn't expected.

"Before I leave, I will bring the machine to you." I replied spontaneously. The eyes of the elder lit up in youthful delight. I too was pleased that I could provide some joy for this old fellow.

Very early the next morning, I was standing with my belongings below the house at the village square. Almost all the residents had gathered, wanting to bid me farewell. The merchant waved me over to him. He had provided a mule as promised and communicated that he wanted me to pay for it immediately. Thrown over the back of the animal was a grimy old blanket that was included in the price. Two other mules and several yaks with their backs loaded up with more supplies also waited patiently for our departure. These yaks, mighty archaic creatures with shaggy manes and huge horns, were very impressive. They exuded power and stamina, qualities essential for anything attempting to survive in this harsh climate.

The merchant was accompanied by two helpers, both of whom eyed me distrustfully, almost fearfully, from a distance. It hardly mattered to the merchant who I was or where I came from. The important thing for him was that he got the price he wanted.

Everyone in the village knew this dealer and wanted to know exactly how much I was paying him for his services. The unanimous consensus was that I had been given a fair offer.

Upon my departure, each person wanted to shake

hands. As I festively handed over the electric razor to the elder, everyone clapped with joy and nodded their appreciation. The elder's oldest son offered a gift in return, a thick coat. He was sure it would be useful at some point. Finally, they wanted to know if I would be passing through the village on my return journey. At this time, I couldn't give them a good answer. I had no sense of my return at all.

The path leaving the village and heading down through the valley was full of stones, but we managed to make good progress, as the merchant continually reassured me. The cold felt harsh to my body in the early morning hours. I soon wrapped myself up in the coat I had been given.

In my imagination, I was picturing my first meeting with this master. I pondered how I would greet him and how I would form the first significant questions I wanted him to answer. I was certain that within three weeks I would have gathered the necessary information and could make plans to return home. Still, I was firmly resolved not to let myself be satisfied with philosophical theories. I wanted to get to the true substance of things, as I had always done in my investigations.

After the midday break, we started to follow a steep, narrow path. This was the beginning of our ascent to the pass. We hiked along for several hours, the snow-covered peaks on the horizon appearing more plentiful and imposing as we climbed. The air became thinner as well. At some point there was no longer a recognizable trail. As I struggled to breathe and sensed the vast silence, broken only by the shrill movements of the wind and the tapping hooves of the mules, a sense of loneliness engulfed me. I had never known this feeling before. I felt lost.

With the overwhelming landscape surrounding me and all of the things my senses were absorbing, something from very deep inside was being brought to the surface, something difficult to explain. Invisible shadows, frightening anomalous feelings, began to crawl up from the deepest trenches of my being. At some point I realized that these were suppressed fears and insecurities that had taken hold within me. I had never been fully aware that I was carrying these things around.

Immediately my way of observing shifted. I saw with abrupt clarity that everything I was taking in from the outside was not and could not be separate from the one seeing, the subjective observer, me. They couldn't be two different things. Yes, what I believed I was seeing outside was in truth something that was in me, something in my own inner being. The thing assumed to be outside was an image formed from my senses of something within, a reflection of my own mind.

But if everything I saw was nothing more than a manifestation in my own subjective consciousness, how could those things have any reality? Could anything I saw be real?

As these questions appeared, I had reached the limits of my mental power. An encounter with an expert in such matters was imminent, so I decided to let this so-called master elaborate on these things when I met him. Perhaps I could eventually obtain some deeper insight. At least I could hope so.

Without my really being aware of it, an increasing intensity of such hopes and expectations was mounting inside me, from one hour to the next. What would my meeting with this person be like? Somehow I had already formed an image of how the master would be. I saw him in front of me and had the intuitive sense that I already knew him quite well, though of course I had never actually seen him.

The merchant snapped me out of these contemplations. With a loud shout he drew our attention to a huge hanging cliff up ahead. A small stone hut was situated beneath it, protected by the extended outcropping. Dusk had gently draped itself over the mountains. We had hardly stepped inside the hut when darkness consumed the last fragments of daylight. The merchant had known exactly how long the trip from the village to this shelter would take. What would have happened if we had still been underway in this blackness of night in these high mountains? I chose not to think more about it.

That night a storm arrived, a storm that raged like nothing I had ever experienced before. The wind howled as if a gaping chasm had opened deep within the mountain, from which countless agonizing voices could be heard, shrieks that rose toward and beyond the surrounding peaks. Then the gates of heaven opened, and it began to pour rain. An enormous amassing of water was released, washing and purifying every nook and crevice in these mountains and valleys. There was something terrifying in these immense forces of nature, and something fascinating as well.

The merchant's helpers prepared a simple meal. Soothing heat spread from the fireplace and expanded throughout the room, pacifying my private tumult. For my fellow travelers, such rapid and intense weather changes were nothing unusual. In the middle of this violent storm, one of the helpers had left the hut to visit the stalls nearby and feed the animals.

The merchant and I talked well into the night, accompanied for a long while by the snores of our assistants. He could hardly believe that I had chosen to undertake such a journey. To think that I would have come to these high mountains to look for a yogi, whose name I didn't even know! Perhaps the guy I had heard about was simply a screwball who didn't want to get married. The merchant suggested this possibility with a comical grin on his face.

I had to admit that after a while I, too, had come to regard my plan as absurd. But I was there, and I was intent on finding this man as soon as I could.

As we left the hut the next morning, the sky was shining brightly, everything around us pure and crystal clear. A very special light reigned at this altitude, offering a mild and friendly luster in steep contrast to the snow-covered giants, which emanated a sense of something unapproachable, untouchable.

We climbed higher and higher, the animals trudging through snow that came to their knees. The air became increasingly thinner. Each movement forward became a strenuous effort. By late afternoon we had finally reached the top of the pass and could begin a slow decent, much to my relief. I was having difficulty with my heartbeat and blood circulation at these elevations.

Hardly a word was spoken along the way. A few commands were uttered to the animals, as they skillfully carted us on their backs through the coarse terrain.

We arrived at a stone hut where we would spend the

night, reaching our destination as planned, just as darkness was overtaking the vast sky above. The merchant explained to me that his ancestors had built this hut many years before. All the men in his family had been merchants for generations. As soon as his three sons were old enough, he wanted to bring them on his business travels, just as his father and his father's father had done. He proclaimed that his sons would have to become so familiar with the paths that they could find their way in their sleep. That was the family tradition. A measure of pride could be discerned from the merchant as he spoke. He casually added that he was the only one of the villagers who made it over the pass several times a year, carrying vital provisions and mail back to the locals.

WARM SOURCE

Inexplicably, anxiety appeared, holding me in its clutches. Was it because of the upcoming encounter with this master? Did he perhaps already know I was coming? A confusing multitude of uncontrollable thoughts flashed through my mind with lightning speed. The helpers had gone off to sleep near the animals. Except for the uneven breathing of the merchant, no sound could be heard.

At the break of dawn our helpers appeared again with the animals. The guide secured the hut with a huge padlock. I was uncertain whether I had slept at all. A cold gust of wind tore me out of this strange mind state. It had snowed during the night. The entire landscape looked as though it was covered with cake frosting, glittering in the pure clear air. The view was immaculate.

The merchant seemed to be in a hurry. He constantly pressed the yaks to keep pace. We hadn't traveled very far when we suddenly came upon a deep gorge. Stretched over the chasm was a primitive, very unstable hanging bridge. The thought of having to make this crossing sent a rush of blood to my head. But I had no time to skulk in my uncertainties. The merchant gave us firm instructions about what needed to be done. We were to take the animals by their halters and lead them carefully over the planks. I knew for sure that this would be a delicate operation. If one of the animals became frightened and jerked back, we were lost. To my bewilderment, the merchant went to each of the large creatures, stroked the animal on the head, and whispered a few incomprehensible words into its ears. We then approached the bridge, and the animals calmly and cautiously proceeded along the weather-beaten boards.

I made efforts to breathe slowly and deeply and keep my eyes focused on the animal making progress in front of me. I didn't dare to look down and navigated my thoughts with feverish desperation toward completely irrelevant mental pictures that I could cling to...it seemed the task of moving over this bridge would never end.

Finally we arrived at the other side. In this moment I knew much more profoundly what it meant to be on solid ground. The merchant offered me a warm glance, and I appreciated the amiable look of understanding in his eyes. My debilitating fears had not gone unnoticed. As I caught his gaze, he gave a slight nod. He then turned and summoned the animals to continue onward. Not another word was spoken about it.

We continued on for a while before coming to another halt. The merchant dismounted again and waved me to come closer. I looked over at him, unsure of what he wanted. As I came near and finally stood next to him, he pointed to the area below us.

Was I dreaming? Could this be real? A small valley lay in front of us, so green, so lush, so magnificent that I rubbed my eyes again to be sure I wasn't hallucinating. I could never have imagined that this kind of abundant vegetation could flourish at this altitude. The merchant, who noticed my amazement, spoke in his laconic style.

"Special place."

As they caught sight of all the green foliage, the yaks snorted loudly and clicked their tongues with anticipation. They would soon enjoy an extended rest amid this thriving plant world as reward for their arduous efforts. For the moment, however, the merchant would have to use all his wisdom and cunning to keep the animals from indulging on the wheat and soft grass along the trail before reaching our destination. To keep the hungry beasts from coming to a complete halt, the merchant spoke to them, whispering soft words, which they seemed to understand. The knowledge that they must continue now, with the reward of a meal soon to be provided, seemed to have been communicated successfully. They obediently resumed their pace, moving toward our destination.

The landscape here was marvelously fertile. There were orange groves and trees with other small citrus fruits surrounded by red flowers, which I later learned were poinsettias. It was a tiny fleck of paradise, hidden in the vastness of this mountain world.

As we entered the village, my astonishment was even greater. The people I encountered had red hair, glittering yellowish eyes, and unusually fair skin. I had seen no one with any features like this since entering these mountains.

There were stark differences in their manner as well. Until now I had met extroverted types who were curious and not hesitant to approach me. The people here were just the opposite. They seemed extremely introverted and shy. And there was something very calm about them. They emanated a serenity that seemed to extend through the entire valley.

I was observed from a distance. I caught their restrained glances, which fell upon me as if I had arrived from another star. The questioning expressions on their faces spoke volumes. Obviously, no one here could imagine what a foreigner was looking for in this region so far removed from the rest of the world.

Near the main square of the village, we turned down a small side street, the merchant guiding his mule nimbly down the road. He spoke to me in an easy tone, "Come on, we are here. I will introduce you to my brother and his wife."

He opened a door, and we entered a small shop where one could find all the necessary provisions for living in this region: groceries, clothes, and simple tools for farming. The woman behind the counter was in the process of selling a sack of grain to an old man when she noticed us. Calmly, but obviously filled with delight, she greeted us and called to her husband, who quickly appeared, scurrying from the back room of the store to meet us. I noticed immediately that the merchant's brother had only one eye. Where the other belonged, there was only a small oddly shaped opening.

The merchant soon explained to his brother the purpose of my journey, which caused him to shake his head back and forth. But he assured me right away that I could stay with them as long as I wanted.

The large living room next to the shop was also the storage room. The merchant's helpers began carefully hauling and stacking the goods we had brought on our journey. The wife closed the shop and sat down with us. She was then informed of the reasons for my arrival. Rather than shake her head, her reaction was a friendly nod in my direction. I took this as a good sign and felt more at ease. Perhaps she could even help me find the person I was searching for. But I had just arrived and held back my inquiry for the time being.

Soon the two men were deeply immersed in discussion of business affairs. The wife went off into a corner of the large room and disappeared. A moment later she returned with a small child asleep in her arms. She handed to me a little girl who I immediately noticed was ill. She was tiny, pale, and withered to the point of being little more than skin and bones. The mother hoped I might have some medicine with me that could help her.

Luckily, I had brought along a small cache of medical supplies. After hesitating for a time, I decided on one that I hoped might do something to help. The mother was overjoyed. She was absolutely certain that this strange foreign medicine would manifest a complete recovery for her daughter. I, too, hoped with all my heart that this would be the case but tried to explain that we couldn't expect miracles. My warnings fell on deaf ears. The parents were steadfast in their conviction that now nothing could hinder the process of healing they so sincerely wanted for their suffering child.

The next day, to my utter surprise, the child was feeling better. The parents were, of course, overjoyed.

As the opportunity presented itself, I finally mentioned my pressing inquiry, my search for the master, and asked if they could help me find him. Instantly, lines appeared on their smooth foreheads. "There is someone like that around here. He lives in a cave not far away, but I have never seen him. Most of the people in the village say that he is a madman. Everyone is frightened of him and tries to avoid him. As to where he lives, I only know that his cave should be over there, on that southern slope." She pointed to the large mountain across the valley, which was visible between the citrus trees in her garden. "It would certainly take four hours of hard walking to get there. I know someone who can guide you." As she spoke, I could see she was pleased to be able to return a favor.

The merchant and his brother came out to meet us in the garden. We sat down in the shadow of the fragrant fruit trees. The merchant spoke thoughtfully. "You are worried that you have made such a long journey, and that it may all be for nothing." He was right. I had doubts. Had I actually undertaken this long, strenuous journey only to arrive at my destination and be confronted with a crazy old man? I would have to find out, and the only way was to meet the person myself.

The wife continued to appraise me with her huge, inquisitive eyes. I asked her about the guide she had mentioned and gathered that he, too, was a member of the family. I wanted to know for certain that he was willing to accompany me in the morning up the mountain so that I could discover just who and what I had come all this way to find.

MAGICAL AWARENESS

We spent the day visiting family members and wandering with them through their lush green fields. Each time we approached someone, we immediately received a warm-hearted invitation to tea and sweets. My digestive organs worked hard to process the assortment of offerings I was putting into my mouth.

Outside the village were several hot-water springs. In places the water spouted up and out, generously covering the surrounding earth with moisture. The villagers had left a few buckets there, collecting water to be used for bathing and washing clothes.

The sun had barely withdrawn its last glimmering rays when the air became abruptly cold. Before I lay down on the simple bed I was provided, the merchant shared with me his plans for traveling back over the pass. He said that if I wasn't ready to leave by the time he departed, I could wait at his brother's place until his return.

The next morning, I awoke with mixed feelings; my heart was filled with anxiety and darkened with a menacing sense of foreboding. My guide was already standing at the door. He was accompanied by a small girl who relentlessly tugged on the maroon skirt he was wearing. The two sat down to eat with us.

As we ate the brother of the merchant took time to

explain why the young girl accompanied my guide and to tell me her remarkable story. She was truly unusual, an enigma to everyone in the village, but she was adored and venerated by all of them. As a child, she had hardly learned to speak when she began to pray at sunrise and sunset. At these times she spoke repeatedly of a great invisible teacher. Because the villagers were convinced that the girl's presence provided protection and brought good fortune, she was always taken along on lengthy journeys.

Fixing my glance on this unassuming, mysterious child across from me, I resolved at that moment to mention her story in my book. I had concluded for myself that this phenomenon must be connected to experiences of a previous life. When I shared my thoughts with the others, they confirmed my hypothesis.

But my mind took a quick turn to skepticism. I became aware of a stream of destructive thoughts. I felt agitated and wanted to question everything I had heard. But I managed to catch myself before I offended anyone and resolved to let go of those initial critical judgments and remain open-minded.

Once again I was aware of the preconditioned narrow views I clung to. I seemed to be held in an invisible straitjacket, as my mind flaunted its attitude of superiority and rational omnipotence with an unbearable conceit.

We had hardly left the village behind when the young girl took my hand. She danced and sang continually as we walked. She was amazing. She shared only exuberance, never showing the slightest hint of displeasure with the world.

We entered a densely wooded area. This forest was like a jungle. Looking out from the village, I had already noticed that the tree line here was very high. The temperature was comfortable, and the damp earth emitted a delicate fragrance. Something of the open and unassuming character of the people I had met had rubbed off on me as well. I felt as if my soul had been given a warm embrace.

The higher we ascended, the more impenetrable the forest appeared. At a certain point the guide stood before a small stream that flowed tranquilly back down to the valley. "From here, you have to go alone. Follow the stream farther up the mountain. The stream runs by the cave where the master lives. You can't miss it." As he was giving me these directions, I could sense uneasiness in his voice.

I was confused. I had assumed without question that he would accompany me until I reached my final destination. I had to express my disappointment. I asked him, "Why don't you go on with me and lead me there yourself?" He only rolled his shoulders, said his farewell. He and the young girl were off before I could do anything to stop them.

Within moments I was completely alone, standing in the middle of an impenetrable and unfamiliar forest. An occasional birdcall and the soft splashes of water against the stones in the streambed were the only sounds that interrupted an almost eerie wall of silence. I had hardly become accustomed to my situation when a creeping sense of helplessness began to gnaw at me. To combat it I began to hum a tune and quickened my pace along the trail.

The cave couldn't be far. I intently followed the path up the steep incline. As I walked, new worries began to turn in my mind like an endless merry-go-round, as I searched frantically for the ideal way to greet the master and articulate the reason for my visit.

Gradually the forest thinned. Like a shadow, I escaped out of the woods and came into a huge clearing. Here, I saw the cave carved into the side of the cliff. In front of the entrance was a fireplace. Next to it sat a figure who seemed to be cooking something. The man had not seen me yet. I thought I would stay at a distance and observe him awhile.

My feet sank into the ground. In a matter of moments, all my senses were drowned in the deepest pool of disappointment. The person I saw hunching over the fire was a small, stocky man with thinning gray hair. He was wearing a faded old shirt and baggy pants. Completing this wretched vision were the filthiest feet I have ever seen. Was this the master I had come to see, whom I had traveled for so many weeks to meet?

I was seized with rage. How could I have been so naïve? How could I have believed those people who sent me here? The man I was looking at was certainly nothing more than a mountain farmer, who had for some absurd reason retired to this place.

For the sake of protocol, I took the final steps of my journey, intending to introduce myself formally. I approached him. But … was he deaf? I was standing right next to him, but he hadn't noticed my coming at all.

As I finally began to open my mouth and speak, he quickly glanced up. "Hey! Go get some water from the stream." This was all he said, and before I could get over my disbelief he had already pressed a pitcher into my hand.

Though annoyed that he would presume such authority, I ran to the stream, filled the pitcher with water, and returned to the cave. He held the jug to his mouth, and in two swallows it was empty. "More," he said, again using a commanding tone. Once again I was on my way to the stream, irritated and confused, holding an empty water jug in my hand.

I was soon seething with anger. I wouldn't allow this guy to boss me around, not again. As I ran back to the cave with the full jug, I began to think up plans for my return journey. I wanted to get out of there as quickly as possible. The villagers had been right. This person was a madman after all.

Once again I was standing in front of him. "Sit down. We want to eat," he said. He disappeared into his cave and returned with a second set of eating utensils, which he set down near my feet. The meal was simple and tasted good. As I chewed my food, my anger gradually began to subside. Meanwhile, the less than friendly cook smacked his lips over and over again, obviously engrossed and contented with his meal. It seemed he no longer was aware of my presence.

I had forgotten all the things I had planned to say, all the questions I had painstakingly prepared. It was as if an invisible windstorm had passed through my mind and taken everything with it. I said nothing. Since this old man wouldn't talk either, I supposed he wanted to remain silent during the meal, believing perhaps that the preparation and eating were a ritual act of some kind.

After the meal, he spoke again. He asked me in detail

where I had come from and why I had wanted to visit. I decided not to ask him any of my more serious questions until he directed the conversation a little deeper. Perhaps there were customs in the mountains that I didn't know about. I didn't want to offend him.

We washed our hands and cleaned our plates and utensils with the water I had brought back in the pitcher. As we were finishing up, I thought to myself in anticipation, "Now is the time he will really want to talk." But he only let out a loud belch and grabbed hold of his stomach with both hands, perhaps to signify the successful gratification of his appetite. Then he lay down on the floor, stretched out flat on his back, and shut his eyes. In a moment he was sound asleep.

I was in utter disbelief. I had never met anyone like this in my entire life. I couldn't understand him, nor could I classify him according to any category of human being I had ever heard of or read about. Once again a huge cloud of anger arose within me, my mind boiling over with the most terrible expletives my memory managed to retrieve. Though I said nothing, I cursed him vehemently. Only after all the nasty rubbish stored in this venomous old closet of indignant words had emptied was I able to be calm again.

But this was not all I was experiencing. I had to admit to myself that his totally unconventional behavior was rather intriguing. I had never witnessed anything like it. I was also baffled by my own situation. How long had I sat there already, waiting for this strange guy to open his eyes!

I knew I had to get out of this place as quickly as possible. But evening was falling. I reckoned it was too late to try to get back to the village. I would stay the night there.

Darkness approached swiftly. Overhead, infinite variations of color and shadow were manifesting. The early evening light cast a gentle spell on me. The sky seemed to represent a massive work of art, endowed with inexpressible beauty.

I continued to wait for the fellow to wake up. My intention was to ask his permission to spend the night with him in the cave. As these thoughts went through my mind, it seemed as if I had shot a message directly into his sleeping brain. Just as this request appeared in my mind, his eyes opened. In an instant he was on his feet. His smooth movements displayed a grace and nimbleness I would never have expected from him. He then spoke to me. "Come, I will show you where you can sleep tonight. It's good that you have a thick coat. It will be quite cold during the night."

The space inside the cave was much larger than I had thought. According to my scan around the small cavern, dishes and cooking gear, some sleeping mats, and a primitive travel bag were all the worldly possessions he had. He rolled out one of the mats in the farthest corner of the room and signaled that this was the warmest spot inside the cave.

I was exhausted and lay down immediately. But within a few breaths, a distinctive smell quickly disrupted the relaxation I had anticipated. I followed the odor back to my host. No way was I going to be able to sleep with this stink in the air. "He reeks like an old mountain goat. Surely he hasn't bathed in weeks," I thought to myself as I lay there, fully awake, with my eyes shut. As my thoughts whirled, one point of reflection offset the offensive stench of my host; I didn't smell like a field of fresh flowers either.

I must have soon fallen into a deep state of unconsciousness, because when I awoke, it was full daylight outside, and the strange fellow I had met the day before was nowhere to be seen.

I waited again. Hours went by. I would have preferred to leave that morning, but I chose to stay near the cave out of politeness. Finally, he returned with a huge pile of dry wood tied neatly under his arms. He nodded to me in a friendly way, walked up next to me, and began to sniff me over like an animal. He spoke brusquely, "You reek like an old mountain goat! Come, let us have a bath." My brain began to erupt. Huge doubts filled my frontal lobe. After only two short sentences, I had become absolutely miserable.

A few moments later he was taking me by the hand. We flew at a breathless tempo up the rugged mountainside until we reached the snow line. I hoped, at this point, that we had arrived at our goal. I had already reached the limit of my endurance. He wasn't unaware of my fatigue, and we stopped to rest for a short time, this weird man next to me content to stand barefoot in the snow. He gazed at me in my decrepit condition, now showing kindness in his eyes. I would never have guessed that he was in such good shape. Looking at the figure he presented, I had assumed the opposite.

I had hardly managed to recover my wind when he silently started off again. I followed along, and soon we were stomping through an immense snowfield toward the top of the mountain. We then crossed an extended rocky plateau, where we had a breathtaking view of the mountains ahead, each taller than the one before. Suddenly we came to a small lake of ice-cold water formed from the surrounding snow.

With two swift hand movements, he was naked. Before I could believe my eyes, he had jumped into the icy water and was splashing around. "Come in. You really must have a bath. You smell awfully bad."

I felt numb inside and out. "He wants to see me fall apart," I thought to myself. I wasn't about to give him the pleasure. He obviously didn't know with whom he was dealing.

"I don't have a towel, and the water is far too cold. Down below in the valley there's a warm spring. I'll have a bath there. It will be much nicer." I spoke in a detached voice, or I tried to.

"You don't need a towel! And it doesn't matter if the water is warm or cold! You have to be clean for your return journey. Come in! Take a bath!" His tone was strong and uncompromising.

"OK, so that's it," I thought to myself. "He actually wants to get rid of me as quickly as possible. Well, it won't be so easy." With that thought I flung off my clothes and jumped into the water.

Oh!!! I felt as if I had been instantly transformed into a block of ice. I couldn't feel any part of my body and could hardly draw air. I lost the feeling of having a body at all. All of my senses, inner and outer, were instantaneously directed to one point, to one thought, "Get out of the water, or you will die."

He stood next to me and laughed. "You are only imagining that it's cold! Breathe deeply and calmly. Let go."

My blood seemed to coagulate. My singular intention held me: "I have to get out of this water!" I struggled to the edge of the shore and pulled my body out. I stood up and began to massage my blue-hued skin. "I hope you won't mind if I stay in a little bit longer," he asked me smugly.

It took me a while to pull myself together. Eventually he came out of the water, wide-eyed and cheerful. "Come along. Let's go back and have something warm to drink." He was smiling.

He continued to speak. "Those of us who live out here in the mountains, in nature, have to be as strong and adaptable as the elements that surround us. In order to stay warm in the bitter cold, or to stay cool when it is terribly hot, we must live where hot and cold don't exist, where neither 'here' nor 'there' belong. Those who are caught on the umbilical cord of the outer world continue to drink from a black cup filled with the bitter water of death. Spinning in time … and lost in the end, they continue to live in pain and darkness."

I was unexpectedly awakened to the fact that this was anything but a joker. The guy was also no simple mountain farmer, as I had falsely assumed. For one fleeting moment he had shown me his true face. I could only partly follow the things he had just said to me. Now I wanted him to continue speaking. I needed further clarity. His words functioned like an invisible stepladder made of pure light, leading me from the finite to the infinite. Already I felt transported, guided on a never-ending inner voyage. In this moment this was very clear to me. A never-ending inner voyage …

Why in the world were such thoughts going through my head at that moment? Where did they come from? Did he somehow plant them in my brain?

We swiftly made our way down the mountain. My clothes quickly dried. Soon my body was warm again.

A pleasant tingling, a sense of great contentment, flowed through my being.

Soon we were sitting comfortably in front of the cave, sipping hot tea. "When are you going back?" he asked me unexpectedly. It was already afternoon, again too late to try to get back to the village before dark. Somewhat embarrassed, I asked him if I could spend the night in the cave again. He had no objection.

As I opened my eyes the next morning, I found him sitting directly across from me and looking straight at my eyes. It was terrifying. I wasn't at all prepared.

"How did you wake up?" he asked me.

"Here on this mat," I answered.

"You aren't listening. I didn't ask you where or when. I asked you how," he said, holding his gaze on me. There was something piercing in his voice, and the question confused me. I took a long time to think about it. Finally I came to the recognition that I had no idea "how" I woke up that morning. For some unexplainable reason, I was suddenly awake.

He had moved to the front of the cave and was making some sort of decorative carving on a wooden stick. His hands moved over the wood skillfully.

"I have no idea how I woke up. I just woke up," I said to him.

"Come, sit down. Explain to me exactly what you did this morning in order to wake up. How did you manage to accomplish this?"

I sat there as if someone had dumped a bucket of cold water over my head. My mind began to race around in a panic, searching for intelligent words. I needed some answer. I had to show that I was a rational, clear-thinking person who had engaged in his share of philosophical discussions. But no matter how hard I tried to formulate a response, I had no good answer for this question.

"I am not aware that I did anything this morning in order to wake up. At some point I was simply awake."

"OK ... but where did you come from then? At least that much should be clear to you, don't you think?" He was pushing me even more. His round face had suddenly taken on a mischievous expression. He was playing a little game of cat and mouse with me.

"I came back from the dream-world." I answered without contemplating.

"You mean to tell me that you were in the middle of this dream-world when you suddenly had the thought, 'Now I have had enough of dreaming; I want to wake up'? Were you then the same person you are here and now standing in front of me wide awake?

"How did you fall asleep last night? How did you manage to do it, to make the shift from being awake to being in a dream-state? And what did you bring over from your awake state into your dream-world?"

His questions took the ground out from under me. I was utterly confused. I felt as if I was in a room with no air in it, crawling around on the floor without any direction.

But he wasn't about to give me a break. "You don't know how you woke up, nor do you know where you came from. And you don't know how you fell asleep. Yet still you are convinced that you are, and that the time you spend awake is the only reality. You are convinced that yesterday you were, and that tomorrow you will be. Are you certain that this is really true, or are you only imagining a yesterday and a tomorrow? Throw off the weight of your cloudy mind and wake up, you sleepwalker! You are caught in the stream of forgetfulness and ignorance."

He was insulting me again. But at this moment I was defenseless. I sat there helpless, completely exposed. It would probably take me years to come to grips with what had been said. With a few questions, questions that I couldn't erase from my mind and that I couldn't answer, my entire existence had been turned upside-down. Now I doubted everything.

"What is your name," I asked him, hoping to distract myself from all this humiliation.

"I don't have a name. You can call me what you wish. Those who are completely filled with the sun's light have no name. Are you here to bring me such dumb, unimportant questions? When do you intend to leave?"

And again he was sitting there, stoic, indifferent, continuing to whittle on a piece of wood. After a few moments he stood swiftly, and then he disappeared into the forest.

I couldn't remember a time in my life when I had felt so miserable. I didn't have any idea what to make of this person. His odd behavior was insufferable. One minute he was treating me like a child, the next like a pathetic weakling, and then like an ignorant fool. And I was now painfully aware of my own fragility. As soon as he got back, I wanted to say good-bye and get out of there.

Again, I waited for him. And waited. Hours went by. Inside me, worlds were swirling by, one scene after another, each filled with peculiar emotions. Where was he? I had to leave soon, as it was already getting to be late in the afternoon. He still wasn't back. I played with the thought of just leaving without seeing him again. But I couldn't do it. That didn't correspond to my way of doing things or to the local customs.

When he finally arrived, darkness had fallen. "Oh, you're still here," he mumbled as he strode in. I sensed immediately that I had again fallen into an embarrassing situation, forced to ask him if I could spend the night there one more time. He gave a quick nod. But he didn't seem to care in the slightest. He treated me as if I was one of the large insects crawling around in his cave. They also came and went without him paying them any special attention.

I was resolved to depart the next morning as early as possible, even if he wasn't there. I wasn't going to wait again. To prove to myself that I would follow through, I let him know that my departure time was decided.

But had he heard me? Unconcerned and appearing quite satisfied with himself, he stretched out on his mat and stared into empty space. "Now he doesn't want to participate," I thought. I took a look at him, and what I saw before me was a big fat hollow larva. At that moment I would have loved to give him a good kick in the butt. That night I was so angry I couldn't get to sleep for a long time.

The next day, as the cheerful chirping of the birds woke me, my mood had changed. I felt terrific. I let my eyes wander around the cave. I then glanced toward the entrance, and there he was. He was sitting out by the fireplace cooking something. I took a deep breath.

"I would like to say good-bye now," were my first words to him.

He turned. "Come, sit down. You should eat something before you go. You can leave after your meal."

My stomach was rumbling. I imagined that breakfast would be a healthy and positive way to conclude my short visit. I also comforted myself with the thought that others must be living like him out here in nature. He wasn't so unique.

He filled my bowl to the brim. When he took his meals, he very quietly put his utensils into his bowls and noiselessly brought food to his mouth. I realized he never spoke when he ate.

Then, suddenly, the silence was broken. To hear his voice before he had finished eating was very startling. "Do you know that yogis can fly? Would you also like to learn to fly? I could teach you."

That was the moment I had been waiting for! Finally, here was something real, something to validate my long journey to this remote place. I was overjoyed. His invitation filled me with enthusiasm, and all the spiteful thoughts and feelings I had held toward him were swept away.

Excited beyond my usual self-control, I burst out, "Oh, that would be very interesting!" In one instant, I had been elevated to a euphoric state. This wasn't a strange question like "How did you wake up?" or "How did you fall asleep?" No. Now he actually wanted to teach me to fly! I had read about these phenomena, but now I was at the scene of the action.

"We can begin right after the meal," he said. My anticipation was so intense that I failed to notice how quickly I then shoved my food down my throat. In my mind, a thousand new considerations manifested as I visualized the bounty of my discoveries here. My friends at home would be amazed when I displayed my newly acquired skills.

I waited impatiently for him to finish his food. But I noticed he was actually becoming more deliberate. His hand movements and his chewing were becoming slower and slower, and he wasn't getting to the end of his food. I didn't dare say a word. In no way did I want to risk a mood swing.

So, I waited … and waited … and waited.

He ate … and ate … and ate.

Time passed at a snail's pace. It eventually dawned on me that something very strange was happening: with each spoonful he was taking more food from his bowl, and yet the bowl remained half full.

I had to rub my eyes. Was I dreaming? From this point on I observed very carefully. There was no doubt that he really was eating!

Hours passed. Sometimes he would stand and go into the cave for a few moments. Then he would sit down and begin to eat again. His motions became even slower. This went on until dusk had dimmed the light around us. Suddenly the bowl was empty. He had managed to eat without stopping for the entire day!

Wholly content, he rose from his eating position and explained to me how imperative it is not to waste food. After washing the dishes by the stream, he returned to the cave. He then laid himself comfortably down on his mat and proceeded within seconds to fall asleep.

Another day had gone by! Again I had waited long hours, full of hope, doubt, curiosity, and bewilderment. How did the old fox manage to keep eating from that small bowl for a whole day? He had deceived me. He was tricking me. But I had watched him all day, and I hadn't been able to expose the nature of his fraud.

Tomorrow I would ask him to show me how to fly before breakfast. I was obsessed with the idea. My expectations became increasingly grand. I was absorbed in envisioning what talents I might acquire and let these possibilities shuttle through my ambitious mind.

I certainly couldn't imagine how this heavyset chap was capable of flying. But everything about the man was peculiar and unpredictable.

When I awoke the next morning, I was shocked. This supposed master was lying on the mat sleeping, and, overnight, the poor fellow had gotten fat, incredibly fat. He must have gained a tremendous amount of weight. I wondered if he knew what had happened to him and was curious about how he would react when he woke up. He was still sleeping deeply, his breathing calm and rhythmic.

I went outside the cave to bathe in the sunlight for a little while. I could feel the life-enhancing energy of nature filling and nourishing me. I wandered down to the stream, where I washed and then meditated awhile. The gentle lapping of the water settled my mind. In this state of deep relaxation I could enjoy a break from my normal self-absorption. Still, certain thoughts continued to rush through my mind and disturb my tranquility. Had the guy woken up? Should I check and see? I convinced myself that some meditation would help me in my efforts to fly. It would surely be necessary to remain calm and concentrated if I was to actually succeed.

After quite a long time, I finally returned to the cave. He was still lying there sleeping, round and puffed out like a well-fattened pig. I thought, "How could a person really gain so much weight in one night? Maybe he's ill. That would be a reasonable explanation."

Nervousness and impatience began to gnaw at me. I paced in front of the cave like a trapped animal. Each time I passed the entrance, I looked in and checked on him. He slept blissfully.

About noon I decided to wake him up. I stood in front of him and proceeded to make a variety of unpleasant loud noises. After continuing these antics for a little while, I began to feel silly. And the fellow on the ground didn't seem to notice in the slightest.

I finally bent over him, wanting to shake his shoulder. I didn't get very close before an inexplicable power sent a shot of energy into my hand, a bolt so strong that I tumbled backward and landed on my behind.

But he hadn't budged. I was mystified. How could this be possible? The source of that electric shock through my hand was a riddle I had no means of solving. I decided to go for a long walk. As soon as he was awake, I was going to demand an explanation from him.

I came back to the cave a few hours later. I had a notion of what I would find, and that is what awaited me. He was still sleeping or meditating there on the ground.

As the daylight slowly gave way to the darker hues of night, he finally woke up. He looked over at me and spoke softly, "It is already getting dark. Let's get some sleep. Tomorrow is going to be a tough day." Without another word, he shut his eyes again and fell instantly into a deep and tranquil slumber. The questions I had wanted to ask him remained with me, caught in the holding chamber of curiosity.

So what was I supposed to make of this person? From

the moment of my arrival, he had done nothing but stick his nose up at me and provoke my anger. I didn't have to keep setting myself up for this. He was an old bamboozler, no doubt, and I didn't know if I should love him or hate him. I didn't know anything anymore. I found myself lying down again on the hard ground of the cave, waiting for sleep to come and carry me off.

When it came, it was magnificent! I dreamed all night of flying. What an overwhelming feeling! I visited friends. I traveled to foreign countries. And, of course, I woke up the next morning to discover it was all only a dream. Again, I was disillusioned in the true sense of the word.

Still, it was my big day. I would finally get the instruction and the experience I had been promised. He owed me. My gaze wandered to his sleeping place. He was gone! No, no, not again! He couldn't do that to me! I again fell into a hole of doubt and misgivings. I wanted to run away. But somehow the prospect of learning to fly, of being able to move freely through the air at will, worked like a magic charm, one that couldn't easily be dismissed. I knew that his promise, at least, was no dream.

As I left the cave, he was walking toward me with a smile on his face. I came to a dead stop. I couldn't accept what my eyes were seeing. Was that really him, or could it be someone else? He had lost masses of weight. Most of his fat was gone, and he looked ten years younger.

"Is that really you?" I asked him in disbelief. To my utter bafflement and dismay he replied, "Fattened-up pigs can't fly." At that moment I would have loved to be able to sink into the earth and disappear. I couldn't grasp the fact that he had just said those words. The night before when, furious and frustrated, I couldn't sleep, these were exactly the words that were going through my mind. But I was certain he had been asleep. There was no way he could have read my thoughts and be sound asleep at the same time. But … that seemed to be the case.

If that was so, then he would be terribly angry with me. But as he stood across from me, it was obvious that he was completely unattached. My emotions hadn't touched him at all. Now a tremendous fear overcame me. I had no idea what to say or how to behave. He had cut me down and crushed me. And he was giving me no chance to explain or apologize. Running away wasn't an option either, not at this moment.

His way of reacting to all my angry thoughts was as peculiar as it was unexpected. For the first time I was impressed with his character. He was imperturbable. In seeing how far removed he was from me in his behavior, feelings, thoughts, and perspective, I asked myself if I was willing to actually learn something from him. Even flying seemed trivial now.

After that episode I wished I had a security guard to watch over my thoughts. I couldn't let them roam around anymore. Like dark shadows, like poisonous, muddy streams, thoughts continued to pour out from the unconscious, unplumbed depths of my being.

But were these depths really unplumbed? I had to find out.

"Come on. It's time to fly," he said in a carefree voice. He displayed absolutely no trace of negativity. This human being was a conundrum.

We hiked down the steep overhanging cliff until we reached a huge sloping precipice. "No, this isn't the right place," he said brusquely. Then he turned around to his right and headed for the trail leading back to the cave, which he proceeded to climb. Everywhere I looked there were small inclines, but no, we had to walk uphill for another hour. Each time we approached another possible spot from which we could drop off, he turned away, returning to the trail leading back to where we had started. Uncontrollable gushes of anger arose within me once again. I sensed that I was caught up anew in his foolish games. Obviously, I was being manipulated.

"Here it is … here is the right place. Come stand here," he finally said.

I ran eagerly to the spot where he directed me. Just at that moment, a huge throng of dark clouds filled the sky above our heads. After a few more seconds the heavens opened their floodgates, and rivulets of rain began to pour from above. I watched the water fall from the surrounding trees like teardrops. This cloudburst had come literally out of the blue and appeared to me to be a direct response on the part of nature to my own inner torrent.

We observed the potent activity of nature from the cave entrance. Long, thin streaks of lightning descended from the gloomy sky like skeletal arms reaching down to touch the earth. The person I had hoped would teach me to fly was sitting next to me, content within himself, enjoying the various moods of earthly activity, centered in the invisible space of eternity.

Again I observed him with new eyes. Had he conjured up that rainstorm? I didn't want to let such thoughts go any further. I had no idea where they would lead me or what challenges I would then have to confront.

As quickly and unannounced as the storm had come, it retreated. Soon we were standing again on the slope, at the spot where he had signaled me to stand next to him earlier. The ground had been softened by the rain and was slippery. I was excited. This was the moment. I started to tremble with anticipation. He promptly gave me my instructions.

"Shut your eyes and breathe deeply and evenly. Feel yourself becoming lighter and lighter. Imagine you are flying. Raise your arms and bend forward slightly. I will now count to three. Then … you jump."

I perceived myself being elevated. I felt extremely light. His voice seemed to be speaking from a great distance away. "One … two … three …"

I jumped.

Instead of being lifted into the sky, I toppled over headfirst, rolling down onto the boulders below us. When my body finally came to a stop, I noticed a fiery pain in my right foot. My arms and my face were covered with scrapes and scratches, and blood was trickling out from the small wounds.

I lay there powerless. I could not and would not believe what had just happened to me. My mind filled with loathing, I looked up at him. He was laughing. "Not a bad beginning," he remarked casually. Then he turned and disappeared into the forest.

He was leaving me behind, without help and all alone. To add to my fury, I was now consumed in self-pity as well.

The fires raging inside my chest fueled my crawling ascent on all fours back up the cliff. With my last scrap of energy I reached the cave. I pulled my wounded body inside. Beaten and exhausted, my body sank into the ground.

How I despised this person! Why had I ever thought to come here? For that, I despised myself. And what should I do now? He had me in the palm of his hand; I knew it. There was no more escaping.

I gradually calmed down a bit. Not long afterward, he returned. He was carrying an assortment of roots and herbs. Silently, as if nothing had happened, he lowered himself onto his knees in front of me and began to examine my foot.

"It looks like you might be sticking around here for a while." Then he made a compress out of the herbs and carefully cleaned my open sores with juice taken from the roots.

Once more I felt as if I had landed in the dregs of my dark feelings and emotions, amid difficult mind states where love and hate were blindly intertwined. He was reaching at my innards, connecting to the place where, invisibly, the energy strands of fate were carrying out their sinister diversions.

I began to ask myself if some greater power had guided me there, to carve out the cosmic path concealed inside me, covered over by so much muck. In order to understand this person, first I would have to open the eye of the heart, that eye of light that could perceive the meeting point of heaven and earth.

In this moment of inner clarity, something peculiar was happening to me. I could observe myself very objectively and was painfully aware of how arrogant, prejudiced, and ignorant I had been acting since I had encountered this man. Without making an announcement or drawing me a sign, he had been able to place a mirror in front of my eyes and had compelled me toward this direct experience of myself. I hadn't come to him for theories. I wanted to know the practice myself. But I hadn't expected this practice.

Within a short time, he had taken away all my defenses. He had pushed me through a sort of temporal window, where I was shown a clear glimpse of my being. Through this portal I could see the states and circumstances in which I was trapped. My fleeting obsessions and the short-lived dramas of the human theater were dangerous offerings for a heart still clinging to the transitory world.

He tended to my wounds with care. He knew that the flying episode and his uncompromising behavior had set off some kind of activity within me. I found these energetic reactions both clarifying and purifying. I was able to peer through previously concealed doorways and have a peek at the radiance that exists beyond the corporeal world, beyond the sensual world. There was an indescribable brilliance, a luminosity that was nothing and where even the word nothing had no place. Earthly eyes could not perceive this light.

Tears flowed down my cheeks. I witnessed the vast desert of the unrealized world and longed to free myself from the earth-bound plane. I felt the fire of the sun burning inside me.

"How long would you like to stay?" he asked me in a gentle voice. Until this time he had asked me only when I was leaving.

"As long as I am allowed to," I answered, filled with an indescribable sense of joy. I could see eternity shining in his silent eyes. It was hard to believe. In a split second, my relationship to him had transformed completely. He had been testing me, continually, carefully, and exhaustively.

"If you want to stay here, you will have to kill the seven demons in your heart. They are the mother of all suffering and the father of all delusions. They lead to the lower paths. As long as you haven't flushed these out of your heart completely, you cannot enter the realm where there are no shadows. You remain unsatisfied, floating in the shallow foam above the true depths."

The fullness of his spiritual power had embraced my heart at its deepest core. He was holding the key to life before my eyes. How unspeakably weak I had been my entire life, and how strongly I had invested in my own illusions! My talent until now had been the ability to organize my own world, a life where only I existed. With this egocentric strategy, I had imagined myself a strong and thoughtful person.

Up here, high on the mountain, the building blocks at the base of my self-styled world had been smashed to pieces and now lay scattered on the ground. I knew it would be impossible to reconstruct myself in the same way. Painfully, I had to own up to the fact that I had never had a true foundation.

I had never thought that this trip was going to bring such a devastating rupture to my life. I had wanted only to gather knowledge and had never intended to let myself be pulled so deep into the liberation process. But how long had I mistakenly trodden the paths of darkness in this human world, where neither God nor soul had a place, where all are caught staring into the cracked mirror of ignorance and heartlessness? That was my life. How wretched and miserable I was. It made me nauseous to think how many half-truths I had mistaken for reality and preached to others.

Everything I knew had been written and retained in the dark barrels of memory. Their contents left a harsh and bitter aftertaste, which unsettled my nervous system.

The false light I had been following had bound me to a heavy chain. The links of the chain were steps in the evolution of death, and each one caused pain. I continued to cause this harm to myself, roaming as I was, in search of some flickering rays. In doing this I had lost sight of what it was to be human. Unknowingly, I had continued to pour the poisonous liquids of a transient world down my throat. This twisted path had bound me to the blinding powers of material existence.

But all was not lost, at least not for the moment. The engraving on the headstone had been removed. I still had a chance to live. Silently, I rejoiced.

AN INNER TONE

During this experience of inner clarification, my eyes had been closed. As I opened them and came back to a sense of my body, the Master approached me and placed the long stick he had been chiseling in my hand. "This will be your third leg for a few days," he said, softening his lips into a slight grin. I thanked him and inspected the wood from top to bottom. Suddenly, I jerked back. Underneath the skillfully formed grip, two letters had been carved. They were my initials. I had never had the chance to mention my name to him. And yet … there was no doubting it. My initials were there, right before my eyes. Perhaps I had made a mistake? Perhaps the letters had a completely different meaning?

The Master did not fail to notice my bewilderment and began explaining. "You still have a name that belongs to the sleeping material world, because that is what the letters represent. It is the name of your prison." His authoritative words penetrated to my bones and marrow. There was nothing ornate or coaxing about them. They went in straight and deep.

I knew that he had carved the stick the previous day. This fact also confused me. Had he already known about my plunge and the ensuing injury? I could not and did not want to believe that. It was still much easier to write it off as a coincidence.

The next days passed easily, almost unnoticed. The body did its work of healing swiftly and economically, and gradually I recuperated. During this time I wondered at the intricacy and refinement of the healing powers contained in the body.

The Master spoke little. The flood of thoughts in my mind eventually began to subside, as when someone stops turning the wheel of a barrel organ. A feeling of equanimity flowed with increasing potency through my strained nervous system, spreading throughout my entire being like fine balsam. The silence and unspoiled beauty of the place, and this master who was wordlessly winning my heart, imparted a feeling for life that I had never known. I was looking less and less at my personal history. At one point the Master discussed this in connection with a question I had been pondering concerning my origins. He helped me to become aware of the dangers in revisiting the past:

"To think about the past is to live in the past. To live in it is to be caught by it. The past is the killer of intuition. Don't live in the past, or in the future, or in the present. Live truly. The past, the future, and the present are all stains in your thinking, empty words, empty shells, like ghosts roaming around. They are restless and eternally dissatisfied. They are the murderers of love."

It was clear to me that I couldn't stop to think about what he was saying, or I would miss a chance to burn off that which he was calling "I" or "the present." If I tried to follow with my brain and find something, I would surely drift back into the realms of yesterday and tomorrow. My intellect was brought to its edge. It was finally clear to me that the thinking mind could not penetrate this wordless reality. The silent presence of the Master was the manifestation of this inconceivable state.

He recognized my transformation, my insight into the almighty power of inner stillness. I sensed the loving energy that radiated from his being. Soon after, he looked at me with a long, warm smile on his face. I could not figure out what he was thinking, but then he spoke to me.

"Everything that once was must vanish. In the ever-present reality, there is no room for things. Here the soul has no form. It has left the realm of the senses and discarded the necessity of thought. In the eternal there is no being, not the slightest division or any concept of existence whatsoever. You have come from far away, but I don't know you as something or someone particular.

"Don't expect, don't hope, and don't create. Recognize the ever-present reality. Don't separate that which has never been separated. Otherwise you entangle yourself in what you have created, through your patterns and what they produce. The laws of habit in this world produce a life of agony, eons upon eons of being held prisoner to a life that always senses an icy chill on its tongue, the flavor of death."

His words expressed what his being is. They were words loaded with the entirety of his inner strength. His powerful spirit was the cause of this rapid transformational process. This unbounded way of living was still impossible for me to fathom. Just being in the Master's presence had shaken my understanding and philosophy of life to the core.

After two weeks my foot had healed to the point that I could accompany the Master on short walks through the forest without the walking stick. I had been accepted. This made me very happy and provided me with greater self-confidence.

On one of these walks I had another glimpse into his unimaginable world. We had been going along for several hours when we came to a grass-covered meadow at the edge of a cliff. There we met a man who was caring for a herd of goats. The shepherd was kneeling on the ground and tending to one of the animals, which was whining pitifully. As soon as the Master caught sight of the man, he made his way swiftly over to greet him. Evidently the two knew each other. Immediately the shepherd explained to the Master that one of the younger animals had broken a leg. Right away the Master approached the wounded creature and began to stroke its head softly. Then he laid both his hands on the broken limb. I heard a soft snapping noise. A few moments later the animal was able to stand and move around. Soon it was galloping vivaciously over to the other animals. It was completely healed.

I was astonished. The herdsman was also taken aback. He thanked us sincerely and invited us to share a simple meal with him.

After my initial amazement, a question sprung up in my mind; if the Master could heal the leg of the goat in just a few moments, why had I been forced to suffer with my injured leg for so long?

We ate and conversed with the shepherd, who took the opportunity to talk about his life and his various difficulties. He paid careful attention to what the Master said and clearly appreciated the valuable advice and suggestions he was offered.

Finally, we began to make our way back. I could observe with silent admiration how alert the Master was in the midst of nature, how he saw eternity in each leaf and felt the sap flowing through the veins of the trees as he tenderly touched them. He could perceive the earth under his feet and feel it as a source of inexhaustible energy. He helped me to observe the glory of creation, which he dubbed "the dress of what one cannot express."

In this deep attentiveness to all things inside and outside, profound hidden secrets were revealed, though not to the intellect, which could only grasp at the emptiness and return empty-handed. It was a pilgrimage to the inner realms, a journey of discovery into the eternal. The intensity was overwhelming. I found myself in an energy field of all-embracing transparency, where exceptionally lucid awareness and remarkably potent powers of observation were possible. The Master could fully perceive each thought and every movement. In this state of incredibly vivid awareness, there was no yesterday, no today, no tomorrow.

"You have to constantly let go of all your experiences and begin again in each moment. If you don't, you will continually live in the past, the old superficial layers. In this triviality there is no depth. You cannot give yourself to the search for the eternal, because the eternal in not an object to be found. The beauty one perceives in the infinite depths of Self-realization is the key. To perceive without words, without a personal interpretation, creates enormous energy and allows a total absorption and selflessness in the moment."

He spoke these words as if in passing, but they settled deeply in my heart. I felt as if I was experiencing my first sunrise, as if a freshly planted seed had just begun to sprout.

Still, to let go moment by moment of all my self-centeredness seemed impossible. It was exactly the opposite of how I had lived my entire life. I could understand the idea of it, the theory. But that wasn't the point. I had enough awareness to know this.

My love for this strange person was growing with each breath. He had led me back to myself, to the inner truth, to the pure radiant fields of real life. The dark lineage in my blood was filled with images of the idols that reign in this fleeting world. But my obsessive attachment to them was gradually waning. Now my fear-ridden heart was feeling the golden seam of life and in some way made contact with true reality. Nevertheless, I was still stuck within this lineage, where ignorance weighed on me like lead--still stuck in a muddy world of my own making.

We arrived back at the cave shortly before darkness expanded to the horizon and established itself as night. We sat in front of the entrance, absorbed in the experience of the natural world and its passage into stillness. The Master lit a small fire, and the flames scattered a flickering ring of light around us. Beyond the circle all was pitch-black.

We sat quietly. It was as if time had come to a halt. I spoke the question that had been burning on my tongue the entire afternoon: "How was it possible for you to heal the broken leg of the goat so quickly?"

The Master said nothing for a long time. A concentrated silence filled the air. I felt as if my question had seeped into him like water, penetrating deeper and deeper, until it finally arrived at the place where an answer was possible:

"The perfect love of God knows no illness. It knows no disharmony. It is all-encompassing and ever-present. To be one with God means to be one with divine consciousness. That means to be one with the limitless power of the divine spirit and to express it in all its immeasurable brilliance. In this light, in this energy, all things must be restored to health. This is because the law of divine love is the healing, the purifying, and the complete regeneration of every creation.

"To express the power of love means to be this love, this power. As I held the injured leg of the goat in my hands, the vibration increased according to this rule of love, and in that instant a healing occurred. To live in God is to express his supreme will, his supreme power, consistently. Healing is actually reestablishing the original condition of all things where no disharmony exists.

"To restore the outer layers of a person or an animal to good health is not the most important thing. The inner person must be freed from the limitations of the flesh-formed outer husk and all the lower forces that he is still attached to. He must be led back to the inner Self.

"The mystical force that moves the sun and the stars is the silent voice of the supernatural. The world is not what you think it is. It is not what you see with your eyes. The cosmos is only the outer robe of the highest of the high.

"The water of life comes from the ever-flowing wellspring of God. This water is the pure light. These emanations of light are filled with bliss, bestowing the purest delight. Bliss is the true condition of all beings. One doesn't try to practice this principle. One becomes it."

The Master looked at me as if he wanted to see how deeply his words had penetrated. He was sharing with me the experience of someone who stands entirely in this light. His words and deeds were his offering. He was holding the original essence before my eyes. My being had severed itself at some point from this essence, and now I was wandering in dark underworlds, a slave to my unconscious. But the light of transformation had invaded this dungeon, providing an unmistakable indicator that this divine world exists! I made a sacred vow to myself that I would not waver. I would overcome and dissolve my old conditioned mind completely!

But I wasn't free of doubts. "Why did you heal the goat right away, after you had let me go around hobbling with a stick for two weeks?" I asked the Master in an irritated voice.

His spoke ironically, "You are not a goat. Goats don't manage with a stick very well."

I swallowed hard. He had exposed my thought pattern completely. Now I was thrown back heavily upon myself. It was obvious that he wasn't going to waste another word on the subject. He had reasons for doing things the way he did and wasn't interested in giving explanations. He had offered me comprehensive insights into the secrets of life, but as soon as it began to feel personal and my ego thrust itself to the surface, the exchange was over. I had to accept and respect this.

The next morning, he didn't speak to me. I asked myself whether I had done something wrong, but I wasn't about to bring it up with the Master. He was being particularly aloof.

"Go into the forest," he demanded suddenly. Then he disappeared into the cave.

What should I go into the forest for? Perhaps he wanted to be alone for a day. I started off, wandering peacefully through the trees, immersed in the silence of the forest. Here I noticed that my powers of observation had increased. I took more time to become aware of my surroundings. I noticed the flies that landed on my hand. The numerous small details of these creatures' forms caught my attention, aspects I had never noticed before.

In the evening I returned to the cave, where the Master had prepared a small meal. He himself did not eat, and he didn't ask me anything. I understood that he did not want to speak.

The next day, I received the same instructions. I again spent long hours walking through the woods. The deep solitude there began to have a noticeable effect. Each day for more than a week the Master sent me out into the dense forest. During this time my relationship to nature grew more vital and intense. But it was not the visible world that I was feeling deeper contact with. It was something more profound, more comprehensive. From every direction, the eternal was whispering to me. It had taken a long time for this dried-up spirit to be truly touched by something beyond the senses and beyond thought. For such a long time my inner being had been laid up ill. I had been in bad shape for so long that all true levels of awareness were subjugated and finally eliminated. Now a shift was occurring. I was gradually cultivating a sense for what life really was.

Weeks went by before the Master spoke again, finally giving another assignment. "Go to the mountain." That was it. He had become mute. I missed having a dialogue with him, but eventually I was able to get used to his wordless ways, and it became easier to spend my time with him in silence.

Every day I scaled the steep slope of the mountain. Very high on the summit I discovered a spot I especially liked. The stones there shimmered soft silver, endowing the area with a magical glitter. I had made a comfortable seat out of grass, and I sat there for hours just looking at the beauty around me.

Every day I returned to that place, and it became more familiar. There was hardly any vegetation that high up, so the rows of piled-up boulders and barren rock faces were my only companions. In the forest I could communicate with the animals, plants, and trees, which made passing the day easier for me. Here there was only stone. I observed the different types of rocks and their formations and noticed how veins had developed in their hard surfaces.

But during all the time I spent with these seemingly solid acquaintances, I knew that something was still not right, something was lacking.

The Master continued to send me off each day. Then one morning he told me to remain up on the mountain for a few days. The idea didn't excite me at all. I knew for certain that I had to do the things he asked of me, but I couldn't explain to myself why. I packed a blanket and some provisions and made my way upward again.

As night approached, a paralyzing fear suddenly grabbed hold of my being and refused to let go. All the positive feelings and deep mind states I had experienced were wiped away with one jolt, as if they were nothing more than feathery dreams. Soon the sky was dark. Around me it was pitch-black, and I had nothing with which to make a fire. The Master had sent me to … death!

Fear of death took command of my being. Wicked demonic faces rose up from the dreg-filled cellars of my soul, sneering maliciously and mocking me. My whole body rattled with panic, and I felt an invisible power gripping my throat firmly, preventing me from screaming.

Soon I was able to recognize the acute blackness for what it was. Thousands of death experiences that I had agonizingly passed through seemed to have collected together within my being, becoming a thick black bundle. But now this bundle was unraveling. As its contents were being drawn up to the surface, I saw how many times I had painfully left this world, forced to take flight through the uncertain gates of death, only to return again, forever a slave of time. This world was nothing more than an enormous mass grave that the tides thrust back and forth from one shore to another.

The primal pain besieging me now was excruciating, almost unbearable. One single thought allowed me to hold on: I must overcome this wheel of rebirth! I wanted to live. I wanted out of this millennium-old nightmare. I wanted to truly awaken, once and for all.

But these thoughts could not hold back the carousel of obscure and vile images continuing to arise within me, images that dated back to a primordial time. I breathed deeply and tried to let go as much as possible.

It was strange to be there alone in nature with no one to share my experiences. Days earlier, from my simple habit of speaking, I had begun to converse out loud with animals, trees, plants, and stones. In the beginning I thought it silly and laughed at myself when I found myself talking without anyone else around. But the more I continued to offer my voice to nature, the more clearly nature spoke back to me. At the same time, the more clearly I could see each living being as equally significant, the more clearly I saw my own arrogance. How rough and insensitive I had been, how blind! Why had I always been so harsh with the natural world?

But slowly, too, this inner severity was beginning to melt, weakening like ice set out before the sun. Nature was now my master. It was able to show me the silence beyond silence, existing within my own being. In one moment of deep insight, I could see with what delight the great architect had descended down through infinite sun-filled planes to create this world. I was exposed to the true equilibrium and incalculable logic with which God was offering his loving expression. My heart danced for an instant on the waves of light flowing from this boundless ocean that has no beginning.

But again the dark voices began to murmur inside me. They were the seeds of my past, the seeds of destiny. There were still traces of regression in my blood. I knew I had to overcome my present state, or I would soon sink again into delusion.

Encased in my own inner darkness, I gathered all the strength in my heart. My lips came together in prayer. From within my breast, a call was sent to God, a call for help. I was certain that I could find him in the innermost depths of my heart. Arising from the core of my being, words appeared as if of their own making, words of reconciliation and words of love.

Simultaneously, with each new breath the darkness began to withdraw, conceding to the glow of light expanding inside me. The murkiness of mortality was clearing. The mold cast by death was breaking open. This new radiance was spreading like soft lotion over my soul. I had stared into the hideous face of death, and now, in the next flashing instant, another energy wanted to emerge from this intensity and triumph. This energy entered my polluted brain, approaching the millions of ill-bred cells inside and cleansing them in pure light. At the same time I felt myself suddenly being transported by a powerful presence that strove to release the shackles that bound my heart. It was the force of the eternal that elevated me with its loving kindness.

Never had I felt so much joy at the coming of dawn as I did on this new day. I felt reborn, completely new. I thanked this silent place where I had sat for so many days, and that had enabled this purification. I had never imagined that something so tumultuous or so dreadful could happen to me here. If I had had the slightest inkling of the experience that was awaiting me, I would most certainly have found a way to avoid it.

It was time to return to the Master. I looked forward to seeing him again. At the break of daylight, I began my descent down the steep slope of the mountain. Two eagles flying high overhead and monitoring the region for possible plunder kept watch over me as I went along.

I took the air deeply into my lungs, filling them with oxygen. I had been infused with a new vitality, and I felt freshness in all my limbs. Soon I reached the edge of the forest and could enjoy the view of lush greenery and the various scents wafting in the air around me.

I arrived at the cave with a sense of anticipation. I

was relieved to find the Master there. He greeted me with a friendly smile and prepared a meal, which I greatly enjoyed. It was the first time in several days that I had received something warm to put in my belly. In the meantime I had lost quite a bit of weight. All my unnecessary body fat had dropped away, leaving my clothes hanging limply over my lean body.

The Master sat at the meal in silence, a silence that continued over the next few days. I accompanied him on long walks, but he never spoke. To spend time like this was magnificent. In my eyes he was a purely cut diamond. My inner eye could clearly distinguish his immaculate light. No word crossed his lips, but his silence during these days had a wonderful invigorating effect on me. I could discern the densely concentrated light energy that emanated from him and spread over the whole region, carrying love and blessings. He was an enormous light field, whose span I couldn't even begin to estimate.

Who was his teacher? Where had the Master lived before he came to this cave? How old could he be? These questions went by in a flurry. I was surprised that they were arising for the first time so many weeks after I had met him.

My watch had stopped long before, and it occurred to me that I also had no idea what month or what day of the week it was. Noticing this felt good and appropriate, but at the same time it scared me. Before I had come here, my daily life was structured and organized. I followed a regimented schedule and thought it meaningful to live that way. I was always on time and expected the same of others. But up here that attitude seemed so ridiculous and absurd that I could only shake my head. I had built my own boundaries. I had handcuffed myself, and now these constraints inhabited my brain like phantoms.

In the scheme of my former life, there was no place for the Master. I imagined a master to be someone wearing a suit and tie and a golden watch on his wrist. I imagined him with his mouth always moving, and always laughing.

This master stood for a moment and glanced at me, looking amused. I knew he had seen the neatly painted picture I was holding in my mind, He chuckled and seemed delighted as he went along the path. I enjoyed his childlike carefree manner. It rubbed off on me. I held that smile for a long time.

One morning I was surprised to receive a new directive. "Go to the water," he told me. Somehow I had expected something to happen first, before I again had to leave the Master's side. I wasn't happy to separate from him. But at this point I understood what had been happening over the past few days. The Master had been helping me to calm down and compose myself. The terrifying experience with death had required more exertion than I wanted to believe. I had looked death in the face, but I was a long way from conquering it. I knew that now.

The next morning I took my blanket, packed some food that he had already prepared for me, and said goodbye. Judging by the weight of my provisions, I would be on my own for a while. "Go to the water." His words reverberated in me like an echo. What was I supposed to see? What hidden secret would the water reveal to me?

As I went along my mind was buried in thoughts. I became aware that the Master had prepared me in a special way in order to make these deep experiences possible. I noticed that many of my deeply ingrained fears had vanished. And it wasn't because I had learned something. It was much more a particular condition of my mind, a change I couldn't explain.

I sat down on the trunk of a fallen tree and resolved to look at this question of fear and get to the bottom of it. What is fear? I sat silently and let this question slowly sink into me. I received no direct answer. Fear is nothing, then; fear is empty. I laughed to myself, and at the same time I sensed the depth of this recognition, which was not an intellectual one.

Fear is nothing. Fear is empty. I contemplated further. It occurred to me that fear is not something that really exists. More to the point, fear was the result of my own misconceptions and lack of clarity. Fear was not a continuous state of mind. It appeared only in particular moments. As I encountered death, I felt tremendous fear, but it was the fear of my own created imaginings. The fear grew out of my identification with my mental pictures. This frightening storm of images had nothing to do with my true divinity. The pure light in me was eternally free from fear and was never attached to a transitory body. The half-appearances of spiritual things, which I had produced myself, were the result of my outlook, which was fixed on a fleeting universe. This deluded view was the agent of my fear and imbalance.

My mechanical everyday mind-set, and the gloomy discontent it carried with it, had obstructed my perception. I had never glimpsed the masterly arrangement of things on this earth. It was all so beautiful. But the chain of fear, the fear of losing something, of saying something wrong, of not being loved--these unholy forces had compelled my soul into exile without my being aware of it.

In the silence of the Master, I had experienced the eternal freedom from gain and loss, from "mine" and "yours," of the pure unattached soul, of the soul eternally unbound to self-proclaiming, egocentric energies. The foundation of my being was this light-filled soul. Now I was feeling a tranquil centeredness, and within this core an inexpressible tenderness. How painful it was to see the debris with which I had covered this over. I was calling this dwarfish small-mindedness life. These old energies, which I was clinging to so tightly, were the cause of all my fear. They were what the Master called "the demons of the heart."

As I resumed my journey, following alongside the stream, the thought occurred to me to look for the source. I decided to seek out the place where the water first bubbled from the earth.

It was a beautiful sunny day. I was feeling good as I followed along the path of the water, although the going wasn't as easy as I had expected. At times I had to use all four limbs to traverse slippery rock walls. Other spots were so narrow and steep that I had no choice but to walk in the stream itself.

After a time I was completely wet and worn out, and I stopped to rest for a while. Had I taken on too much? How far could it be to the source? My foot hurt. The ascent had been too strenuous for it. It needed some time to recover. I began to look around for an appropriate spot to spend the night. I eventually found a small area that I liked, surrounded with low-lying trees and bushes.

I remembered how the Master had used the leaves of a plant to make a medicinal fluid and tend to my foot. I decided to look for the plant myself. After a short time, I was able to find it. This little discovery gave me a feeling of accomplishment, and I was in high spirits.

I made a compress to cover my foot for the night. The next morning, the swelling had disappeared, and the pain had disappeared with it. I decided to allow three more days for my trek toward the source, and no more.

Along the streambed, many flowers and herbs I had never seen before were growing. I took time to examine them more closely. My powers of observation were unusually heightened. I could look upon external forms and perceive the firm linear expression of nature's spirit.

One of the herbs had a pleasant gentle odor. I quickly broke off a twig, but not without first apologizing and expressing gratitude. The inner matter dwelling within the plants spoke a foreign language, concealed in a complex code that was difficult to understand. The Master had enabled me to notice this. When I returned to him I would ask about the healing benefits and possible applications of this plant.

I understood now that all things having a body are bound to the never-ending round of mortality. But even in death, this deathless light lives. This magnificent radiance is alive in everything. This light remains untouched by all the transitory things of this world.

I managed to walk the entire day. The consistent movement of water that accompanied me day and night was sharpening my ears to the different colors of sound: the hissing, the gurgling, the murmuring, and sometimes the roaring. I developed an ability to listen deeply and discern the rich symphony of nature that accompanied me along my path. The stream offered its broad repertoire joyfully, sensually, happily, freely, and with an overflowing heart. I listened quietly, thoughtlessly, and became internally more fluid and at the same time more calm and collected. The swirling water shone like pearls as I reveled in a love song composed by the earth itself.

I sat in this condition for a while, submerged in my own consciousness. I listened to the voices that spoke out through this untamed region. That place where the infinite and the finite touch each other was almost palpable here. It drew my soul back and down through the mighty corridors of boundless existence. The call was there. But along with it was the arduous agonizing passage through time, where the obstacles of fate and mortality resolutely occupied their positions.

Three days had passed, and I hadn't found the source of the stream. I decided to look for a spot where I could relax. Soon I was standing in front of a small waterfall. Underneath it a small lake had formed. The tapestry of sound was much louder and more forceful here. A carpet of moss covered the earth encircling the water. This was the spot!

I knelt down along the shore, formed my hands into a chalice, and drank with delight from the crystal-clear water. I then took off my clothes and stretched out in the stream, letting my body fall under the surface. "Go to the water," the Master had said. Now I was not just at the water, I was in it!

For the next few days I sat at the shore and observed everything that went on around me. But nothing noteworthy happened. The following days began to pass more slowly.

I started to feel heavy. A dreadful monotony thickened the air around me. These clouds of stagnation brought drowsiness, and soon I was sleeping most of the day as well as through the night. While I was draped in this boredom, gnawing doubts roamed within my mind. I languished in these idle thoughts, pondering whether there was anything up here in these mountains left to find. Perhaps there was nothing more for me to gain by staying?

One day I was awoken from my napping by a loud thunderclap. I hadn't noticed that a huge storm had covered the sky above me. Within a few moments the rain began to pour down in buckets. The stream, which had flowed so smoothly through the ravine, was transformed in the blink of an eye into a monstrous torrent. I was not protected and had to move quickly. Frightened, I scurried up the bank to avoid the furious waters swelling beneath me.

Moments before, I had been sleepy-eyed and lackadaisical, my mind drifting toward a dead end. The storm had been like an alarm from the gods sounding right above my head. With one strike I was awake again, and at this moment the poison of boredom had taken flight. I spent the night in a small cave I discovered nearby.

The next day, the water was slapping softly against the banks of the stream, just as gently and pleasantly as before. My clothes and blanket dried quickly. Again I sat by the water observing the current, feeling calm and alert. Suddenly, my perception was altered. The flow of the water had somehow moved from the exterior world to my interior one. My being had entered the stream of true existence. I knew this stream would lead to eternal life.

I sat drenched in light, in a state of superb delight. I could taste the divine nectar. Suddenly I saw the planet

Earth as a pure sphere of light hovering in front of me, transparent, subtly vibrating, and immeasurably beautiful in the light of the eternal sun.

Basking in this light, I perceived countless correlations between human beings and Earth, between Earth and the sun, and between the sun and the central stars of our Milky Way, which I could also see in its connection with still greater constellations. Everything was tied together and inter-dependent.

An immense intelligence was continually at hand in order to create. This intelligence supported every single one of its creations. Overflowing with love, it dissolved each creation as well. Those things initiated and extinguished by this intelligence would become the highest consciousness, the purest light. They radiated the ever-increasing and everlasting splendor, the glory of the one beginningless God.

This pure light was no system, no form, no coming or going. It was not subject to birth or death. I thought, "My light-soul is this untainted light. My body is born bearing its load of consciousness, and according to the laws that govern it, must die." And I knew that I was the one observing it all.

With this entry into the stream of life, I had taken my first steps out of the ephemeral and into the enduring, from mortality to immortality. The profound insights that accompanied these strides released potent chain reactions within me. I felt as if my insides were imploding. Outwardly, I was overflowing and expanding beyond all previously set boundaries.

Yet, these deep experiences were just the beginning of the journey. I knew intuitively that I was only in the preparatory stages. That is why the Master had sent me here. I had come to know the sweet and the bitter in their extremes, but I had not arrived at the gateway to ultimate liberation.

I remained at my spot for two more days, reflecting deeply. How terribly easy it would be to slide back into the sluggish lethargy of living unaware!

Finally, the time to return had come. I headed for the cave of the Master.

It was late at night when I arrived. The Master looked straight into my eyes, staring deeply. He then spoke to me. "The oceans of the world have only one taste, the taste of salt. Divine law has only one taste, the taste of complete liberation." He continued, "You have had some important experiences now. You have faced some difficult situations and brought them under control. But to control them is different from truly rising above them. This is the beginning. Experiences are important. But in the end, such knowledge is of no use at all. You know this yourself."

In saying these things, the Master had spoken exactly what I was sensing. I was like a small child who had learned to take a few steps, but who wouldn't get far before landing on his little butt again.

The evening was magnificent, filled with immense beauty. Soft light combed the landscape like gentle fingers, caressing the trees, plants, and stones before withdrawing. The shadows became longer, offering a silent lullaby escorting nature to sleep. Something magical was happening during this entry into the world of night. My surroundings were continuously reaching out and touching me, moving me in the most intimate way.

The Master and I sat for a long while facing the dancing flames of the fire, talking late into the night. Shortly before we lay down to sleep, he asked me casually whether I would join him on a long trip. He was unceremonious. He said he wanted to visit some friends. I had assumed that the Master spent his life completely alone and knew no one. His suggestion surprised me so much that I gulped unintentionally and began coughing. Once again he had toppled another of my assumptions. Now my brain began to think rapidly, searching for a logical explanation. Originally I had not planned to spend more than three weeks here. It had already been much longer. I had been here for more than two months.

"How long would we be traveling?" I asked him timidly.

"I can't say exactly," he answered. "I am sure I will be gone several months, perhaps a whole year. I know you'll have to think about it. Sleep with this question, and give me your answer in the morning."

SHADOWS OVER PARADISE

That evening, I had a strange dream. A small girl and boy took me by the hand and led me up a steep mountain. We stopped at the top, and as we stood there, the two pointed up to the sky, directly at the sun that was beating down on us. I looked up through the blinding light and could decipher a person. His being was pure light. His face shone more brightly than the sun itself. His saintly body was the expression of majesty, the glory and invincibility of the entire divine universe. A mere thought arising in his mind could send ripples across all the oceans of the world. After this powerful glimpse, we descended again, the boy and girl skipping along, laughing innocently until we finally arrived at the threshold of the cave.

When I awoke, I found myself again nestled into my sleeping spot on the ground. It was already light outside … how could that be? I had laid down just a moment before.

The Master was sitting nearby with the old bag in his hand that I had always seen back in the corner of the cave. I had often asked myself what might be inside. Now I got my answer. The Master opened it. I leaned over and looked inside. The bag was empty.

What was he keeping it for then?

He turned to me, amused. The bag didn't belong to

him, he explained. Even the dishes and utensils were in the cave before he came there many years ago. He owned absolutely nothing, and nothing owned him. He seemed to enjoy telling me this.

"I would gladly join you on your journey," I said.

I was a bit shocked at how suddenly the words flew out of my mouth. I hadn't knowingly decided anything yet. Something deeper had made the decision and put it into words.

"Very good. Then let's go right away," he responded.

I hadn't expected that. I had assumed we would be leaving in a few days. But I had become accustomed to having my assumptions turned upside-down when the Master was involved. His spontaneity was extraordinary. This natural way of doing things was intense and penetrating, in complete contrast to the rigid mental preparation I was used to. We set off.

The valley was still covered with shadows as we moved deeper into the mountain wilderness. The Master had explained that we wanted to arrive at an ancient temple that night, a place where unusual things were said to have occurred.

The immaculate gleam of perpetual snow atop the mountain peaks was purifying. But our path was long and grueling, leading us over many stony cliffs. The Master slowed the pace so that I could follow him. He was barefoot but easily moved past every obstacle without the slightest injury. The soles of his feet were tougher than the soles of my shoes!

In the late afternoon, we came into a valley. A shallow stream flowed through it, and high rock walls lined both sides. The stone layers of these massive uplifted rock formations were exposed and jagged, weather-beaten over thousands of years. Suddenly, a deafening thunderous groan sounded from above, leaving me quivering in my tracks. Apprehensively, I looked up at the cloudless sky. Avalanche!

At that moment I felt the Master reaching for my hand. The next instant, we were standing five hundred yards farther along the trail. Piles of stone more than ten feet high now covered the place where we had been standing.

It took a while for me to comprehend what had happened. My whole body was shaking. It was gradually apparent to me that the Master had just saved my life. Horrified, I looked back. Without the Master's help, I would be back there in a deep grave.

"How could we have gone such a distance from one moment to the next? How is that possible? I don't understand." My voice was shaky. I was falling apart.

The Master answered me with unwavering calm. "In such instants, one has to apply a higher principle, which overtakes lower ones and eliminates them. The vibration is then raised to a very intense level, more intense than that of the physical body weighted down against gravity. When your spirit is completely unbound, each thought moves faster than light and has the power of a volcano.

"God's creative force is unlimited. No human eye could have seen this movement. What we experienced took place outside time. Normal human awareness, with its limited instruments of perception, belongs to the lower principle. In this case it was completely overtaken by the higher law. Space, with its barriers, was dissolved."

But how does one attain such transcendent capabilities? That was what I wanted to know. I was awestruck, completely blown away by what had happened. I would never have believed that something like that could actually be experienced.

The Master continued, "The true person is limitless, free of boundaries, one with divine awareness. What you just experienced is possible for each person. You only have to overcome your inner barriers and limitations completely and come to live in pure light. You know, the word impossible belongs to the lower principle, to the weight of death. Here, one is trapped; one is a prisoner.

"In the higher, divine law of light, the word impossible doesn't exist, because within this principle all creative powers and possibilities are unlimited and accessible. Absolutely everything is possible." I could feel the care he felt for me as he spoke.

"I thank you. You saved my life! Without you I would be dead, squashed and buried under a million stones!"

"True life is deathless. You cannot keep life, nor lose it. The body is born and then fades away again, but the true life-essence remains completely untouched by this coming and going. There are people who have purified every cell in the body. When the time comes for them to leave the earthly plane, they bring that physical body with them. This is also possible. In all cases, it depends on how one wants to shape one's own God-given life. The state of death belongs to the lower principle."

"A moment ago, I temporarily untied the bonds of energy holding you to destiny, bonds that belong to the lower principle. Because I raised up the vibration, these forces lost their power over you. By doing this, I was able to prevent you from having to abandon your body prematurely."

I was astonished. Clearly I should have been dead. Not so long ago, I had looked death in the eye up on the mountain. But I could see in this moment how tightly I still clung to my body and to everything connected with it. I knew that it was ephemeral, but still I clung with my full will. Over time I had come to the awareness that this clinging was an inner mental state that actually had nothing to do with the body. As a personality, I inhabited this body of flesh and blood. I used it to express myself on the earthly plane, so that I could be active. And it was just these actions, each and every one of them up until this moment, that I now doubted. My life appeared to be so superficial and silly. I had no guidelines to help me work through the question I held now; I wanted to know the significance of my existence in its true expression. Until this moment I had always managed easily to avoid the matter.

The Master could sense my uncertainty. "You are trapped in the old law again, lost in the superstitions of mortality, of coming and going. Look how your thoughts fall into line with the idea of destruction, and you see exactly what you think. What you think: that is what you live. Remember the words of Master Jesus: 'He who wants to keep his life shall lose it, and he who loses his life in my name, he will live.' To say this another way: he who believes in death, in coming and going, he who clasps on to these superstitions, will die. He who gives his life over to the light of God will live forever."

The Master had shown me what it meant to overcome the lower mandate with the higher mandate of God. His demonstration penetrated deeply, and it was clear that this way is available and possible for all who patiently dedicate themselves to this eternal divine life. He was expressing this divine law in its full breadth and was showing me that it was only thoughts that separated us. His simplicity and naturalness impressed me all the more.

"Come," he said, "we want to keep going. Otherwise we won't make it to the temple before it gets dark."

A thick blanket of clouds covered the sky as we hiked up the narrow path. High above us I saw the small temple, which was built along the steep edge of the valley. Just as we arrived, rain began to fall.

"Gaya, are you there?" called the Master. His voice reverberated throughout the temple.

A voice responded, "Master, it's you!"

A woman with youthful energy wearing a long ocher-colored robe stepped out of one of the neighboring rooms and approached. She greeted us with radiant eyes and folded hands. She then put a reverential garland of bright flowers around the Master's neck, their gentle fragrance filling the entire room.

As the evening progressed, I understood that Gaya was a longtime student of his. She lived in the temple in complete solitude. She told me how she loved the silence and purity there. She seemed to anticipate my questions and described for me the conditions of her life. She told me of a small village, four hours away by foot, where she would go once a month to buy goods and see friends. She told me also that no one knows how old the temple is, and no one knows who founded it.

We entered the small room where she lived, which

was very modest. It appeared that she had very few possessions. A small butter-fueled lamp emitted a faint light. Yet the extraordinary vibration I felt as I entered was vital and luminous. I was shifted into a meditative state almost instantly. Time did not exist. It was difficult to even raise a thought in this place where the deeply spiritual atmosphere held reign; there was no room for the intellect here.

The Master lay down to rest, as did I. Soon I was fast asleep.

It was pouring rain when I awoke the next morning. A dim melancholic mood had descended upon the region. The clouds hung low and clung to the mountains. It was cool outside, and everything was damp.

Gaya brought a cup of hot tea, which warmed me. I took a look around but could not find the Master.

"He has gone off for a couple of days. He has asked me to look after you until he returns," she said, smiling.

"Where did he want to go in this weather?" I asked. But she couldn't answer. The Master had simply said good-bye and left.

As the morning passed, I asked Gaya how long she had known the Master. "Two hundred years," she answered. I was certain I had not heard correctly.

"Two hundred years" was again her answer after my second questioning. She grinned as she added that she herself was no less than 112 years young.

It was impossible. I had estimated that she was fifty. Gaya seemed to take pleasure in my utter disbelief. She laughed and tried to help me understand. "Where the soul orients itself is where it expresses itself. True life has no age. Even the body, which is subject to the laws of change, is deathless. When you free yourself from the idea of being captive to your physical form, the aging process slows down. It can even be brought to a complete halt.

"Those who live completely in this most eminent divine energy vibrate at a very elevated level. This speeds up the chemical processes in the body, inactivating the tendencies of solidification and accumulation. This is not a goal. This is simply a characteristic of the way of liberation.

"There are masters who are so completely united with the divine light that the aging process of the body is eliminated. Their being is this light: pure, unchanging, and unending. Each cell, each atom of their physical existence, expresses the eternal majesty of God. The Master's teacher is one of these realized beings."

My ears pricked up. "Have you also met the teacher of the Master?" I asked. This was exciting.

She had not yet seen him, but she knew he lived somewhere in these interminable mountains. "You can't find him," she told me. "He calls you." There was great reverence in her tone of voice.

We stood in front of the temple under the eaves. Outside it continued to rain. Water trickled down lightly from the three magnificent trees in front of us, gently falling from the tips of the leaves and seeping into the earth. Silently, with great sensitivity, I observed the natural world around me. I was absorbed in a timeless gaze where the seen was untainted by thinking. Silence, vast and limitless, had swallowed me.

But it wasn't long before an unintentional inner impulse reactivated the thinking process. Instantly, the undivided clear perception I had experienced was dispersed and scattered. Again, dark shadows encroached on my paradise.

Suddenly I recognized something: There is no outside and no inside. Nothing is separated. The internal creates the external, and the external forms the internal again in a continuous rotation. This was the game I was playing. The movements of my thoughts determined everything. They formed the internal, and from there the shape of the external appeared. This constant back-and-forth routine had marked my entire life. Further, this disastrous drama directed by the senses had been on stage for thousands of years. I saw how the external formed my internal world, how the inner activity shaped all the life-forms of my external world. In this closed circle of movement I saw the cause of my attachments and confusion. I had created a horrifying penitentiary for myself.

An overwhelming feeling of helplessness now consumed me. I could not imagine how I could possibly escape this vicious cycle.

But the Master and Gaya were my proof that it was possible. They had burned away all that clung to time and space. I couldn't linger in doubt. I had to witness and penetrate this process of incarceration and then rescue myself from its control. This was the reason for my being, the meaning of my life on this planet Earth. In that moment I could see the state of indifference I had sunk into, and the recognition was painful, almost unbearable. What had I been doing all these years? I had been basking in superficiality and egoism for too long. I had become a dullard!

It was now dawning on me for the first time that I had no idea what true life was. I had no idea how to live freely, to be receptive to life's immeasurable beauty and intensity. At the same time a deep feeling of gratitude emerged. I was thankful for the Master and Gaya, and I was thankful for the spiritual forces that had guided me to them.

Gaya and I sat in a large round room inside the temple. Except for the rugs and cushions that covered the floor, the space was empty. Small openings in the walls invited a gentle light that illumined the room.

"This is the Temple of Light. Many siddhas have lived here, and others seeking God. When you enter this timeless silence totally, you will hear the heartbeat of the universe." Gaya's words echoed within me.

Quietly, with half-closed eyes, we sat and immersed ourselves in the infinite. At times I would glance over with amazement at Gaya. She sat in perfect lotus posture, completely relaxed, every muscle and nerve suffused with perpetual calm. An enormous energy radiated from her.

Then, the endless stream of light took hold of me. The gate to the inner universe stood wide open. The limitations of ephemeral consciousness dissolved. My soul experienced a "close-up" of the ultimate, the absolute. What I felt was so powerful, so sublime, that words could neither name nor describe it.

It was not an inner point or place I had arrived at. It was not a state. It was not a perception. I could only label it as "IT": "IT," in a particular sense, or "THAT"? "God" might do, but no, "God" is also only a word.

But I was thrown again into the world of desires by a confusing urge to hold on to THAT, to not lose IT again. I recognized that a huge inner process of transformation had to take place for me to free myself of all the concepts and images I was holding on to and allow THAT to be, and only THAT. A burning pain tore through my heart. I was so unaware, so trapped! Yet I knew that the inner realm of limitations had to be fully overcome. When that inner realm disappeared, only the eternal remained, the absolute, the ever-present THAT.

I quietly left the temple and stepped outside. It had stopped raining, and a hushed wind had opened a gap in the cloud cover, allowing the sun's rays to shine through. My legs were stiff from sitting such a long time, so I started to walk around. The temple was built just at the edge of the forest, so I had to hike up the mountain awhile before I could look down on the green valley sprawling below. It was spectacular, being surrounded by snow-covered 24,000-foot mountains towering up to the heavens, glimmering under the brilliant rays of the sun, with the broad tree-lined valley at their base. The unspoiled beauty of this place brought me into a kind of rapture, as I satiated my senses on those divine works of art.

Who is this almighty spirit who hides away, creating this space, this world of outer appearances? Who molds these shapes that inebriate my senses and delude me with their incredible charms? Where does the source of this sacred embryonic energy first arise, this force through which bodies appear and disappear?

With what outrageous incomprehensible magic has the eternal law found a body and brought about this immaculate, incomprehensible creation? What hand was it that crafted the finite from the infinite, fashioning all from such a flawless blueprint? The depths of this divine spirit were unlimited, unimaginable, unthinkable.

As I was absorbed in these poignant queries, my heart quivered. I was contemplating from a place far beyond my shallow attachments. Inspiration poured from my insides like celebratory wine.

"Isn't this a beautiful spot?" Suddenly Gaya's voice sounded from behind me.

"I can understand well how people looking for God find their way here." I replied. "It truly is a sacred place! Still, I think about how all this beauty will not always be here. It makes me sad somehow."

She took my hand gently. "Awakened souls do not grieve for the dead, or for the living. I myself was never nothing, and you were never nothing, nor were any of the souls in this world. We will never cease to be. Appearances only seem to be appearances, the transitory only seems to be transitory, for the eternal truth is always true and is always unstained by passing images.

"When you become completely unmoved by objects, by others, you will recognize the source that produces these thoughts. When your own physical form appears illusory to you, you will learn to let go of yourself too. When the soul awakens, it is blind to all the delusions of the flesh."

We remained sitting in silence on a large boulder while above our heads night softly enclosed the heavens.

When we were together again that evening, I told Gaya about my life and my project of writing a book about a master who lived in the wilderness. When I told her my original plan of staying for three weeks, Gaya laughed until tears began welling up in her eyes. I couldn't help but laugh myself. Many weeks had already passed, and I had written only a few vague sentences.

My intention to make notes daily had fallen away

and become irrelevant. The Master and Gaya had opened something deeper in me, and this something now had my full attention. I wasn't going to let it slip away. I knew that in the future I would have to dedicate my life to activities very different from the superficial role-playing I'd always busied myself with in the attempt to pay dues to the social order.

At first, the simplicity with which these people lived, without any of the comforts I was used to, was appalling. But gradually I discovered their true riches; they were absolutely unattached, and they were thoroughly independent. They were free from the world on every level. They were truly human, humble and generous. There was nothing I could give them, which created a situation that I had never known before, and one that was difficult for me. It was easier for me to give than to receive.

Their souls were soaked in the light of eternal life, while mine was still held captive in the jail of a troubled conscience. In this prison of mortality, in the world in which I was stuck, my deepest inner voice was screaming out for light. I had to abandon this cave of inertia! I was literally torn between light and darkness. Damaged, crippled, bleeding with countless open wounds, my soul yearned for healing.

The next day, Gaya showed me some of the wonderful carpets she had woven with her gifted hands. She took the articles she made to the nearest village to exchange for food supplies.

The weather was bright and beautiful, and we went off on a long walk. We came upon an area where I could smell goats, but no animals were to be seen. Gaya told me about the local shepherds. She said they were often gone for weeks with their flocks. Some of these lonely wanderers were, without knowing it, on a deep spiritual path, distinguished by their simplicity, honesty, and friendliness.

After we returned, I spent some time alone in the Temple of Light while Gaya collected herbs in the forest. She had encouraged me to spend as much time within the high vibration of the temple as possible.

This place seemed to me like an invisible window to the eternal world of light. As I inquired more deeply, I eventually came to the insight that this perception originated within myself, that the Temple of Light was only the outer equivalent of my inner state. It was only a reflection. And within me was also the threshold where form dissolved into formlessness. The silent truth of this light was the unlimited inner Self. The outer physical form was only shadow.

The longer I sat, the more absorbed I became, and I could see something else more clearly. I had a goal here. I was after something. With my will I was eagerly trying to create a spiritual result. I was bent on attaining something that was inaccessible. There was no path from the world of time into the world of the timeless.

I awoke to another painful fact: the insights I experienced did not come without leaving traces. A subtle pride was growing within me. This sobering observation felt like a severe blow on my backside. I was back at the beginning again, as ignorant as ever.

At this point I figured it would probably be best to just go home and keep this trip a pleasant memory. I wasn't ripe, or perhaps just not cut out for the path of liberation they wanted to show me. I was chagrined that there in the Temple of Light, where I held such high hopes, only this disappointing fact would come to light … I decided it was time to leave.

I didn't know how I would explain myself to the Master and Gaya. I decided to wait until the Master returned. I felt miserable and ashamed as I lay down to sleep early that night. Gaya had noticed my dejected mood and could sense that I didn't want to talk about what was bothering me.

In the morning, when I woke up, the Master was already there. He greeted me with a ripe piece of fruit. He peeled it carefully and placed it in my hand. I told him I would like to share it with him and Gaya. But he let me know that he had brought it just for me.

"What can I offer you? Is there anything at all I can do for you?" The words leaped out of my mouth. But he just smiled. He remained sitting silently in front of me.

During all my time in these mountains, I had never come across such a fruit at any market. I knew it could grow only in tropical regions where the land is flat. Yet it seemed to be fresh off the branch, incredibly sweet and juicy. Where did he come up with that? I wanted to know, but I didn't yet dare to ask.

"Did the Temple of Light speak to you?" the Master asked. The question took me by surprise. How should I tell him about my intention to end my travels?

"Yes," I said. "It spoke very deeply to me. And I must tell you of a decision I have made. I must …" I couldn't finish my sentence. In the blink of an eye my tongue and voice were rendered mute and useless. I tried again and again, but to no avail. Not another word crossed my lips.

"The dialogue with the Temple of Light has obviously been a deep one," said the Master as he smiled. "Divine light always shatters the 'I.' That is the only way a great inner transformation is at all possible. The Earth is the dark valley that stands before the light. In order to know the light, you must diligently work to release the darkness. Don't hold to one spot. But stay aligned with the indestructible source, the source of the all-embracing wisdom and invincible power of God. The soul can only grow, literally, after it has been disillusioned."

He stood up and went to Gaya to help her with the preparations for our meal. Once again he had known exactly what was going on inside me. And again he had said just the right words at the right moment, words that went straight to the heart. Now there was some higher power active within me that had prevented me from voicing my resolution to go home. And I was at a loss as to how this was happening.

Any residual thoughts of ending my trip soon vanished. I stood and went over to talk to the two of them. Gaya began to sing a song in Sanskrit. Although I couldn't understand the meaning of the words, I could feel the power living inside her. It was a hymn praising the highest divinity, praising the light that takes away all darkness, the light that transports the soul from ignorance to wisdom, from mortality to immortality. After the Master explained this to me, he joined in the singing. Soon the pure energy of these two souls giving vibration to these potent words filled the whole room and then expanded outward in waves over the entire region, penetrating everything, elevating everything, blessing everything.

The Master tapped on his thigh with his right hand to

intensify the rhythm even more. Their shimmering eyes and smiling faces mirrored the energy contained in the lyrics, which were no longer separate from the singers. They had merged completely with the song. The ambience that permeated the room was incredible.

After the meal, the Master told me that we would be traveling again soon. He asked Gaya if she wanted to continue on with us. She seemed less surprised by this suggestion than I was. I had heard from her own lips that she had not left the temple in the past twelve years, except for her monthly visit to the neighboring village. This was the moment I noticed how deeply she already lived within my heart, and that I dearly wanted her to say "Yes." But I held myself back from saying anything. It was not appropriate to try to influence her with my personal wishes. She would make the right decision on her own.

She remained sitting peacefully. Had she even heard the invitation from the Master? I was anxious to hear her answer, but she wasn't showing the slightest reaction. She finally got up and moved to where she could clean the eating utensils. The Master proceeded into the main temple room.

I had expected an immediate response from Gaya. But both she and the Master behaved very differently in this situation than I would have expected based on my everyday life. Their way of communicating was incomprehensible to me. I went into the main temple room and, finding the Master there, seated myself next to him.

I was sad. To me, Gaya's silence meant that she wasn't going to be able to come with us. "Why are you unhappy?" the Master asked. I told him my feelings, and also that I couldn't understand why Gaya wouldn't answer or speak at all.

"She answered from the silent depths of her soul. Didn't you hear it? She will come with us," said the Master.

A wave of joy flooded my being. Still, a response that sprang from the silence of the soul was bewildering. I asked the Master to say more about it.

"When the soul is freed from its limitations, then it is one with the mind. All misunderstandings rooted in duality are absent, so the idea of 'your soul' and 'my soul' doesn't exist. There is only the one divine mind, which inhabits every soul, which is everything.

"The person who has awakened the mind is fully receptive to everything divine, and is completely unreceptive to the dark and evil-spirited, the hell-realm of egomania.

"Every thought is an impulse. It contains a power filled with a particular purpose. It is a vibration, a wave that moves toward the person receiving it with great speed. If one has the necessary sensitivity and openness, he can receive the images and information sent to him with ease. He can read them and understand them. This kind of communication doesn't depend on proximity.

"This is how I stay in contact with certain people in this vast mountain area. There is no place here for chatter. Silence reigns. But this deep silence is also dynamic. We who live here are continuously connected to each other in divine light.

"A word is a very powerful creative energy that expresses the will of God. We are very aware and careful in how we use this gift of using words, because what we create is what we are.

"The choice of words offered from a pure soul reflects the clear and noble state of its consciousness. On this level, we are fully aware of the great responsibility for the spoken word and its enormous power. Spoken words can start world wars, or they can bring world peace. They can destroy, and they can heal. When the soul vibrates in its utmost purity, when it is clear, unattached, and illuminated, then words can be filled with the absolute power of God. They become uninterrupted revelation, the fulfilled glory of a radiant mind.

"Those who give themselves completely to the divine don't act with their own purposes. Thus they have no good or bad intentions. They work through the light, with the light, and for the one who lights the light.

"Awareness is the most important thing. You should never forget this. To understand really means to understand without being caught on the one who understands. The sweet-talking voices of delusion try to put those people looking for God under the spell of comings and goings. Stay awake and uncover all delusions with the power of the inner-dwelling universal light of God.

"The 'un-manifest' lives within you. Don't look for it. You already are it. Mindfully peel away everything that is temporary and limits you. Separate out these delusive mind states, because they are the house in which death dwells. Insight and intuition are the necessary instruments for accomplishing this.

"What I am explaining to you is no theory. Theories are absolutely useless. Knowledge and memory belong to the dualistic world of death, with all its temptations and illusions. Life in the light of God means to drink constantly from the bottomless source of the spirit. Life is a tremendous journey of discovery, full of beauty and power. The whole meaning of our lives is held right here, in the journey. You came to me as a dead man. You will go home as a man who is truly alive. Come now, let's go to Gaya."

As we stood up, I thanked him for his words. But the last sentence he had said, that I had come as a dead man, troubled me.

Gaya was sitting in the small kitchen sorting out medicinal herbs. We sat down next to her and offered to help. "I am happy that you are coming with us," I said to her.

She nodded. "It is the right time for me to leave this place again. But I would like to visit the village and tell my friends I will be away for a while. Otherwise they will worry unnecessarily." The Master nodded in agreement and said he thought that was a good idea.

The next morning we began our descent down the trail. Slow-moving layers of fog crept across the valley. The small village appeared almost empty as we arrived. But before long some of the locals stepped out onto the lone street, greeting us with bows and folded hands.

We came to a large house in the middle of the village. As we neared the entryway, we found a cow standing there, tied with ropes to a pole. Its calf was lying next to it on a bed of straw. The small animal was terrified, staring at us with fright-filled eyes. Gaya went over to it right away and gently stroked its head.

A middle-aged woman came out of the house and greeted us cheerfully. She had hardly said a word to us when a flood of children came running out of the house and zealously grabbed on to Gaya. They were obviously old acquaintances.

We sat down to tea under the pale light inside the hut. Gaya gave our hosts some instructions. She unrolled a cloth on the ground and laid out a variety of healing herbs, which were to be distributed to certain people in the village.

The hosts listened intently. They also asked Gaya questions. Evidently, she came to the village not only to shop. She was a healer and counselor as well.

SEARCH FOR YOUR "YOU"

We left the village, and by late afternoon we had made our way through much of a sparsely wooded valley, walking over earth covered with heavy grass. As evening neared, we came upon an empty hut where we were to spend the night.

The room heated up soon after we entered, just as a ray of sun quickly brings warmth to a place cooled from having been in shadow. This confused me. It was pleasantly warm in the hut, even though an icy wind was blowing in through the cracks in the walls. I looked over at the Master, trying to figure out what was happening. It was immediately clear to me that it was he who, with full awareness, was regulating the temperature.

He laughed. "Don't you remember your bath up in the mountains, in the lake? What you think is what you become." He said nothing more. I was aware that he had implemented a higher principle but knew he didn't want to talk further about it.

I fell into a state of deep contemplation. In order to survive within this immensity of nature, in the face of its tremendous power, one needs an enormous individual power as well. Otherwise one would be crushed by imposing worldly forces. Hidden within the hermetic loneliness of these peaks were the gates leading to the divine.

From era to era, epoch to epoch, these huge masses of stone were always present, immovable and imperturbable. The plateaus and valleys below were available to human beings, offering a place of refuge, a sanctuary where they could experience intimacy with the powers dwelling within themselves.

Destined to search, humans have been driven by a predetermined purpose to their own boundaries, so they could clearly recognize those limitations and overcome them. It is the intensity of this ancient recollection that compels humans with primal force back into the beginningless, eternal landscape of the soul. The silent caress of the eternal allows one to recognize a true relationship with the divine. Now it was more apparent to me just how important it is to completely overcome the self.

Allowing these thoughts to flow within my mind, I experienced the marvelous energy felt when the soul is born in boundless light. Here, my eyes bowed their gaze to the eternal flow, delighting in the radiance of the inner world. The infinite had taken hold of me and was expressing itself through me. I was drinking from the source of life. For the first time I felt the stream of white light within.

We traveled for several days, eventually traversing a pass and entering a broad green flatland. Looking ahead, we could see a large village centered among diffused green fields. My senses delighted in the peaceful scenario as we approached. There were splendid deciduous trees, colorful fruit trees with branches spread wide to display their delectable confections, and villagers bent over at work in the abundant rice fields.

The Master spoke to me. "There is an important destination for pilgrims nearby. Many people have visited there over the centuries. We'll go there later. First I have a few things to do in the village."

We were not far from the edge of the village, stomping through a meadow with high grass, when suddenly a snake shot its head up right in front of us. It was hissing and poised to attack. Paralyzed with fear, I stood like a stone, my feet rooted in place. Gaya was also frightened for a moment, but shook off the abrupt tension of the situation in a few seconds. The Master remained as tranquil as ever. He was not intimidated for even an instant. Apparently he had overcome fear at every level.

We stood motionless facing the serpent. It didn't move away.

"Don't kill it," the Master said to me.

What did he mean? All I wanted to do was start running in the other direction! The only thing holding me back was my paralyzing fear, believing that the snake would attack if I moved in the slightest way.

We remained stationary for a long time in this silent face-off. Gradually the fear that had gripped me subsided. I regained my composure. And I could now see from direct experience the enormous power of fear, how it had taken hold of my consciousness and nervous system and left me incapable of functioning.

What was I so afraid of? A snakebite that might kill my body? Or was it simply the strangeness of the situation?

In spite of these observations, I couldn't convince myself to let go of all vestiges of fear. I knew I had to understand its power more deeply, a power that didn't belong to my essential spirit, but one that certainly still clung to my being. I hoped the Master would let me ask about it as soon as we were freed from this situation.

I noticed something altering within me. The longer I looked at the snake, the more the antagonistic feeling, the aversion that was so ingrained in my being, dropped away. It dawned on me now what the Master had meant when he said, "Don't kill it."

And then something unbelievable happened. The Master approached the snake. Even though it remained steadily concentrated in its aggressive posture, he went right up to it and began to pet it gently on the head. Then he spoke to it in a very soft voice. I couldn't believe what my eyes were seeing. How could this be? Soon the snake retreated under a bush, and the Master walked back to us. He must have hypnotized the snake; otherwise, it would have bitten one of us. At least that is what I thought.

"You are pale," the Master said to me and laughed. "Your own fear got the best of you. Your fear is the true poisonous snake, which kills you over and over again. Your fear of losing your life, your holding tightly to the belief that YOU are the body--that is your big mistake. The spirit lives in the body, but the body doesn't live in the spirit! Live in accord with the divine and you will see that fear is hollow and without substance."

"Did you hypnotize the snake?" I wanted to know.

"Absolutely not! The snake saw no enemy, and I saw none in it. Love undivided, complete respect for all creatures--that is the higher principle. Don't kill, whether in thoughts or feelings or actions. If you cultivate yourself in this way, immeasurable beauty and boundless creativity will be revealed to you."

As we continued down the trail, the farmers in the fields waved to us. Many townsfolk were waiting as we entered the village, offering tea and gifts of food. As a symbol of hospitality, they laid garlands of fresh flowers around our necks. Obviously, they were acquainted with the Master.

We were brought to a large guesthouse and offered spacious rooms. Our bedding was already laid out. A pitcher of fresh water and a bowl filled with ripe fruit had set out on a table for us.

A young man, whose job it was to look after new arrivals, asked me to come with him. He led me through the garden behind the house and proudly showed me a building with a large open room inside. The sweet aroma of incense filled the air. The boy explained to me in an animated voice that the Master would speak there tomorrow. He would perform healings for the sick and ailing. The Master himself had been here a few days earlier to announce our coming.

I asked the boy if he could be mistaken in saying that the Master had been there "a few days earlier." I thought this might be just his manner of speaking. But the boy assured me that what he said was true. We had been traveling for more than a week to get here. But I was being told that he was here only three days ago. Once again, I was confused.

By late afternoon the women of the village had finished the food preparations. They provided us and the rest of the community with a humble but tasty meal served on banana leaves.

In the evening, each small space in the large room had a body filling it. All the inhabitants of the village were there, sitting pressed up against one another, the women on the left, the men to the right.

The Master gave a talk. He spoke about the meaning of sharing, about harmony in the community, and the importance of integrating diverse energies within a group. He explained that one should not cling to material possessions, which are to be utilized by us only so that we can learn more deeply. He pointed out the underlying nonreality of objects, the transience of material things, and the immortality of the true person.

Respect for all creation is respect for the Creator, and this implies the holy mandate: love the one next to you as you love yourself.

He reminded us that God's quiet mind is itself emptiness. Here all things unknown to the intellect are revealed. Right here in the unconscious is where the eyes should be looking. Behind the known is the unknown: God's reality.

The voice of the soul--which awakens, which rises up, which penetrates all darkness--is the path leading to the eternal. Fixing our gaze constantly on our own selfish ambitions is the way of death.

Finally the Master asked us to dedicate ourselves completely to the path of divine justice and to live a wholesome, God-pleasing life, as this is the only way to know true being, eternal and boundless.

We were all moved deeply by these words. Everyone could feel the importance and depth of the Master's teaching and what meaning it held for our lives. The great power emanating from the Master had raised the whole community to a new dimension, as if we were riding on wings of light,

Afterward people asked questions, and the Master gave a thorough answer to each person who approached him. Then someone brought out a harmonium. Devotional singing went on for hours. Wonderful voices offered themselves deep into the night. The Master and Gaya knew all the lyrics and contributed with great joy and enthusiasm. Obviously the Master loved this singing.

It was very late when people finally made their way home. The many children who had fallen asleep hours before were carried back to their dwellings in their parents' arms.

When I returned to my room, I lay down on my mat and gazed out the open window at the star-filled sky. I couldn't recall any time in my whole life when I had felt so happy and fulfilled.

The following day I sat near the Master and Gaya as they took their place in the hall. The line of people coming to see the Master seemed endless. They came either to be healed or to ask advice. There were women with their children, frail elderly folks, and many young people whom the Master supported in word and action. It was fascinating to watch how he healed people. He rarely touched anyone. His hands passed over certain parts of the body, always at a distance of about fifteen inches.

The transfer of energy in each encounter was brief but intense, and the effects were immediately perceptible. The Master spoke to me at times. "Healing is the blessing of the soul," he said. "When divine light is present, the soul reacts harmoniously. This is how the higher principle is set in motion. This is where our inner-dwelling powers of regeneration and healing are activated, and where these processes can take place on every possible level. A true healing and complete recovery can take place only when this happens.

"Illness, rightly understood, holds within it a deep learning process. One doesn't take illness away from people. One makes them aware of its essence. This supporting energy helps them to recognize and understand very thoroughly, so they can experience an inner transformation."

Later in the afternoon, when all had left the hall, an elderly couple entered. The man was crippled, having the use of only one leg.

The Master listened for a long time as the two aged village dwellers spoke. One could tell that they had not had an easy life. The man's handicap was the result of an accident. The Master asked him to put his leg up. He then knelt in front of the man and laid both hands on the badly damaged leg, closing his eyes.

The Master spoke a prayer in a very soft voice, using words that I couldn't understand. Then something inexplicable happened. I saw how the leg of the man began to change while beneath the hands of the Master. Gradually, the limb returned to its original healthy form.

The old man had kept his eyes closed. He was apparently asleep and had not even noticed what had happened to him. His wife, however, had experienced the healing and began to sing out the name of God. Her voice trembled, and tears of gratitude flowed over her cheeks.

The singing of his wife awoke the old man, and as he opened his eyes and saw what had happened, he threw himself down at the feet of the Master. Overwhelmed, he could not utter a single word. He reached down to touch his leg again and again with both hands. He stood up and walked around the room without difficulty and without a stick! Supreme gratitude brought the man repeatedly to the Master's feet, though the Master helped the man to realize that he should be thanking God instead.

After the two elders had left the hall, the Master explained to me that the last karmic traces clinging to the man had been removed. He said that both people had lived long and profoundly religious lives.

That evening also marked a turning point in my life. The Master turned toward me, put his hand on my forehead, and spoke. "Healing is blessing. Blessing is awakening."

Then my whole body began to vibrate and radiate, as if the power of the sun was expanding from within. I was submerged in a sea of light and serenity. Every cell of my body disappeared and merged with the infinite. Only after several moments did I emerge again in a physical condition, in the world of clearly defined forms.

In silent awe, I sat and looked at the setting around me. I had an odd feeling, as if I had landed on a strange planet. The threshold where boundaries and the boundless converge had melted away.

The absolute power of the spirit had ripped away a mask. I had witnessed the spirit in its unadorned sparkling brilliance, like a star exposing itself on a dark night. The supernatural gateway to God had opened for an instant, and for a brief moment I could distinguish the origin of all things and the hidden energy that permeated them.

I had not yet overcome my earthly constraints, but the power of God had altered my being and taken its hold. I would have to pull away completely from the embrace of the transient world and travel along the river of the soul in this territory of the highest infinite bliss. I knew now very clearly from deep experience what the Master meant when he spoke about a higher principle that canceled and eradicated the lower principle.

With a strange sense of certainty, I knew that I had embarked on an endless journey from which there would be no turning back.

The Master touched my hand softly and repeated the words, "Healing is blessing. Blessing is awakening." Only at that moment could I even begin to fathom the depths of these short phrases. He had bestowed upon me a deep healing and true blessing. I felt in my deepest inner being that a meaningful transformation had taken place, though in exactly what measure I could not yet comprehend.

The Master was ready to lend a hand when I needed to stand up. I staggered like a drunkard at first. It took some time before I could coordinate the movements of my body again. We walked about for a short while. I discovered that the village was not as big as I had imagined, for very soon we found ourselves at the other end. The villagers we met treated us as if we had always belonged to their community.

On the way back a farmer approached us. He was the man whose leg had been healed through the facilitation of the Master. He asked us to make a short visit to his stalls. One of his cows was sick. The attitude of selfless assistance exhibited by the Master had no limits. We entered the small stall. The cow was lying next to the door with her calf nearby. She looked up at us, her large eyes filled with doubt and fear. The Master knelt down next to her and immediately put her head on his lap, grasping her below the throat. He then put his hands directly over her heart.

The Master spoke to the farmer. "She had a short period of weakness, but she will be healthy again. She will live a few more years." The words pacified the old man. The Master left his hands resting on the cow's heart for a long time. Suddenly the cow stood up, let out a loud Moooo, and began to stroke her calf affectionately with her tongue

The farmer beamed with joy. He invited us to return with him to his modest quarters. There we met his adult children. All were speechless when they saw their father walk into the house without a stick. They expressed their gratitude to the Master, both for his words and for his inner guidance. One of the daughters proudly showed us her three small children, opening a curtain behind which they lay sleeping.

I was continually amazed by the Master and the way in which he encountered each living being in such a humble, uncomplicated, loving manner. He treated each person, each animal, and the entire natural world with the same gentle care, the same unconditional compassion.

I had to laugh at myself as I remembered those first days spent with him. How thoughtful and uncompromising he had been with me! And I, who could hardly tolerate him for a minute, had wanted to run away! He had thrown me back upon myself from the first moment of our encounter. I had to face my arrogance, my hatred, and my doubts, and I had to bring an end to them myself. He didn't do it for me, nor did he meddle in the process. But he never neglected an opportunity to lead me along the course of direct experience. He was able to guide me patiently along this inner path of liberation in a most uncommon, remarkable manner.

In listening to the conversation with the farmer, I learned that the Master visited this village and others nearby each year for a few days. His stay was always a special event.

As we entered the guesthouse again, the Master immediately retreated to his quarters. Gaya and I sat together and talked awhile. I expressed my wonder at the Master's simplicity and modesty in each situation, at how he truly mastered every moment.

Gaya responded, "The Master has cultivated the power of God to a very high degree, and can apply it with unlimited capacity when he thinks it is appropriate. No one knows the full measure of his capabilities. He never speaks about it. When I asked him about these supernatural powers, he said to me, 'Beware of the deceitful beauty of the false light, which lives in the cracks of the soul. It will seduce you and bind you in sugarcoated knots. You will be tied to cravings for power and domination. The souls that follow this light become the slaves of illusion. They are damned to the lower world of demons. If you want to enter the true and pure light, close your senses off from all desires leading to manipulation and power, and end the chain of impulses that lead you to think you are something special, or that you could become someone special. Extinguish that flame inside, and the divine will manifest within, without you doing anything.' These words were a gift, a clarification that set me free at that time, and I am happy that I can share this experience with you now. I was guided to a very high level of awareness.

I became more awake, more mindful and humble. This was the first moment that I saw how numerous the dangers that lie in wait actually are. I saw what temptations threaten to distract and disturb us and take us prisoner."

I had listened very intently to Gaya's description. Her words initiated a kind of tumult within me, which only gradually settled down. The immeasurability of the universe was increasingly more apparent to me. My conscious perception of the human being as the universe itself was becoming clearer. I had never thought so deeply about these things, about how easily one can become consumed by the false light, engrossed in the seductive glimmerings of the senses and the multiplicity of subtle whisperings coming from the egocentric mind.

I had to admit that, until this time, I had almost exclusively followed this false light. But now something had changed. A new facility of discernment was opening gently within me. An inner eye perceived things in a fresh light. I felt tremendous gratitude. How marvelous it was that Gaya was traveling with us!

I remained lying in my spot for a long time. As I breathed in the ambience of the night, my thoughts wandered back to where I lived, the place I had left only months before. I thought of my friends and my work there. I felt a slight terror, noticing that weeks had passed with no thoughts arising that connected me to my earlier life. It was strange to think that that existence used to define my place in the world.

Before sunrise the next morning, the Master came to my room and seated himself next to me. Wordlessly we watched how the approaching day embraced and ultimately dissolved the darkness with its radiant light. Then he spoke to me. "It is important that we take a moment of awareness to see what is infinite and beautiful in this universe. There are thousands of galaxies with suns, stars, and planets. There is a tremendous abundance of life. In an extended curve on the outer edge of the galaxy we call the Milky Way, which even though it is one of the smaller galaxies still has billions of stars, you find the planet Earth, where we live.

"The fact that plants, animals, and human beings are born here is no coincidence. It is the deliberate impulse given by an intelligence that cannot be measured. This intelligence underlies the universe. Everything produced from the orderly, life-generating powers of Mother Time demonstrates a great plan, a divine order in which each person and each being is rooted. This plan is the principle that underlies all creation. Nothing exists merely for itself. Everything is contained within this great unity. Every being is connected and dependent on every other being.

"This universe was born, and therefore it carries the seed of its final end. But beyond this universe there is an intelligence that is so superior and flawless that human consciousness can never understand it. Humans can have only an idea of it, at best.

"When humans live in harmony with creation and the one great underlying principle, they discover the inexpressible: that which was never formed, never gathered, never separated, and never born. This is the origin of all existence.

"This origin is the source of your own being as well. You are the formable, creative, living power of God itself. From now on, always be aware of what responsibility you have toward nature--animals and plants as well as humans. Observe your thoughts, feelings, and actions. You see, you have a clear and direct influence on everything there is.

"The egoistic self and the divine Self can never meet. Before the mystical powers can make a god out of you, the self of the ego must be totally dissolved. So don't be upset about your karma. Don't worry about your fate or trying to understand the ways of the transient world. Overcome your boundaries and your limitations, and the treasure chest of divine light will open up for you by itself. Then, your heart will sparkle like a diamond in sacred sunlight. Only the eyes of the soul can look into the world of God, enter it, and unite with it. Then the spark becomes a fire."

The sun had ascended and covered the whole region with a golden hue. The Master, Gaya, and I set out to hike up a very steep mountain nearby. I was deeply absorbed in my thoughts and hardly paid attention to my laboring body as it made its way up the mountain. The perspective that had been shown to me was incredible. For the first time I experienced that the entire universe was in me, and that I was in the entire universe. This was revealed to me with an explicit clarity. I recognized that behind the visible, ever-changing universe there was an unchanging, formless universe. This was no theoretical idea. It was my direct experience, into which I had been guided with enormous energy.

The Master stopped at one point and pointed to the mountain across from us, which rose like a snow-covered pyramid up into the deep-blue sky. "On the right side, down below at the foot of the mountain, is a pilgrimage site. We will visit the place for the next few days. For centuries people have gone there to revere and worship God. Many yogis live there. The monastery, with its purity and energy, provides great support for their special exercises."

The Master continued to speak. "The strength to do good things in the world, having the competence and resolve to accomplish what one has set out to accomplish, and to do it fully, this is the way to God."

Gaya had been standing next to me. She nodded silently. The Master had spoken from his heart. When he left us for a short time to observe the unusual trees nearby, I turned to Gaya. "I sometimes have the feeling, when the Master looks at me, that he is looking right through me, at something beyond, something I can't see myself. Each time he does this something deep inside me shifts, but I can't really understand what is happening."

"Yes," said Gaya, "the Master sees what the worldly eye always fails to see. But still, this reading of the human body serves only to offer the healing support a person needs for the process of liberation. The Master looks into a person for one and only one reason: in order to transmit divine energy and insight.

"Those who have come to a place where they think with the heart and see from the eyes of the soul have also stopped creating limitations for themselves. They are cosmic human suns. The Master is pure unconditional love itself." She put special emphasis on the last sentence.

Just as the last words were spoken, the Master waved us over to him. He was standing next to a tree. He explained to us that the sap from the tree's bark contained great healing attributes. He demonstrated to Gaya how one first excuses oneself to the tree, then asks it for a few drops, and finally takes the sap without harming it.

Then he asked the tree for a small piece of bark. He took a piece and pressed some juice out of it with a stone. He then spread the resinous liquid over the place where he had taken the sap. Finally he expressed gratitude to the tree.

He looked over at us and gave a short instruction. "If you place a few drops of this on your tongue, let it mix with your saliva, and then swallow it, it will clear up any problems you have with your metabolism. The medicinal qualities of this sap are many. But we will talk about that another time."

Gaya listened carefully. She didn't miss a word and followed every movement the Master made. Her whole-hearted concentration was apparent, and I was deeply impressed.

Then the Master turned toward me. "Many millions of years before humans appeared on Earth, the trees were already here. They provide the foundation from which humans are able to survive on this planet. They produce the oxygen we inhale, and they inhale the toxins we exhale. Humans and trees are completely interdependent. Mankind is bound to this exchange, bound within the circular movement of nature. We can see that there is no individual freedom on this level, as many mistakenly believe. Trees are very vital and sensitive. We have to approach them with love and respect."

In the evening, as we returned to the village, the Master told the new assembly that we would be continuing our travels the next day. I expected that more than a few would express their disappointment. The Master had brought so much light here so quickly. Surely they would ask him to stay a few days longer. But nothing like that happened. Just as they rejoiced in his coming, the villagers celebrated his departure.

My structured Western mind with its emotionally driven thought patterns could not understand their behavior. There was a depth in this culture that seemed inaccessible to me. I didn't sense the slightest sorrow or frustration. An awareness of our short time on Earth was much more present in these people, and their attitude toward impermanence was more palpable. They seemed to embrace the fact that we are guests on this planet for only a short time before we submerge again in the unseen world. Their behavior communicated this. They never held tightly to the things of the world that come and go. They didn't pile up unnecessary things in their homes. The entire village had given me a profound lesson in how to live life.

I would have loved to stay there longer. I had already accustomed myself a bit to their simple way of life, which was sparse but not poor. Nevertheless, the Master saw to it that I had no chance to habituate myself to anything, or to cling to any place. He taught me through experience that things are always moving, that to become inactive, to come to a standstill, would mean being trapped, being a prisoner bound to the wheel of rebirth, a trek from one death to the next.

As we left the village the next morning, a large troop of men from the community accompanied us for part of the way. But soon the time came to say good-bye one more time, and we were alone again.

The weather had shifted during the night. Thick clouds were moving idly over the mountains, and it had gotten chilly. The gray mood that draped the landscape was mirrored by my own disposition. I thought to myself that we should have stayed a few more days in the village and let the bad weather pass. But the Master was unwavering. We carried on.

Gradually conditions grew even worse. Thick fog was creeping up from the valley, and soon our vision was obstructed to the point that I was convinced we couldn't go one step further. Still, the Master showed no intention of stopping. I had to concentrate single-mindedly on the ground below me in order to keep from falling. Only my deep trust in our leader allowed me to stave off fears that we had lost our way or that we might slip down a ravine. The Master did not slow his pace for a moment, although we couldn't see more than two feet in front of our noses.

I suddenly heard his voice. He was speaking to me. I could feel his strong presence, although I couldn't see him. "Pay attention to your footsteps. You are going through your inner world, through your foggy mind state. Don't lose your confidence. Keep your faith in the inner-dwelling power of the spirit that guides you. The danger of losing your way in the dense fog amid the many labyrinths within you is greater than the dangers in the outer world. The inner fog is difficult to perceive. It keeps you lazy. So, be bright and clear inside. Then it will also be bright and clear outside. Do you understand what I am saying?"

I pulled myself together and let his words sink in. Then, suddenly, I was able to understand what the Master was really trying to say. Although I could not see him, I was truly following him blindly. I had complete trust in him and none in myself. This weakened me and had led me into an undesired dependence. I hadn't assumed any true responsibility for my actions. Until this moment, I was convinced that I had been perfectly aware of all my responsibilities. Now the superficiality and self-centeredness with which I had constructed my life were painfully obvious.

Once again the Master had guided me to an experience that deeply clarified my thought process and realigned me within. More profoundly than ever before, I saw how tremendously important personal responsibility is.

Instantaneously, the fog outside disappeared. It was as if a mysterious hand had swept it away. Heavy rain clouds still hovered above. We stopped to spend the night outdoors, under an overhanging rock face. Soon a warm fire was blazing at the base of the huge stone.

The Master offered another explanation to me. "Nature is a step on the majestic ladder of being. In the direct experience of beauty, the heart is offered the gifts of energy, joy, and insight into the wondrous and blissful realm of the one God. All that is seen is the prayer of the unseen. The natural world is the subtle harmony of the unseen manifested by spiritual light, a powerful revelation of the deathless.

"Nevertheless, everything that comes together disperses again. The inner-lying principle works this way."

The fire rose up for a moment, and the next gust of wind blew it out. In a gentle solemn tone, the Master continued to speak. "Just as the flame was put out by the wind and disappeared without a trace, the one who is truly free disappears and is impossible to find. Now, does one who is liberated cease to exist, or does he continue to live eternally?"

The question was addressed to me, but I was incapable of an answer. After a slight pause, the Master continued. "When all elements of the limited ever-changing individual being are completely overcome and dissolved, then all attempts at description are also extinguished. The calculating intellect, which tries to determine whether the liberated being exists or not, is gone forever. This question and the desire for an answer to it disappear, because the desire for such understanding arises solely from the limited components of the limited individual. When no component of the limited individual remains, there is no more of this kind of thinking, nor any more attempts at description.

"One can be certain as well that the person who has become completely free and who no longer exists in the limited world has not been negated. The liberated person enters a condition beyond the seen and unseen, beyond all borders and boundaries of space and time, beyond the confines of 'this side' and 'the beyond.' In those spheres, the power of death is still not expelled. There are no human words that can possibly grasp or describe this condition."

A huge energy was released while the Master spoke, a force that blessed, transformed, and liberated everything that existed. Nothing was left untouched. Here was evidence of this inexplicable spiritual condition.

The Master added, "The word is a powerful force. It creates worlds and supports them. Most people are not at all aware of this, because these worlds are not visible to the physical eye." These final phrases added clarity and support where they were still needed. The Master could undoubtedly read the slightest movements within my mind. His words guided those movements out of the darkness and into the light.

In the meantime he had again stoked up the fire. He glanced at me with a profound, yet playful grin on his face. The Master himself was constantly stoking the vibrant spiritual fire, which not even a hurricane could extinguish. Where there is light, darkness must retreat. This is true on every level. Through the spoken word, this consummate master had expressed the entire light force of the divine universe. This force could truly move mountains. He communicated this to me with his smile.

THE MONASTERY IN THE VALLEY

We started off the following day as soon as the morning light silently offered itself and allowed us to distinguish all of nature's manifestations. Our pace was brisk as we moved through the unadorned landscape, contoured with brilliant mountain peaks. In this vast isolated region, where only a few small bushes could survive, the air was noticeably thinner.

We ascended a mountain face and continued along a narrow ridge. We then descended again, hiking parallel to the jagged green-blue tongue of a glacier. We had to loop around the toothy ice mass, as crossing it would be far too dangerous.

Hunger and thirst were distracting me, along with an assortment of other inconvenient desires. My imagination began conjuring up an assortment of tempting fantasies. The clearest picture was of a piece of cake, my favorite, and a warm drink. It had been many weeks since I had enjoyed something like that, and I thought about how many months it might be before I would be able to enjoy my favorite foods again.

We continued on for six straight hours, finally coming to the bottom end of the glacier. The Master decided it was time for a break. My feet hurt. We had hardly spoken since morning. I sensed that the Master didn't want to disturb the silence and purity of this mountain world with unnecessary conversation.

We sat down on a large stone. Gaya took a pitcher to the tongue of the glacier and filled it with the clear water that was trickling from beneath this ancient mass of ice. She offered the pitcher of water first to the Master, then to me, and then took a drink herself.

"You are hungry," the Master said to me. I was embarrassed, because the two of them almost never ate while we were traveling. I didn't know if Gaya had brought anything with her to eat from the village.

"Yes, I'm hungry," I conceded. As if on cue, my stomach sent out a loud groan as testimony.

"Do you see the tree over there?" the Master asked. "There is something waiting for you on the other side of it. You can go and get it now."

This unusual suggestion puzzled me, but I stood up anyway and went over to the tree. On the far side of it, at its base, I found a hole in the trunk. Since we had only just arrived here, and none of us had been to that side of the tree, I wondered how the Master knew that the hole was there.

Now I was nervous and unsure what to think. I reached my arm into the hole until my entire forearm was inside. I felt something sphere-shaped and grasped hold of it. I pulled my arm out. I was holding a beautiful round mango in my hand. It smelled wonderful.

"It's yours," I heard the Master call out. "Unfortunately, I couldn't gather the ingredients for your cake." He was laughing.

A storm of thoughts and feelings moved through my mind as I walked back with the fruit. Gaya, who had been observing the scene, offered me a friendly smile.

But I couldn't believe it! It was totally beyond my capacities of understanding. How did this freshly picked fruit appear up here in the hollow trunk of a conifer tree? I couldn't think anymore.

I reached out my hand to my companions. I wanted to share my mango with them, but they refused. They smiled and told me they didn't need anything. I should go on and enjoy it myself.

Eventually I recovered from my bewilderment. I asked the Master how something like what had just happened was possible. Nobody would believe a story like this. Anyone I told would probably think that it was all a daydream of mine, or that I was hypnotized, or that someone was playing a trick on me.

"You don't have to tell anyone a story," the Master said with a laugh. "But there was no magic and no hypnosis necessary to pick a piece of fruit. The imagery of your desires was so strong and obvious that a tremendous turbulence was created in the pure silence high up here in the mountains. I decided to quiet those thoughts and satisfy your desires for the moment, until you have overcome them.

"Look and see the mechanical process of desires within yourself, and observe what power they hold over you. Your feeling of hunger created all these images. Now that it has been gratified, you are calm again. The images and the desires they carried have received a satisfactory response."

He continued to speak. "Tension and a relaxation of tension on this level mean an endless wandering from one death to the next. The cake is not really so harmless, when you see all that is tied together in this lower prin-

ciple. I already explained to you that thought itself creates, inhabits, and supports invisible worlds. Thoughts
are powerful magnetic clouds, bipolar fields of energy
that you discharge into your environment. These energies
interact with other energies and come back to you. These
energetic relationships are the field of being, where you
live out your existence. An energetic emission takes place
when thought occurs, which has a reactive effect on the
thinker. That is the magnetic principle. And this closes the
unwholesome circle. Here, you are a convict in a magnetic
prison.

"The thinker and that which he thinks, the inventor
and that which he invents, are inseparably bound with
each other. You have to break through this endless cycle
ingrained in the world of death if you want to enter the
timeless world of the divine. Through proper insight and
realignment, toxic clouds and their poisonous contents
are diffused and ultimately dissolved for good.

"All humanity is connected on this level of magnetic
energy, each person bound to others by powerful hidden
force fields. For millennia these killing fields have been
relentless in creating soulless, egocentric worlds reeking
of death. These deceitful places carry the foul odor of the
ancient past."

The ties and attachments that the Master held before
my eyes had never been so apparent. My psychic state
of consciousness continually emitted magnetic energy, at-
tracting others to it. I was lost in this game of exchanging
energies, a prisoner in the world of death indeed. I recognized also that the structures of these force fields were
the subtle formations, the outlines of "the beyond", which
exists alongside "this world." The entirety is a perfectly

matched system, a monstrous magnetic dungeon, a massive double-tiered cemetery of the soul, which has been chained to humanity for thousands of years.

An inner voice expressed itself within me. "Look right there, right there where you are thinking. Exactly there is the threshold separating captivity and liberation. Every expressed aspiration that comes from the higher principle will be instantly manifested from original essential matter."

"Everything that manifests must vanish again," said the Master, who had been observing me and knew exactly how I had reacted to the words he had spoken. "All desires are completely extinguished in the awakened person. There is nothing that he could desire, as he lives in the joy and bliss of the un-manifested." It was important to him that I understood exactly what he was saying.

He had taken me through powerful realms and dimensions. At this point I realized that I had lost all bodily sensation and found myself in an ecstatic state, with the sense of being completely free. But all too soon the shadows of captivity cast themselves over my soul. The black shawl of death was upon me again. And yet, for a brief moment I had experienced that I am something beyond the body.

"Could we continue? I would like to reach the monastery before darkness sets in." The Master was ready to move on. I was unable to formulate any words, and simply nodded.

Gaya took me caringly by the hand, and we made our way toward the valley. Gaya began to sing in Sanskrit. The sound of her wonderfully robust voice made me feel as if we were flying toward our destination, riding aloft on graceful wings.

A subtle awareness opened within me now. I could distinguish the individual rays of the majestic sun above. I saw the beauty and the perfect form of all things, the embodiment of interchanging thoughts. I could hear the whisperings of the wind and feel the currents of timeless energy flowing from the trees.

The inner eye in the center of the heart recognized the transitory character inherent in birth and death but rejoiced in the eternal and unchanging essence beyond them.

We reached a wide plateau, where we found a soft grassy meadow with cows and goats grazing contentedly. On the shore of a small deep blue lake stood several tightly packed houses surrounded by hedges and large trees.

A farmer was guiding his ox over a field. The large animal towed a wooden plow, creating a furrow in the stony earth. Small children played by the edge of the lake, while their mothers washed clothes nearby. The lake provided a perfect mirror, and I observed the clear reflection of the large trees in its still clear water. What a wonderful place!

Without disturbing this idyllic scene, we made our way to the opposite edge of the water. In the distance I could see our destination: a large three-story building situated on a small hill. Numerous windows seemed to pop out like eyes from the whitewashed facade. A few houses were nestled next to the wall that encircled this monastery.

In two more hours we had reached the narrow path that led up to the entrance. In the inner square a few monks were busy with their various chores. We saw many fruit trees and an expansive garden. The place was certainly well tended. One monk was drawing water from a well with a large wooden bucket.

The monks noticed us immediately. Some of them ran up and greeted us. One led us inside the main building, guiding us through the narrow hallways that led to the Abbot's chambers. All the monks had shaved heads and wore long ocher-colored garments. Their uninhibited sincerity was heart-warming. I didn't feel like an outsider at all, not for an instant.

The monk who was guiding us knocked on a door upon which a large mandala was painted. A strong deep voice called us to enter. The Abbot was a dignified older man who radiated concentrated stillness. His eyes sparkled like two glittering stars. The fire emitted from his gaze testified to profound experience. Compassion, kindness, and warmth flowed toward us immediately, gently embracing and supporting us.

"Welcome! Have you eaten? I'm sure you haven't." The Abbot answered this question for himself and gave instructions to one of the monks to have food prepared and to guide us to our rooms afterwards. The Master and the Abbot were obviously well acquainted.

As we sat down to tea and spoke about various topics, the joyful laugh of the Abbot penetrated every cell of my body, transporting me to a euphoric state. The energy released through this laugh was the luminosity of a being liberated from this world.

I hoped secretly that our stay here would be an extended one. I wanted to stay as close as possible to the Abbot for as long as I could. From the moment I met him and felt his naturalness and simplicity, I knew that I could learn a great deal by his side.

During the tea the Abbot explained to me the daily routines of the monastery. The information was nothing new for the Master and Gaya. Wake-up was before sunrise, followed by two hours of meditation and then a simple breakfast. After the meal the chores of the monastery were carried out, and when all was clean and in good order, time was dedicated to study of the scriptures. The main meal was scheduled just prior to midday. Only liquids were offered afterward. Early in the evening the Abbot gave teachings, and at ten o'clock activities ended for the night.

I was exhausted as I lay down on my mat to rest and fell asleep immediately. But the loud banging of a gong tore me out of my deep slumber. It seemed as if I had fallen asleep only a moment before. It was still completely dark outside. I was soon up and following a row of monks through the hallway. Each step along the cold stone floor made me feel more awake. In the monastery everyone goes barefoot.

We arrived at an adjoining building through a narrow passage that they called "the Hose." The second building was where the meditation took place. For the first time I saw all the monks who lived in the monastery gathered together.

One of them pointed to a spot where I should sit. There was a precise order to the seating arrangement. Gaya entered the hall, and she was shown to a place near me. She was the only woman in the monastery. We were told the night before that this was a men's monastery, but the Abbot took in everyone. All were welcome.

I looked around, but I couldn't see the Master anywhere. I thought perhaps he had overslept, or was busy doing some other business. The Abbot was the last to enter and seated himself among the other monks. He had hardly gotten settled when the reciting of sutras began. Afterward, there was only silence in the hall.

DEEP WITHIN

The power of the sacred scriptures being chanted by the monks led me into a state beyond the corporeal, beyond the limits of time and space. I felt like a flake of gold moving through an unending ocean of light.

At some point I noted the subtle ringing of a bell in the distance. I opened my eyes and saw that the monks had stood up and were silently walking around the room. They went along wordlessly, with slow steps and great awareness, hands folded, stopping at each corner of the room, where they would stand for a short moment and bow, acknowledging in turn the four directions.

The ringing of the distant bell was perceptible again, and the monks sat down in their places. The absorption of the entire assembly went still deeper. This sacred ritual was repeated four times. The concentration of spiritual energy in the room gradually rose, and I noticed the walls of the monastery becoming transparent. Our bodies were so thoroughly infused with divine light that we started to vibrate at a higher level of consciousness, coalescing with a force of energy that spiritualized everything and everyone and led all things back to their originally intended purpose.

Later at breakfast, I had an unusual experience. A person was sitting eating and drinking, but the inner being remained uninvolved with the outer person doing the feeding. I was that inner being! I sat there and simply observed myself absorbing food and drink. What I was experiencing was no splitting of the personality, and this was not an out-of-body experience. Through the meditation I was so deeply immersed within my essence that the outer shell of my body was perceived as a fleeting shadow on the periphery of my true being.

Following the morning schedule of the monastery, I found myself in the garden house sweeping dirt from the floor. The condition I had experienced earlier that morning gradually faded. Once again I was the entire body, with all its ephemeral attributes. But I noted how this subtle energy was having its effect within me, setting off chain reactions that were melting away my inner boundaries.

When I met Gaya in the afternoon, I asked her about the Master. She didn't know where he was either and was wondering herself what had happened to him.

Later the Abbot asked us to join him for tea. He wanted to have a talk with us.

"The Master has instructed me to tell you that he will be away for a short while. He wants to visit a friend," reported the Abbot. He then told us about one of the Master's disciples who was a very developed spiritual being. He had lived with the Master for eighteen years. Afterward the Master had sent him to live at this monastery for eight years. Then he was sent to a cave in the mountains to live for eight more years. During this time he was not allowed to speak a single word.

"He has been up there for almost five years already," the Abbot told us. "Our monks take him provisions of food every two weeks. Whenever the Master visits nearby, he goes to see him. The Master initiates him in the highest cosmic teachings. He teaches him how one reorganizes living atoms and explains the metamorphosis of elements and the energies that determine the direction of all life. Such an understanding can be achieved only through deep cosmic insight and the highest revelation. This is how human beings are transformed into living suns."

Gaya was surprised by the Abbot's explanation. She had known the Master for many years and had never heard anything about this student.

Before we left, the Abbot offered us the chance to visit him every day for tea if we wanted. We gladly accepted.

I was tired and wanted a chance to sort some things out in my mind, so I went back to my room early that night. I looked out the window, at the green expanse below me. I could see also just a bit of the deep blue lake we had passed on our way to the monastery. As dusk arrived, the sky covered itself in yellow, then red, finally blending ever so slowly into navy blue. Like a gentle caress, with exquisite tenderness, everything was transformed. Before long, night had subdued all colors.

That is the fate of this transient world, I thought to myself. But nothing was capable of covering over the highest power, that core of the universe within a human being, after that person has seen and tasted the majesty and splendor of the Nameless. I thought for a long time about my life and its significance. I had not sought out the events taking place in my life now, nor had I held a yearning for them. A higher power was carrying me, a power from which I couldn't release myself, a power that determined how and when my whole life would be transformed.

Countless stars, shimmering like diamonds, filled the sky. I lay down but couldn't sleep. It seemed as if I had been away from home for years, here in this mysterious world between heaven and earth, between dream and reality, inhabited by human beings different from any I had met before. I liked them. I was moved by the quiet dignity and authenticity of these uncomplicated people who lived in such harmony with nature.

I had hardly fallen asleep when the large gong sounded. Moving like a sleepwalker, I stumbled toward the meditation hall. A monk who noticed my sorry condition took my hand and led me to the courtyard and up to a well. He took a bucket half filled with cold water and motioned for me to bow slightly. He then upended the bucket, swiftly splashing the water over my head. In a moment's time I was wide awake.

The monk handed me a towel from a small chest behind the well. He asked me to dry myself off quickly. We had to hurry if we were to reach the meditation hall on time. As we walked he explained that the monks also use such means to wake themselves up. The Abbot allowed no sleepiness in the morning practice. We entered just in time. A moment after we seated ourselves the Abbot entered the hall.

Gradually I accustomed myself to the daily rhythm of monastery life. Gaya and I enjoyed our conversations with the Abbot and felt the grandeur of his boundless patience and generosity.

On the sixteenth day the Abbot led us to a huge underground vault. It was a library where old scriptures were preserved. "This is the treasure of our monastery," said the

Abbot. "The secret knowledge of the hidden world is engraved on these long wooden panels. The wood is prepared according to various methods for seven years, so that it will not decay and rot. Only then can it be engraved upon."

A small Buddha made from pure gold stood in the center of the room on an altar. The composure emanating from this statue attracted me. The Abbot acknowledged my curiosity and said, "Do you see the smile? He has his eyes only half-closed. That means he has transcended both the seen and the unseen worlds completely. That is what his smile is expressing."

He continued, "The Buddha is holding his robe in the left hand. This expresses his complete mastery over the material world. And with the formation of the fingers in the right hand, he is setting the wheel of life in motion. This statue is very old. A monk brought it here two hundred years ago. He later became the abbot of this old monastery. This building has been renovated over the years, and many other buildings have been built. But this basement where we are standing remains from that time."

The Abbot lit three lamps, which spread a pallid light across the room. He then removed two fine white spotless gloves from a casket and put them on. He went over to the shelves and carefully pulled one of the engraved wooden plates out and laid it on a table in front of us. Even before he said a word I felt a wave of calmness embrace me. After a short prayer, the Abbot started to read aloud:

"Only he who has the will of the sun can enter and penetrate the fathomless depths of the Nameless. There is only light and the absence of light. Therefore, Awakened One, see what is to be done. The eternal knows neither ethics nor morals. It is pure nonbeing.

"Look, oh Limitless One. See the secret in the atom. Each central part contains another central part. This continues endlessly. Leave the exterior circle of appearances. Release your hold on the periphery of passing things. Turn back to the central point, where causes arise. Awaken the sleeping power within you. Then you will act correctly.

"The power thus revealed will purify the components of your material being. It will change and transform them. In this way a new world of light will be created within you. This is called Nirvana. But this is only a name and should not be held on to. You cannot see the infinite. You cannot understand the infinite. You cannot enter the infinite. This is because the infinite has no relation to the finite. The finite is nothing but illusion.

"Release all your shadows and live in the eternal. Live and breathe in everything you perceive. Live in all things, for all things are the Nameless. Be in harmony with all beings and each being, for each is the Nameless. Remain in the sun. Never return to the land of shadows. Nonduality is life. Duality is death."

The Abbot carefully returned the thin wooden plate to the shelf. "There is also a century-old manual of herbal medicine here, which is very extensive and is being continually updated. If a monk's internal nature is suited to studying medicine, he is educated in this part of the monastery. Those monks must study for many years to become qualified. Then they go out to the villages, where they can help sick people. Through true sympathy and compassion for all beings they can forget the egoistic self and achieve liberation.

"Other monks choose different forms of renunciation.

It always depends on the disposition of the individual. In truth there is only one path that leads to complete liberation. That is the pathless path."

The Abbot extinguished the three lamps, and we departed the darkened vault. We returned to the Abbot's room. Once we were seated, he began to speak again, his voice full of bright wit but also great depth. "Just as the gentle light in the vault was extinguished, never to be found again, so it is with the liberated person. He is extinguished, never to be found again. But before he vanishes, he makes sure that no glowing coals are left, nothing that could set the flames of the illusory world burning in him again."

The Master had said the same thing to me using other words. I now understood the importance and ultimate significance of complete liberation from the twofold realm of death, the realm of "this side" and "the beyond."

Later, Gaya and I were greeted by a young monk who had not been in the monastery long. The Abbot had arranged for him to escort us to a large workroom that we had not seen before.

Several monks whom I had seen in the meditation hall and at meals were sitting or kneeling on the workroom floor painting. Their works in process were deeply meditative concentrated mandalas, produced in a variety of sizes and colors.

A very thin older monk was giving instruction in this way of painting. We greeted him. He approached us with a friendly laugh and asked us whether we would like to know more about mandalas. We were very interested.

The old monk excluded nothing in his explanation. "Each monk here in the monastery paints seven mandalas in seven years. This is part of their education. In this way they learn the comings and goings of the world from their own mind. From the mandala, the monks can know and recognize the transient worlds of the seen and the unseen located in the four directions. These worlds exist with their good and bad aspects, and are attached to the painter, so long as he is not completely free of them."

He pointed to a small circle in the center of a mandala, where a Buddha was painted. "He exists outside the picture. The mandala begins with the circle around him, spreading outward. This clearly determines that the Buddha does not exist within the born, the accumulated, the formed, the created. Seeing it in this way, the monks can absorb themselves, recognize their true condition, and cultivate their minds.

"When the monk begins to paint, he first confronts his own lower world, filled with demons. Next, he confronts the world of the gods. His awareness must always be in the center, resting in the state of Buddhahood. Only in this way can he know the difference between the transient and intransient worlds.

"Each monk keeps his seven mandalas. In the eighth year there is a great purifying ritual. The monk offers his painted works to the fire and allows them to burn. In this way he learns that everything that has been gathered and given form is subject to passing. This is the nature of things. He learns not to mourn over things that pass away. He also learns not to accumulate earthly possessions. It can be viewed as an analogy. Just as the eternal spirit of this world of appearances creates and destroys, the monk has also created a world from his life force and painted it onto paper, only to give it back to the fire in the end. What remains is only this energy, without form, without birth, without beginning. The entire eight-year process offers a powerful growth of awareness.

"The wisdom and freedom the monk cultivates over these seven years is eternal nature itself. He has achieved the end of being. Our entire life is a great mandala that we must come to understand."

The Abbot gave me permission to spend a couple of hours each day alone in the meditation hall. I needed time to process all I was hearing and experiencing. Each day I was also immersing myself more fully in the cheerful easygoing atmosphere of the monastery. The strong clear vibrations of the wisdom and compassion surrounding me penetrated each cell of my being.

During these days, I had recurring experiences that revealed to me the "I" of my personality, the one I had acknowledged and related to throughout my life. In every case I witnessed its form as a hollow construction subject to passing. My ideas of life and death, my scheme of reincarnation, of "this side" and "the beyond," all these things belonged to this construction. They were incorporated in the ever-changing contents of my knowledge-based consciousness.

Seeing this with such clarity was shocking. With one glance, in one instant, my entire world was reduced to a pile of ashes. But an imperceptible energy was urging me to look deeper. I still had to understand what this leftover pile of ashes was.

At one point during this thorough inner cleansing something shifted within, a movement transcending all my earthly limitations; now, the sunlit inner universe was unveiling itself. The flow of grace that flooded my being was so strong that each and every part of my body trembled. Tears of joy and gratitude ran down my cheeks.

For the first time I recognized my true internal home. But still, at this initial encounter I could only sense it. As long as the age-old foundation and walls of my previous interior dwelling were not completely annihilated, this infinite realm of the sun could not completely reveal itself and manifest within me. I couldn't enter this inner realm. The intensity was too overpowering. My body felt as if it was in flames. I was at the limit of what I could handle. I stood up and went around the room, doing the sacred ritual of offering greetings to the four directions, as the monks did every morning. It was clear to me that I was not yet purified enough to accept and abide in this powerful universal energy.

Suddenly the Master appeared. I saw him from my inner eye. His calm presence softened the turbulent waves of energy. I heard his voice speaking inside me. "Be patient. It is patience that allows the soul to mature. For the power of God to be perfect, the vessel must be purified and polished. Otherwise it will be perish in the divine fire. The celestial robe must be carefully prepared.

"Patience, attentiveness, correct insight, simplicity, and love are the means by which the vessel is purified and prepared. The most important thing to understand is that words are deeds. When we understand this, the great illumination and sanctification of all humanity begins."

"Love and love alone is the great energy that brings realization to each moment. When the thoughts and words people express are not in unison with the deeds to which they are connected, then this energy of love that offers realization in each moment is absent."

How fantastic it was to have the Master in my life! How uplifting to hear his words! Although he was far away from the monastery, he hadn't forgotten me. He was keeping a watchful eye on my inner state of being. Knowing this gave me tremendous strength and confidence.

In the meantime, the Master had been away for more than a month, and I had already been asking myself if he had a particular reason for leaving me at that place. I still found his way of thinking and dealing with things very peculiar. He never committed himself to anything, nor did he speak about his plans or intentions. He lived what he said and managed to accomplish things in an extremely dynamic way. The synchronicity of word and deed that he employed without the slightest gap was the key to his unlimited spiritual power.

Soon I went looking for Gaya. A monk told me he had seen her in the large workroom. I felt anxious to tell her about the visitation of the Master. As I entered the room, I saw her kneeling on the ground. She had just begun working on a mandala under the instruction of the old monk.

I sat down next to her and watched as she calmly drew the first lines. Still reeling from my experience, I was doing all I could to keep quiet. It was obvious this wasn't the time and place to share what had happened. I dared not disturb her during this meditative activity. My impatience was clear to me in these moments. But I had no idea how to conquer it, or even reduce it. The words of the Master were still reverberating in me. "Patience is the virtue that allows the soul to mature."

My strategy of suppressing my restlessness and creating a peaceful outer appearance was failing. One of the monks was instructed by the old teacher to bring me a cup of tea, and then he took me to a corner and showed me some of the different mandalas they had painted.

It was extremely quiet there. I became aware for the first time that no one in the room spoke except the teacher. Painting was a deep meditation. Each monk was confronting his inner world.

As Gaya stood up, she waved to me. We left the workroom together and went to my room, where I could share my experience with her. I had expected some kind of special reaction from Gaya, but she didn't respond as I anticipated. She said casually that the Master had also contacted her, telling her that he would be away a while longer. This form of communication was evidently nothing new or special for these people.

More days passed. I was often busy with several monks doing repairs on one of the roofs. My admiration for their inner calm and stability increased during this time spent together. We rarely spoke about philosophical things. They lived the path of liberation with simplicity and clarity.

There were periods when I didn't see the Abbot for days. I had no idea whether he was in retreat during this time, or whether he had left the monastery completely. Then he would appear and invite me to tea again. He was interested in what had moved me to travel to the Himalayas and how I had come to meet the Master.

When I told him that I originally wanted to stay with the Master for two weeks, and described how the Master had received me and what I went through, the Abbot broke into such raucous laughter that I was sure everyone in the monastery could hear it. He encouraged me to share each detail of my time of initiation and took great pleasure in all my accounts.

"He is a good master, a good master," he repeated again and again. Now that all those events were months old, I could also laugh at my follies. But actually, during that time, as the Master chased me through the cauldrons of alternating feelings and emotions, there hadn't been much to laugh about. I told the Abbot this. His smile remained, but he nodded with a sense of understanding and said, "All those who travel this road of liberation must go through this experience sooner or later. This is the test for the soul, to know whether it is ready to follow the steep path of liberation in this incarnation."

A couple of days later the Abbot asked me, "Would you like to visit the room again where the scriptures are kept?" I blurted, "Yes." I would have made this request before, but I didn't have the courage. The Abbot was always so busy whenever I saw him.

After breakfast the following morning, the Abbot led me into the vault. Gaya didn't come with us this time. The austere old monk insisted that those who work on mandalas finish what they start. The painting practice was a developmental progression that admitted no interruption.

The soft light of the small lamp flickered as the Abbot laid the wooden panel on the table. Then the Abbot turned to me. "Today I will read to you from a very old text. The subject matter is difficult. Please listen carefully."

The stars sing with the voices of eternity. Their song spreads throughout the entire universe. The seven rays of the twelve perpetual light-streams penetrate the seven chambers and bequeath a song to each of them. This song carries the message of the eternal inner kingdom of light.

The Twelve Lords of Destiny, who give life to the lower principle of time, exist in the seven chambers as well and also play music. The melody they raise is the song of all things time-conditioned and passing.

The lower principle does not know the higher eternal principle. There is no path that leads from one to the other. Those whose beings have been transformed by pure light into an ether gown within the higher principle are completely free from the lower principle, from the gravity of time. They possess the power to enter the timeless eternal kingdom. The secret behind the blazing wheels of fire adorning their new ether gown reveals the abundant wealth of the universal light-realm.

The solar power of the eternal illuminates, liberates, and blesses all worlds and beings. Awakened One, you must be a sun as well. May the radiance and bounty of God be revealed within you and expressed through you.

Although I listened intently, I could decipher little from these mysterious words. The encoded offerings within this message were beyond the grasp of my awareness and interpretation. I felt like a child starting his first day of kindergarten only to find himself at a university lecture.

Without a word, the Abbot put the wooden panel back on the shelf. He took off the white gloves, put out the lights, and requested me to accompany him back to his quarters.

As we walked along, I tried to recall the words from the scripture, in case the Abbot asked me about it, but found it absolutely impossible. I felt as if an invisible hand had reached into my head and pulled out a plug.

Although I had understood nothing of the texts, I noticed how the fiery words had a powerful effect on me anyway. I felt as if a tube of light had been burned into the deepest regions of my being, a tube that led from darkness into utter illumination. Divine light streamed through my nerves and blood, causing all voices of darkness and limitation to lament as they dissolved in this radiance.

An extraordinary power purified all the cells of my body, which had previously been vibrating in the lower principle of desires. Stubborn millennium-old energies struggled resiliently, thrashing and crashing against themselves in their battle with this brilliant light force. But their defeat was inevitable. Gradually this light defeated all shadows.

New insights filled my mind, as if a row of doors was flying open, one after the other. I saw clearly how I held myself back from these resplendent heights of eternal being. I failed to take the rope and swing upward. The core of the self-centered, self-proclaiming mind was obedient to its own principle, a force that tethered even the gods.

I felt as if I was standing before a solid but transparent wall, looking at the causes of my present condition, seeing God standing there clearly before my eyes, but still separate from me. I wanted to blast my way out of my deep-rooted limitations, but they were too heavy, too strong. My habits of identification and attachment were too deeply embedded within me.

I nursed the hot tea the Abbot gave me in silence. He sat across from me, looking over at me without speaking. The glimmering light in his eyes seemed to shine with particular intensity during these moments. I knew that the text he had read to me had also touched him deeply, although he had read it countless times before. He had surely come to a deep realization of its inner meaning.

He got up and stood next to the open window. "Come, look at this fertile green valley and this magnificent mountain. And look, there in the distance, at the deep blue lake. Do you feel the tranquillity here?

"Without the sun there would be no life on this planet. Its life-supporting energy is immense. Try to sense the greatness, the almightiness with which it creates and maintains so much life.

"The planet Earth is not a permanent home, not at all. It is only a station to be passed through, a step for human beings, who are called to a higher plane. They must overcome the transient world and enter the pure light.

"When you are not caught on ideas and concepts, unattached deep within from all that comes and goes--when you are capable of this, you are capable of passing through the gate leading to that place which cannot be expressed in words.

"The text I read aloud to you was written by people who had transcended all that is transitory and subject to death. That means they had fully transcended the planet Earth as well.

"With their clear instructions, they handed down a ray of light that can be followed when one is internally free. The text points out that behind the universe we can see, the universe that comes and goes, another universe exists that has no beginning, that is eternal. Both of these universes, the transient and the intransient, exist within us.

"Twelve pure light streams reveal the eternal light, universal love, wisdom, and power. Still, the source of light that is the source for these streams is forever untouched and unaffected by all revelations.

"The transient universe that we can see must comply with the twelve emanations, the Lords of Destiny, who manifest themselves in the world of time and create all things that are conditioned by time. These twelve-layered energies divide themselves on the atomic level. All things with a body, whether they appear solid or whether they consist of the finest, most delicate substances, originate here.

"Things that appear on this level express and reflect the manifesting powers that create the complex world in which we live.

"Because people are completely trapped in the delusions of these time-conditioned forces, they have forgotten the meaning of their existence. And this happens even though the knowledge of the eternal light-realm is implanted within the heart of every single person and is vibrating there.

"It is this primal remembrance, this primal force, that moves us to search so diligently for the original limitless reality. In order to reawaken this eternal light-realm in our hearts, to recognize it, to enter it, and to become fully ONE with the eternal again, a great devotion is required of us, an absolute faith in this eternal divine power. Also required is full compliance to the process of dissolving all the old energies of the past. Those who have followed the path of liberation know from their experience what an enormous task this is.

"The powers of the visible transient universe, which together form the human being, tend to maintain a strong grasp. They do not let go easily. Those of us who want to be free, who must be free, because we have rediscovered our true condition, must have strong and unwavering resolve. We must have great intensity and great patience so that we can continually recognize and overcome all of our limitations and restrictions.

"I have no words to say to you concerning the gown of ether or the wheels of fire. But if you really follow the path of true liberation, these deep mysteries will gradually be revealed to you.

"In this respect, one cannot force anything. To do so would only nourish and revitalize the self-proclaiming 'I'-centered energies. Many fall into the trap of wanting, having, and possessing. They follow their craving for the attainment of power. Without being aware of it, they attach themselves even more firmly to these threads of energy and their patterns. People identify themselves with these patterns and are ultimately trapped for eons in the world of death.

"To let go of the image of the world that vibrates in our consciousness completely, without replacing it with another one, is not so easy. This is because the foundation, everything we have and everything we know, belongs to it. We have created it.

"This image we carry and give life to is an assembly of massive energies that have us trapped. When we question these forces, when we begin to free ourselves from them, our actions call forth a chain of counter-reactions. The pressures of doubt, fear, and insecurity compel us, trying with all their might to hold us back from continuing along the path of liberation.

"As soon as we become steadfast, there is a calming of these energies. There is a temporary sense of balance, a sense of peace that is still artificial and inauthentic, and we must recognize it as such. But the person truly seeking liberation continues to go forward without making a faulty step, without being afraid. In doing this, he releases magnetic cyclones and powerful storms. These powerful energies try to destabilize him and to convince him to turn back. But he stands like a great stone in the eye of a hurricane, strengthened through his recognition that these storms are transitory phenomena and will pass.

"Going about it in this way, he successfully arrives at the edge. He reaches the summit of the thunderclouds and, by advancing over them, becomes calmer and more peaceful. He has entered the eternal light-realm at last.

"Everything he has left behind in the storm weakens and fades until finally it has all vanished. He has entered a realm that is completely beyond the comprehension of the thinking mind or the perception of the senses. No human words can describe this eternal realm, which is hidden even from the gods themselves.

"One cannot wish for this light-realm to appear, for the will of humans belongs to the limitations of time-conditioned consciousness. The will is always connected to an object, and through this object it becomes attached. Each object of the will is something constructed, and therefore something transient.

"Where the true power lies, the true power that will certainly get us through all storms, is not in the will, but in the dissolving of the one with the will. Do not doubt yourself. Do not believe you are too weak to completely realize this path. The weaknesses you suppose exist are the whisperings of the restricted magnetic conditions that make up this world of death. Don't listen to them and never let them influence you. It is not about ability or achievement. It is about letting go and not clinging to anything.

"I have explained many things to you today. The Master had expressed his wish that during his absence I should speak to you about these hidden aspects of life.

"Now I would like to tell you about the two ways, the two possibilities. It is important that you look at this in connection with what I have already said.

"Humans have different tendencies and intentions. They choose their preferences according to one of two ways. I have already spoken to you about the first way, the way of nonwilling, of nonbeing, of totally dissolving and overcoming all limitations.

"The other way has a completely different form. The seeker on this path studies the magnetic energies of this world and behaves in harmony with them. He learns to have command over them and to make full use of them. He connects himself consciously with the energies of the earth and succeeds in acquiring great power in this world. This is the way of the will, the way of achievement and power.

"These two ways have absolutely nothing in common, as you can now see for yourself.

"There are communities that correspond to each of these two paths. There is a universal 'Brotherhood of Light,' which exists beyond time and everything that is transitory. And there is a brotherhood within the time-conditioned world, which rules over it. Due to its self-seeking motives, it tries to keep this world as it is. Due to our weaknesses, humanity is exploited and enslaved in this world and in the world beyond.

"The brotherhood of this world has developed its

moral and ethical virtues to a very high level. In fact its members have reached the limit of their possibilities in these fields. But they can never go beyond this boundary.

"The first brotherhood, called 'the Brotherhood of Light' or the 'Lodge of the Transcendent,' uses only the powerful forces of the divine in order to liberate the world and transform it. Its members bring spirituality to the world, offering companionship on higher levels of integration.

"Unfortunately, many seekers go another way. They are subdued by the intoxicating pleasures of power. They are trapped in this matrix and bound to its principles.

"At this point you should not follow the temptation to see these two ways as bad and good, black and white. Do not judge or condemn either of them. Both tendencies are found within us.

"Only after the soul has endured many setbacks and disappointments, only when it is exhausted from its experiences and endless partings, only after countless rebirths that have chained it to the wheel of time, only after the continual passing of loved ones, who go through the gates of death, only when all these things have caused a great crisis, only when it feels impossible to keep living, only then, from deep disillusionment and sobriety, can one embark on the great journey, the path to ultimate liberation."

A great silence filled the room as the Abbot finished speaking. Many things of which I had had only a vague notion were now clear. He remained sitting with closed eyes, as if sleeping. His breathing was deep and steady, and he was totally relaxed. Time was standing still.

I had heard so much information that I couldn't digest it all at once. I felt a sudden need to take a few days alone. I was like a vase filled to the brim. A few drops more and it would overflow! When the Abbot opened his eyes, I told him of my desire. An understanding smile lit up his face.

"Up on the mountain, about two hours from here by foot, we have a small empty house. That place is exactly where you need to be now. When would you like to go?" he asked me.

"Tomorrow would be good," I answered.

"Very well. After the meditation tomorrow, a monk will accompany you. You can go to the kitchen and supply yourself with everything you need. Next to the house there is a well, so you won't need to take any water."

I spent the evening with Gaya. She also had great empathy for my resolution to take time away. I told her about the text the Abbot had read aloud to me, and about his detailed explanation. She remained silent, just listening. She had no response to any of the things I told her. The things that seemed so profound to me were apparently of no great matter to her. Did she know all this stuff already? Perhaps she didn't like this particular form of teaching. Perhaps that was the reason the Abbot had not included her when he talked to me.

I didn't want to hurt Gaya's feelings in any way, so I didn't ask questions. Maybe she had forged a different path to liberation. I could certainly imagine that as a possibility.

"How is the work going with the mandala?" I asked, trying to help the conversation flow again.

"Good," she said curtly, without budging from her concentrated stillness. Obviously, she didn't want to talk about any of her experiences. I decided to excuse myself and returned to my sleeping room.

I was delighted with the thought of being away for a while, as I had been around people for a long time, though it had been a rich time as well. During this period I never felt restricted or pressured. I felt that my destiny had very unexpectedly invited amazing people into my life. I found that these people had a resonance with my own inner rhythm, and the teachings I received from them matched this rhythm perfectly as well.

In relation to the spiritual process, until this time I had been only a collector of theories. This was the actuality. I had taken the role of outsider, a bystander who could then write something of spirituality. But I had figured out by then that this writing would never happen. The spiritual energy that had led me to these people demanded more than mere lessons in observation.

The time had come for me to make a final journey through the great hurricanes and storms, to endure them and survive them. I was already right in their center. What was in store for me? What would I have to go through until I could cross over the inner barrier and enter the luminous land of eternal peace?

I had every reason to maintain faith. Upon my inner journey I had come into the best of hands, and I had nothing to fear. I knew that the Master was following each of my steps into this hidden territory. He was there, accompanying me with love and patience through the shadowy gloom of this mortal world. He was my adviser and my guide, the one who lit my path. But I had to walk the path myself. The Master had instilled this in me, and I saw it clearly.

I sat in a corner of the room and looked out through the window. I gazed into the night sky, which hung low, heavy with clouds. The silver moon beamed a stream of light through a slit in the cloud cover. I hoped the weather would be friendly for the next few days. The weather patterns here were extremely unpredictable.

The next morning at the meditation, I was not concentrated at all. My thoughts were already restlessly planning and organizing. I had great trouble just sitting still. I couldn't hold my body up and kept falling, which was terribly embarrassing. I had the exasperating sense that I was disturbing the whole group.

On that day the Abbot didn't come to the meditation. I would have liked to say good-bye. Gaya went off with the thin elderly monk to the workroom, also distancing herself without a parting word.

Eventually I made my way to the kitchen and stocked up on provisions. As I was sorting them and putting the things into a small bag, I noticed that the young monk who was to accompany me was watching me with an amused look on his face. Soon we were on our way.

Many weeks had passed since I had entered through the monastery's wooden gate, which had a wheel painted over it. During that entire time, I had never stepped outside. It was now strange to me that I had not even been aware of this.

Life inside the monastery had a very distinctive quality. The monks of the community had created their own cosmos, a very special and pure energy field. This dynamic of focusing the internal and organizing the external around one common goal, namely the liberation for all beings, created the opportunity for each person there to ripen in his spiritual development. Exceptional human qualities were cultivated and transmitted in this special place.

We stepped between the two houses that stood outside the monastery. People quickly appeared, crossing paths with us from every direction. All greeted us kindly and respectfully.

The young monk explained to me that at least one son from each of the families living there would eventually put on an ocher robe and become a monk. He himself was from a local family. His parents, who had passed away while he was in the monastery, had brought him to the monastery when he was twelve years old. From that time, the Abbot and the community of monks had become his family.

He was excited to tell me his story. He described to me how proud his parents had been when they saw that he could read and write and recite the sutras. He showed me the small stone house he had grown up in. An older brother lived there now with his family. His other brothers and sisters had left the valley. They had moved down to the flatlands and into the cities, where they sought an easier and more affluent life.

When the houses were well behind us, the young monk spoke to me in a soft voice. "Many members of my family have fallen into the delusions of the material world." A quiet sadness was noticeable in the tone of his voice. But the next moment he had gathered himself fully again and expressed more of his thoughts. "Each must follow the path he or she can see. It will take time before they can recognize that transitory things bring only a transitory happiness and satisfaction, to see that because of their attachment to these passing things they themselves are the source of their own pain and suffering."

These words flowed out of him in a natural way. What he spoke was not theoretical and had no stink of borrowed knowledge. Here there was only shining clarity enhanced with simplicity, compassion, and deep insight.

We soon began a steep and rocky ascent. The morning sun flooded the landscape with light. I felt the supportive energy of warmth entering through my back. We stopped often and could still see the monastery in the far distance and gaze at the deep blue lake beyond it, bordered by meadows and the outlines of cultivated fields. We followed the long looping trail, circling over the sloping rocks until we reached our goal. It was almost noon. The ascent had taken longer than I had anticipated. I was mesmerized by the amazing view!

Along the way we had occasionally seen small thorny shrubs, but nothing bigger. Upon reaching a rocky plateau we found an assortment of conifers and deciduous trees. Beyond them, as far as the eye could see, an endless chain of majestic white peaks, framed by distant ridges, stretched along the horizon.

A small stone house had been built on the plateau. Next to it a small stream flowed gently down toward the valley. I couldn't have wished for a better place to have my retreat.

The house was sparsely furnished. Several oil lamps stood on one shelf. Bedding lay in a pile on a roughly constructed bed. Next to it was a table and two chairs.

"We call this hut 'The Eagle's Nest.' Monks come up here often to take retreat. I've used it myself was several times." He continued, "In winter, when the storms come, there's a lot of snow here. Usually we close the hut and do our best to leave it well protected so that the strong winds don't damage it. But there are monks who come here during those months, sometimes staying the whole winter alone. The old monk who instructs us in the painting of mandalas spent more than one winter up here. By doing that he was able to gain especially deep insights, but he never talks about it. He expresses his wisdom through mandalas."

He changed his tone abruptly. "I am going back to the monastery now. Work is waiting for me there. Be well. All the best!"

The vivacious monk quickly vanished, and I was alone. I hadn't even had the chance to thank him for his help and companionship.

I arranged my things in a short time. I then went out and sat in front of the house under a large tree. I found a badly worn mat and laid it on a large flat stone. I sat upright for a long time and wondered how many hours the old monk and the others had spent in that place. What had they done to fill their days? What did they contemplate? What did they realize?

I remembered one of the Master's sayings: "There is a creative nondoing." I had never fully understood what he meant by this. For me, creativity was doing, connected to clear physical action. Perhaps this was a chance to find out what "creative nondoing" was. A whimsical smile came over my face at this thought.

Soon I stood up and went to find some way to occupy myself. Looking closely at the house, I thought perhaps there was a useful chore for me to perform. I was relieved to discover a few repairs that desperately needed my attention, and I resolved to work on them the next day.

Soon I began to feel a strange pressure, a mysterious restlessness pushing me around. I would not allow myself to become bored. I wanted to use the time up there well, but I actually didn't have a clue as to what I should be doing. How had the others spent their time? Surely they didn't just meditate … or did they? I now began questioning my motives for coming on such a retreat.

Surely I could get a lot of sleep. I could rest and have a peaceful time at the very least. If anything went wrong I could simply return to the monastery. I knew the way. But now I was being complacent. It would be a failure if I canceled this experiment too early, a retreat that I myself had asked for. I wanted to maintain my resolve and stay at least a few days.

I sat under the tree again. Breathing deeply, I exhaled slowly and evenly, as the Master had taught me.

My senses basked for a while in the unspoiled beauty. But as time passed, my being was beaten down repeatedly with all kinds of withdrawal symptoms, which assaulted me with uninhibited force. I remained calm in my sitting place and observed the flow of feelings and irritations twitching and jerking around inside me. I perceived the habits, mechanisms, and mental concepts that were connected to these disturbances. I could witness the entirety of my inner turmoil, my chaotic madness.

This extroverted energy held me in its claws, dragging me helplessly through the empire of death, pursuing the concepts of "this side" and "the beyond," the two valleys of death making up the one world in which I was trapped.

In this melancholic desert of loneliness, I saw myself as a withering flower. It was obvious that I was the source of this fear and loneliness, and that only I could overcome them. But the root of this misery ran deep. I had managed to wear down and discard many old dusty layers, but the core of these depressing energies remained. The core of it couldn't be meditated away.

Patience and attentiveness were the keys to freedom: that is what I had been told often. I settled myself deeply into following this valuable advice. I vowed deeply not to pause until I had freed my inner being and conquered the powers of death. Those forces had always knocked me off-balance and left me anxious and impatient.

I set aside my desires and longings for success, for achieving something, for arriving at a goal. The immensity of the universe was not to be seen or understood through the means of an enforced will.

Twilight advanced over the region. Golden shadows heralded the advent of night. The day was mooring in the harbor of sleep. The dwindling light offered me some moments to reflect on our limited time, and how eventually life within the body fades away. In spite of the all-consuming energies of the fleeting world, the timeless was now awake within. The inner eye was more consistently aware of that light within. Within this inner glow was the voice of immortal powers.

Covered in warm blankets, I lay in bed and waited for sleep to come. I don't know how or when this transition occurred but at some point, as the minutes and hours passed, I was asleep.

In the morning I was awakened by a loud noise. It was pouring rain. The stream next to the house had become a raging river. It was considerably cooler outside as well, so I spent the entire day inside the house.

I contemplated my long journey through those mountain valleys separated from the rest of the world. There, the window to my soul had opened, and I caught glimpses of the possibilities. Energy bubbled from the fountain of love within my heart. My yearning to finally submerge myself in the ocean of divine light was overwhelming. But still I hesitated to enter the wide-open gate in front of me.

I spent the day doing small chores and gave myself long breaks between them, during which I meditated. The rain didn't let up for even a moment. Instead, a strong wind rose up, which by early evening had managed to pull a huge thunderstorm along with it. All around the hut I heard the sounds of the natural world howling and crashing. The noises became so intense I feared the roof would be torn off. Primal forces flaunted themselves with brutal force. I felt helplessly isolated, anxiety and fear creeping into my psyche. This great unease forced me once again to look closely at my inner condition. Fears, like shadowy figures lurking in the night, crawled up from the unplumbed depths within.

I had never been confronted with a storm of such tremendous power. Confounding emotions surged over me like a flooding river. Unrecognizable urges attempted to control my mind and lead me down constricted passages. But I was not completely swayed. I saw clearly that something in me had been liberated. Something had shifted. This stormy night resembled the one I had experienced when the Master had sent me to the confrontation with my own death. What was different was my inner core, which remained calm. Although fear was running rampant inside me, my being was untouched by it. The first time, the Master had sent me into the tempest. This time it was I who, without consciously intending it, had entered the storm of my own accord.

I took refuge within myself, returning to a still place of neutral observation that was unmoved by all outer circumstances. It was a state that no words could describe. To my astonishment, I saw how the multilayered fears and insecurities gradually receded, just as ice melts under the rays of the sun.

It was a wonderful glimpse of light. Ever more clearly I saw the path to ultimate liberation. I saw how it could really be done. "It is truly a pathless path!" The words burst out loud suddenly, my mouth moving with an uninhibited smile.

The storm outside continued to rage. Its strength had not weakened in the slightest. The raindrops were pounding even harder on the roof above. Undisturbed, I continued to sit there. Oddly, this untamed energy that had caused me so much fear now accompanied me like the sweetest music. Something had transformed within. Something had happened that couldn't be achieved through practices, meditation, or rituals. It was something that could not be managed or directed, nor did it have anything to do with skills I had acquired. It was an inner releasing, an awakening within the timeless.

Now I had a sense of what the Master had meant when he explained to me that clear and correct insight is direct experience. It is the inner liberating act itself. This time I had overcome the limited "I" with its magnetizing powers. At the same time it was absolutely clear to me that this experience should not be overestimated. The delusion of false security or the feeling of having achieved something special could easily arise. The subtlety of releasing the ego was not to be misjudged. Now I was clear about this. There was still too much inattentiveness and ignorance working within me, though these forces were becoming increasingly more perceptible and transparent.

"Eternity is a perpetual beginning. The path itself is the goal." The Master had made this clear to me.

Gradually the storm withdrew and, with it, the rain. It was almost dark as I stepped from the door and deeply inhaled the cool air. The natural world before me was fresh and radiant. Just as the rain and wind had washed and purified the atmosphere, my insights and clarifications had cleansed my inner being.

The ground surrounding the house was saturated and had become slippery. A large branch had broken off from the tree under which I had sat the day before.

So where was the Master now? What had he been doing during the storm? Where was this advanced student that the Master had been staying with? What was he teaching him? Question after question came into my mind. I was surprised to be suddenly aware of just how much I missed being near the Master.

After a look around the house I was relieved to discover that the storm had not damaged the building. I hauled away the branch that had fallen. Then, in spite of the dampness, I brought out two mats and laid them down under the tree. I sat upright and began to breathe deeply and calmly, keeping my eyes half-closed. The Master had joked to me at one time, "You have to keep the eyes half-closed, not half-open!"

My heart attempted to sense the heart and pulse of

the nature around me. Immense energies were invisibly at work up here. Only a tiny particle of this infinite whole had been revealed to me, a small facet of mysterious reality that had alighted within my consciousness. The past has no beginning. The future also has no origin. Between them exists a center point where the transient world withdraws, a narrow gateway to eternity.

Darkness had arrived. I nestled into my thick coat and threw a few blankets over me. The leaves of the trees murmured gently in the wind, which carried the dry fragrance of snow down from the mountains. Occasionally, the sheet of clouds would part, and through a fine silverlined opening the moon would appear, almost full. It cast its soft glow down on the tranquil flow of the stream, the light glittering on the water's surface, reflecting fluid forms of the moon's image.

Although I wasn't feeling very competent, I made the best of my solitude in this powerful mountain world. I did manage to push back the feelings of being left behind, but I was by myself, and not ALL by myself. I forced myself to remain seated and practice patience until this strange feeling subsided. An invisible hand soon took the cloud cover away, revealing the sky's sparkling countenance, abundant with stars. In the immeasurable beauty of this universe, I felt the one and only power, the sacred sun that reflects this universe's majesty and allows it to be perceived by the senses through an infinite variety of forms.

I thought, "This divine order is perfect! None of these expressions arrived by mere coincidence. The script written by the stars above is testimony." My soul devoured the nectar that was nourishing it

Shooting stars raced across the evening sky. "You can

make a wish," I thought to myself with a smile. But what should I wish for? I waited half in jest to see if something would occur to me. It came. "I wish very much that the Master were here with me. Perhaps... he can hear me."

THE UNEXPECTED

It was late as I gathered my mats under my arm and returned to the house. I had hardly gotten my bedding out when I was startled by a gentle knocking on the door. I thought I must be mistaken. But the knocking came again, this time louder and more distinct.

This was highly peculiar. Who could have climbed up the steep mountain path in the middle of the night? Did someone else live in the area, someone I knew nothing about? Or was it someone from the monastery? I would have liked to turn back from the door and pretend I didn't exist. But the door had no lock. The person on the other side could come in at any time. I had no choice. Hesitantly I walked to the door. My breath froze as I slowly opened it. My heart almost stopped from fear.

In front of me stood the Master. He casually asked me if I wouldn't like to invite him inside.

Although I had wished for him to be near me, his arrival in the middle of the night was mystifying to say the least. It took a while to pull myself together.

"How are you? How are you getting along up here?" he asked me. A great tenderness filled his voice. I stoked up the coals in the fireplace. Soon water was boiling and I could offer the Master hot tea and some small biscuits I had brought from the monastery.

I had waited to answer his questions until an answer had formed inside me. Then I told him about the turbulence of emotions and feelings that had overtaken me, and also of the insights that came from the experience.

Soon, though, I could no longer hold myself back. I had to ask! "Please tell me … how did you get here in the middle of the night? I thought you were staying at the home of one of your students …"

"Come, sit down next to me," he requested. "It is true that I am staying with a student. He is actually not a student anymore, for he has become a master himself. I am only coming by for a short visit. I will be going back tonight."

I was determined to protest and ask him to stay at least one night with me. But with a movement of his hand, he signaled to me that words would be superfluous. As always, his resolve was clear and undeviating.

"In order to understand how I've come here, you must look in a new way at that which you call material. What you perceive through your senses, an impression of density and heaviness arises, which you interpret as material. In reality what you are reading and interpreting are nothing but different frequencies, which retain specific qualities. The frequencies themselves have no origin. Because of the identification of the senses with these dense lower vibrations, human beings have adopted a distorted vision of reality. The subtle ether body of the Earth suffers under the weight of the unawareness and confusion of its human inhabitants. It's hampered by the destructive developments that threaten the spirit of the planet, and obstruct the spiritual processes intended within the higher principle.

"The entire development of human life, clinging to this distorted worldview, has chained people to a long past. The majority of human beings live and create only from images of the past, and thus they create their future. In this way they remain trapped in the same circle of action.

"When people feel divided and starved for love due to these misunderstandings, the higher principle can neither be recognized nor applied.

"Pure unobstructed love, together with the unlimited creative power of the divine will, enables humanity to go far beyond its supposed capabilities. When the conditions of human limitations are overcome, then the conditioned world with its restrictions and constraints fades away as well. That world is extinguished.

"The pure heart is empty. It desires nothing and possesses nothing, because there is nothing that it is not. The pure heart is light itself. The body is light. Light is unlimited. Light penetrates everything and travels at tremendous speed.

"The conditions from which you have shaped your life lie within you. Evil is born within you, and evil ends within you. Goodness is born within you, as is the way of goodness. Through your confusion, your imprisonment begins; by ending the confusion, you end your imprisonment. Complete freedom comes from you, for you are complete freedom yourself!

"You create your own limits and boundaries. The limitless originates from you. Through the liberating experiences you are having, you are reorienting yourself, and through this process a new way of living is born within, a way of life that has nothing to do with any of your previous attitudes. Have the courage to think new thoughts. Allow yourself to feel the new wings born from your new experiences and let them carry you into the depths of the divine universe.

"In the world of the spirit there is perfect order. Therefore it is important that you stop creating disorder in your life. Disorder comes from you. You are responsible for it, as you have seen for yourself."

Immediately following these words he said, "Thank you for the tea. I am going now. In a few weeks we will see each other again at the monastery. Then we will go off to visit the pilgrimage site I told you about. Will you see me to the door?"

I had followed his words with undivided attention. They had brought me into a deep meditative state. It took a few moments for me to grasp that he wanted to leave.

"Will you see me to the door?" he asked me again. As for my question as to how he had gotten here, he hadn't actually given me an answer. It was likely that I wasn't in any condition to fully understand the answer anyway. The Master again was consistent and insistent. I should take personal responsibility and rely on my own experience.

Finally, I stood to accompany him. Perhaps I could at least observe his mysterious departure. A meek hope began to poke at me inside. I had hardly opened the door when the Master walked out into the darkness. I stood in amazement as I became aware of a powerful light emitting from him. I thought, "This divine light blesses the entire region, yes, the entire world." This recognition was my profound and direct experience.

"I am leaving now. I'll see you again soon!" He turned

back toward me and waved. At that moment an intensity of light emerged instantaneously with such blinding force that I could no longer distinguish his physical form within the field of light. Suddenly the light disappeared. There was no trace of the Master either.

Astonished, I stood there and stared into the dark night. I had somehow envisioned our parting occurring in such a way, but to see it with my own eyes, to witness the Master vanishing through an invisible gate of light, was unbelievable.

Once again my powers of imagination were overburdened. How was something like this possible? What exactly had happened? Again my thoughts were relegated to the realm of speculation.

As I lay down in my bed, I began to envision all the things I could do when my cultivation had reached such levels. What else might be possible, when one could move invisibly from one place to another!

A spree of bizarre ideas, like an extensive fireworks show, ran through my head. But these notions soon caused me to reflect; all these wishes and dreams reeked of a craving for power. They were egocentric and extremely superficial. These thoughts had to be acknowledged. They couldn't stay buried any longer.

Right here was the source of the self-inflicted limitations that ruled my life! With these wishes and hopes I was creating huge gray areas, where the pure light was falsified and discolored. Only the complete eradication of that which was calling forth these grey zones within me would allow the pure light to completely penetrate.

Sleep finally allowed me to slide into a dream world, a world with its own rules and regulations, a world that was not any more real but also not any less real than the waking world. I found myself meeting people from many different cultures. We sat together in a meadow near a forest and listened to a powerful being that was standing barefoot up on a cliff. His lips moved, but no sound could be heard. Still, the movement of his lips held a power strong enough to move mountains. Each atom was pulled along in a surging stream of light and redistributed into an imperceptible higher dimension.

Suddenly I could understand his words, though I didn't know if they were meant for me or for everyone.

"The farther you go along the path of liberation, the more you must be bound to the ropes that secure you. Delusions lurk, becoming ever more subtle, and it becomes even easier to be pulled onto false paths. But the path originates in the fire of the heart. The more you risk, the more you will transform. But the more you follow your fear, the more the fire in your heart will be suffocated, and the light that guides your path will be extinguished.

"This fire can guide you on its own. When its light is blocked, a thousand terrifying deadly shadows arise to put out the flame. If all self-absorbed, self-serving thoughts have not been let go of, then the light of the soul cannot conquer the angel of death. Give up the identification with temporary forms! Deny the sources of darkness of all their power, until they are completely wiped away!

"Once the heart is pure and unstained, and the battle between the higher and the lower is finished, then the field of battle also vanishes into nothingness. Still, this is not the end of the 'Path of Fire.' This is just the beginning. Be careful; be awake. Don't close your eyes. The original source of all things is without beginning. All is without beginning, forever One."

I awoke the next morning fresh and revitalized. On the horizon, a line of mild crimson announced the new day. The words spoken in my dream by that forceful being had traveled with me into my waking state and were now accompanying me as I went about my day. The mysterious indiscernible barrier dividing states of sleep and wakefulness didn't have the power to block them from my consciousness.

Who was it that I had encountered in my world of dreams? It was not a dream in the usual sense. I had experienced it as if I had been awake, though I was certainly asleep. I felt a great longing to encounter this powerful being once again. But I certainly didn't have the ability to manifest such a meeting myself.

I stepped out of the hut and went to the spot where the Master had vanished through the light-gate the evening before. I closed my eyes with the hope of sensing this invisible portal, perhaps even catching a glimpse of it. But no matter how hard I tried, there was nothing to see.

The increasing light in the morning sky foretold the sunrise. It was cool, so I started to do a few yoga exercises that the Master had shown me in the cave to soften my stiff body. As I did the postures, my breaths were deep and consistent. The Master had taught me a special breathing technique, whereby one takes in the prana of the sun out of the air and then consciously lets it flow through the 72,000 nadis, through the nervous system and all the organs, in order to fill them with greater vital energy. This was a great gift for my physical health.

After I finished my exercises, I stretched out naked in

the ice-cold water of the stream. "Don't forget to breathe!" the Master had called out to me at the freezing cold mountain lake. At that time I had no idea what he meant. Now I applied the breathing technique that I had learned and lay there for half an hour, without feeling the sensation of icy water. When I got out, I sat a while and allowed the morning wind to dry off my body. I felt free and invigorated.

Later in the morning, I wandered away from the hut for the first time. It seemed important to get to know my surroundings better. I hiked along the face of the cliffs, stacking dry pieces of wood I found along the way, so that I could locate them again later and bring them with me to the hut on my return.

In the basin of a valley, I was surprised to spot another person. It was a shepherd, who was tending a small herd of goats. The animals picked leisurely at sparse clumps of grass. I didn't want to scare the shepherd, so I raised my voice loud enough to be heard from a distance. He understood my friendly greeting and waved me over enthusiastically.

The first thing I noticed about him was the pair of glasses he was wearing. The frames had been repaired with rubber bands on both temples, and the glass was cracked on the left side. Two tightly braided pigtails hung down from underneath his colorful knitted cap. I had hardly sat down when he reached into his well-worn knapsack, unpacked his simple food, and set it out for me. He was surprised to have a guest from a distant land but seemed delighted to have me join him for a meal.

We sat next to each other quietly and watched the grazing animals. We spent a few hours there, chatting about various subjects. But during this whole time he never asked me where I came from. He didn't try to find out why I had come to this foreign land, nor did he ask how I arrived in this reclusive valley as a solo traveler. He seemed to be completely free of curiosity or any covetous thoughts.

His manner also made it impossible for me to ask him anything about his background. Without him being aware of it, he was offering me an extremely profound teaching. His simplicity and sincere companionship touched me deeply.

Our talking ended, and as we sat together in an atmosphere of unprompted silence, I sank into an unusual meditative state, where there was room neither for the knower nor for the known. The power of silence, unlimited nonbeing alone was the substance of this timeless state. Timelessness, eternity ... these were only shaded words within this powerful reality. Formless liberation was showing me its infinite depths. From within, a stream of love overflowed and engulfed me, transporting me into a state of ecstatic serenity. It was the first time I had consciously experienced a condition of perfect equanimity with all existence.

At some point consciousness of my physical body, which I had fully transcended for a short period of time, returned without me noticing. The shepherd was busy milking the one cow he owned and spoke to it in a gentle voice. "Excuse me mother, for taking a little of your milk away. I know it is meant for your calf." The calf stood next to him and stared at him with huge eyes. The shepherd continued to speak. "Do you like it here in this place I brought you, Mother? Look around. You can eat all you want. We will go soon."

He came back to me with a small bowl of warm milk. "Drink this. The milk will be good for you!" I drank it gratefully and asked myself if he realized that I had fallen into a state where my body no longer existed. He sat next to me and chewed on a dry piece of bread. His peaceful manner fascinated me all the more.

Only glowing coals remained from our small fire. Sunk within my thoughts, I observed the shepherd as he moved around the cold ashes. His small eyes caught mine, and then he said cheerfully, "Buddha says to us that as long as we are not extinguished and cold like these ashes, we are caught in the cycle of rebirth. So we should try to let go of all our desires, because they keep the fire burning.

"We must use all means to forget ourselves, to not make ourselves so important. It will take a long time until I am free. But I have all the time in the world."

His paradoxical play with words inspired a spontaneous flow of laughter. He was evidently pleased with himself. I had understood as well, and laughed along cheerfully.

In this intense mountainous world, far from any civilization, my life had changed drastically. Actually, I was having my first inklings of what life really was and how the shadows of death are produced by humans. My encounters with people here had placed me in front of a great mirror. In this reflection I could discover myself in a new way. What I saw surprised me and was not especially pleasing. I had to face my self-seeking ways and my clinging to the material world. I was able to discern the games I played, using manipulative, strategic maneuvers to attain power. It was painful and upsetting to continually observe the deceitful subtlety of self-interest concealed within my mind.

But a noticeable change had occurred. I had ceased to act or react as I did before. I was more relaxed, less forceful, less weighed down. I was clearer.

Will that change when I go back home again? This thought, arising spontaneously, startled me and sent a ripple of fear through my being. This mountain world with its simple, deep-rooted inhabitants had become my home. Yet, inevitably, I would have to leave this land that, once so foreign to me, was now so dear. That day must come.

The shadows grew longer, forerunners of night. Without thinking of it, I had spent the entire day with the shepherd. Even if I hurried, I wouldn't be able to get back to the hut by nightfall.

The shepherd was pleased when I told him I needed him to host me for the evening. He led me to a small shack nearby. The ground inside was covered with a thin layer of straw. Then he held out two old dusty blankets for me to cover myself with.

The night was cold. A biting wind whistled through the cracks in the walls. I was freezing, and there was no way to warm myself. My whole body was sweating. I thought I was probably becoming ill. The shepherd had fallen asleep the minute he lay down. I scolded myself. Why hadn't I left for the hut earlier? I felt as if a fever was encroaching and spreading through my whole body.

I didn't know how long I had slept. Suddenly it was day. I flung open my eyes. The shepherd stood in front of me and said a greeting. My legs were wobbly as I stood up. I followed the shepherd outside. He had prepared some buttered tea in front of the hut. When he heard me complain of an oncoming fever, his only comment was, "That will pass." As far as he was concerned, the topic was over.

I felt much better after drinking the warm tea and eating a few snacks. The shepherd was tending to his animals, again speaking to each with a calm, friendly voice. He stroked their heads and rubbed their necks. There was obviously a great trust between him and his herd. They appeared to have a way of communicating with each other that I could not grasp.

Finally the sun delivered its warming rays into the valley. I said good-bye to the shepherd and started to make my way back. My limbs were aching as I plodded toward the mountain hut.

On my outward journey I had chosen various spots to leave signs so that I would have no trouble finding my way back. After I had picked up as much of the piles of wood as I could carry and had walked for several hours, I managed to reach the hut. I was so exhausted that all I could do was let my load fall on the floor and lie down. I fell asleep instantly.

When I opened my eyes again, the sun was already positioned at the horizon, looming just above the mountains. I had slept the entire afternoon. I felt better and decided to sit down under the tree for a while to gather myself. I contemplated my encounter with the shepherd and the simple insightful words he had spoken. After a while, the flow of thoughts weakened. A deep and soothing silence settled within. I took respite in the all-encompassing universe. Words surfaced within me from fathomless depths, forming a prayer. I listened, fully immersed in this bottomless source of expression within me.

"You should carry all things within you, so that all

things may transform. Infuse everything with my radiance and my love-energy. Meet everything with your unfettered pure soul, which has been transformed by the light. In this way, elevate all things to my immeasurable heights. You will realign the arrangements of atom-clusters with the flame of your thoughts. Look in the secret mirror of the spirit, where all of nature finds its origin. There, discover the core of my eternal light-heart, from which everything flows and to which everything returns."

I let this revelation, which had its origin within my own being, settle deeper. I didn't want to forget one word.

The dark blanket of night spread itself over the region. I lay down but couldn't sleep. I tossed and turned, but could find no way to calm my thoughts, which were urging me to return to the monastery and see my friends again.

During the next few days I moved some things around in the hut and gathered firewood. It was important to me that I leave the hut as I had found it. I pondered which monk would be the next to take refuge in this solitude.

I continued to visit the location where the Master had said his farewell and disappeared through the invisible light-gate. This little spot of earth had become sacred for me, and I wanted to adorn it somehow. I sought out small stones and washed them in the stream. After I had gathered enough of them, I asked myself what I should represent with them. I sat there for a long time with my eyes closed, waiting for a sign or symbol of some kind. Whatever was willing to show itself would be it, but it shouldn't come from my own thoughts. It had to come from beyond them.

I stood up a few times, loosened the tension in my body, and went over to the stream to drink from the fresh water. I inhaled deeply, letting the fresh air fill my being. After much time had passed, a circle appeared before my inner eye. Within that circle were two smaller circles in succession. I knew intuitively that this image was the correct one and started working on it right away.

As I carefully laid out the first circle, words surfaced from deep within my spirit: "If you want to see the truth, then look through the mirror. The first circle is the external, the consolidated, the corporeal."

Quietly, I continued to work. As I set out the second circle, the following words formed in my consciousness: "The second circle is the perfect mirror of the first circle in the realm of the unseen."

And as I laid out the third circle, the voice said: "This third circle has transcended the first two. It is open, but imperceptible in the realm of the seen or the unseen. This most central circle is the sphere of the Illuminated. The first two circles are attached to each other. The third is the realm of the unattached, the realm of the un-attachable."

An unanticipated vibration began to hum within me. I had realized something, though I could not completely understand it in all its depth, which was frustrating.

I sat myself under the tree again and went into silence. No distracting thoughts presented themselves. My spirit was calm. I was in accord with the greater equilibrium. It dawned on me, finally, that I had laid out a mandala, which represented the divine, liberated, all-pervading human being.

With a flash I recognized the higher association of the three circles. I recognized how a human being is trapped within the two spheres of "this side" and "the beyond." I saw that when he transcends these two, he becomes a divine being. In just the same way as the spirit of the planet Earth is unified with the sun, and the sun is united with the divine cosmic fire, the human being who surmounts the first two circles is completely one with the higher unfolding processes in the realm of the infinite.

I thought to myself, "The entire consciousness of these cosmos, which reveals itself through humanity, must be purified, clarified, and infused with spirit. Only the human being can complete this divine task, for each person is both creator and creation. The Master had pointed this out to me and was a living demonstration of it. If people would realize the true depths of their beings, then the world, as we know it now, would completely cease to exist. All creation would have made a quantum leap out of the finite and passed into the infinite."

But at the same time, other words of the Master echoed in my mind, which tempered my grand flow of thoughts. "Creator and creation exist only in the sphere of the conceivable, only where cause and effect can have influence. In the final realm of truth, those two do not exist. Unity is neither a cause nor an effect. Otherwise, it would not be unity." The Master's uncompromising teachings were impeccable. Through them my life was endowed with ever-deepening understanding and ever-deepening significance. He continually exposed me to new ways of seeing what it means "to be."

I resolved to leave the next morning and make my way back to the monastery. I had a feeling the Master would also soon be returning there. I sat under the big tree for a long while, observing the scenery now decorated with shadows under the glossy glow of the moon. I knew the contours of the region so well that I could see the entire landscape before me in my mind with my eyes closed.

The mountaintops stood like citadels of silver, a cosmic diagram, unmoved through countless ages. I thought to myself, "The face of this planet Earth is so sublime, so marvelous. And what a wonder the orb of the moon is, how it circles around Earth with such precision, how it raises the sea and lets it fall." I sat fully enraptured in the stillness of the night, aware that I was a part of this passage and movement, vibrating with it since before the conception of time.

My heart called out to God with an invitation for him to live in the world of human beings in complete abundance. God had no place in the speedy structured world from which I came, where I was captive to the restrictions of time. I felt painfully aware of this dull, meaningless mind state marred with complacency, which allowed humans to trample in haste from one death to another. Now, as my inner eye was slowly beginning to open, I saw that I was gradually emerging from this inner state of darkness, that I had really begun to free myself of it. An intense compassion for all of life was burning in my heart like an immense flame.

It had become clear to me over time that the complete liberation of my being, the complete overcoming and dissolving of my entire limited self, would be the greatest way of helping mankind and the planet. But in the end, the wish for Self-realization itself and each thought concerning enlightenment had to be put to the fire and turned to cold ashes. If not, the concept of "I" remained, the thought of "me and my enlightenment," and it was exactly this concept of "I" that, through the aspect of mental separation contained within it, produced the duality that darkened my soul.

A strong wind had begun to blow as the sky pulled a thick dark cloud cover over itself. Soon my hut and I were overtaken by an ominous gloom. I quickly moved inside. Wanting to leave the next morning I was hoping that the storm did not signal a drastic shift in the weather.

From within the protected walls of the hut I listened to the howling wind gusting relentlessly through the mountains. The time of isolation had been good for me. Many things had clarified, and I felt ready to take on whatever was coming next.

I slept deeply without dreaming through the night. I awoke before sunrise, feeling rested and rejuvenated. I went and sat for one last time under the tree and meditated. My mind was calm and clear. This deep tranquillity held a powerful depth and extraordinary energy, which took on a dimension in which neither time nor thought existed. This energy is the light within the darkness, the white light that expels everything peripheral, transient, and restricted.

In this white light I saw that my past as well as the past of all humanity was in this moment within me, in its entirety. These records existed in my consciousness and in each cell of my being as living information in the present. And this present was also the future, for the present content of information was in constant motion. I was trying to understand my present state, but other than the vast load of words and ideas from the past from which I continually constructed and lived, I found nothing.

The light of the soul revealed that what I called life

was generated in my mind from moment to moment, and how all things generated in this way were constituents in the current of death, a force I was unconsciously tending, nurturing, and energizing. When I thought about my life, it meant only that I was contemplating my past, and trying to forge a plan that could possibly be realized in the future.

A wave of great solemnity and sobriety came over me. My captivity in a world of death and decay was glaringly apparent, providing a jarring jolt of reality. My good intentions and spiritual efforts collapsed like a house of cards. What horrified me most was not having been aware of the heartlessness and arrogance with which I had lived my life.

But it was pure love and nothing else that had ripped off the mask of heartlessness. This I knew.

I stood, thanked the tree under which I had attained so many insights, and started on my way. Something profound and yet impossible to understand had changed within me, but I didn't want to figure out exactly what it was. I wanted to let the things I had let go of go, and in no way replace them with something else. I didn't want to feed my understanding by trying to hold on to the experience.

I rambled down the path in this weightless, untroubled state of being, the light of which guided my steps. "Separation, time, duality; these forces move and sustain the two worlds but exist only in the hearts of the blind." These thoughts sprang forth from my being. My heart beat loudly, as if expressing its desire to imprint these words directly into my bloodstream, never to be erased.

Deep red covered the morning sky and a cool breeze greeted me on the path. The loud rush of the nearby stream volunteered as my constant companion. Small stones rolled under my feet as if they wanted to see who could get down the slope fastest. I was simply happy, happy without a reason to be happy.

The fine veil of fog down in the valley slowly surrendered to the warm rays of the sun. I stopped often to bask in the beauty and power of an untainted world high in the mountains, where my body had accustomed itself to the thin air and severe climate.

Early in the afternoon I caught a glimpse far below of the green valley and the small deep blue lake. I noticed that my steps began to speed up, but I reminded myself to take it easy in the manner I had come to appreciate in the Master and Gaya, whose every movement, every action, and every word were expressed consciously, and with great serenity. Nevertheless, I knew that this calm was not something I could practice, or I would inevitably fall into the trap of imitation. Obviously the mind state I would arrive at in this way could never be authentic. With Gaya and the Master, this serenity, this ease and equanimity were expressions of truly liberated minds.

The moment when the Master had disappeared through the invisible gate of light appeared in my mind. This memory transported my being into a state of pure delight. The event had triggered something deep within me. Something had been touched, and something had been released. He had awakened a primal intuition that had been slumbering in the deepest layers of my being. The Master had not been performing, or displaying some artistry, nor did he want to prove anything to me. What he allowed me to experience had cracked open my intellect. It had cut through my notion of what I perceived with the senses, what I thought possible and impossible. In a moment's time every concept I had held was exposed and broken down.

Thus I was forced to look at my life, or at least what my conditioned mind had thought it to be, and view it in a completely new way. It had been shown to me that the level of the perceiving mind, the mind that viewed, experienced, and identified itself with the bright and dark aspects of the material world, was very relative. On this level, the measure of truth was based in the perceptions and interpretations of the intellect, all of which are relative. This ruinous manner of misunderstanding was the cause of suffering in the world.

Before I had left for the mountain, the Abbot had explained something very important to Gaya and me. He said, "Pure intuitive awareness is not tied to the concept of a subject and an object, and so it is not restricted by the relative thinking mind, which sees and experiences the material world through its instruments of the senses and identifies itself with those things. Just as I use my clothes in order to cover my body, you should use your transitory thinking mind with all its contents as an instrument. Don't identify yourself with this thinking mind or with the things that fill it. Be free, and know that freedom is the condition of the Nameless."

Again and again I was reminded of these words, which brought me back to a state of great attentiveness. My life had become so intense with things happening so fast! Sometimes it was almost too much, and I craved an extended break, during which I didn't have to hear anything more. But I had come to understand that this break could not happen, not until I had overcome all my limits and boundaries completely.

In the early afternoon I strode through the large front gate of the monastery and into the main building. I saw several monks, and they greeted me briefly. I had to ask myself whether they had noticed my absence at all. I went down the narrow hallway and entered the room I had been assigned by the Abbot. I lay down for a while to allow myself some rest after my long descent. Later I wanted to see if I could find the Abbot or Gaya and announce my return.

I drifted off to sleep. A knocking sound woke me. Opening the door, I found Gaya and the Abbot happily welcoming me back with hot tea.

The Abbot affably inquired whether my retreat had been enjoyable, and if everything had gone well. The mischievous flashing of his eyes told me that he knew very well and had no need for my personal account. As always, I felt safe and supported in his presence. His heart radiated great warmth, which was the result of a lifetime of dedicated work for all beings. He tirelessly modeled this path that led to great bliss and final liberation. But this time I sensed something deeper, a sensitivity that couldn't be expressed with words. Perhaps it was a sensitivity that dissolved all divisions, unveiling a wonderful silent radiance. The Lord of Time no longer held any power over him. The Abbot had stripped him of his control through the power of unconditional love.

After a short time he left us. As always, he was very busy.

"How are you, Gaya? I missed you," I said, turning to

my fellow traveler. She gave a quick laugh and said, "Never have you arrived, and never did you go anywhere. But it is nice that you are here again. Tomorrow the Master will return, and I presume we'll be moving on soon to the famous pilgrim's destination he promised to show you. It's really an impressive place. I was there many years ago, but I don't suppose it's changed much since then."

Gaya led me to the room where she had painted her mandala to show me her work. As no one else was there, we sat and Gaya explained her painting to me. The first thing that struck me was the small golden Buddha, which sat in perfect lotus posture beyond the outer circle, centered at the top of the picture. His image was close to the circle but was not touching it.

The world of appearances in the spheres of the four directions was portrayed in multilayered colorful images. Everything was represented with its twofold aspects as they appeared in this world. Gaya explained the many details to me.

Suddenly the gaunt old monk was standing behind us. He spoke in a soft voice. "The human being is like the lotus blossom, which is born in muddy water. It grows in this cloudy water, until its pure white chalice can rise above the surface of the water and unfurl. At this point it can no longer be stained by the slimy mud. The way of liberation for human beings is just like this."

The monk had guided Gaya through all the components of her mandala and had communicated to her the deep insights that correlated to each aspect. He sat with us so that he might evaluate Gaya's work more closely. He was not a man of many words, but his concentrated stillness spoke much.

After a long silence he added, "For humans, everything but our true shining essence passes away. The pure light inside is covered on the outside by a lazy lump of flesh. This inner illumination moves this flesh for a while and shows it the way toward the gate of great equilibrium. The light-body is not made of flesh and blood, nor is it built from the basic elements that create the forms of nature. It is Buddha-nature itself. The light-body calms all storms and realigns everything that falls out of balance."

An everlasting kindness radiated from the eyes of the old monk, an eternal essence that shone from his body, blessing us and aligning us as well. His presence filled everything around us with a profound fragrance of silence and peace. He was empty of the illusory world, a nothing with a body, which after his death would be a nothing without a body.

My inner eye held a vision of him sitting under the tree up on the mountain in front of the hut, wanting nothing ... nothing wanting nothing. He was life itself, unfathomably deep, ceaselessly creating and flourishing. He embodied an uncomplicated simplicity of eternal truth. No power on Earth or in any other world could diminish or destroy this simplicity.

We remained sitting in stillness. My spirit was calm, relaxed, and extremely receptive--not to words, but to the pure illuminating power that filled the room. A younger monk entered whom I had seen before. His walked with gentle steps to his teacher and passed something to him.

The old teacher stood, nodded to both of us, and left with the young monk. I wanted to say something, but a subtle energy restrained my tongue.

Later Gaya and I went out of the monastery together and followed the path to the lake. As I absorbed the beauty and abundant plant life surrounding me, I felt as if some force had put me under a spell of enchantment. An elevated awareness and a tender feeling of compassion for all living things were vitally alive within, a heightened emanation of the love-energy that pervaded our encounter with the old monk.

But thoughts soon made their way into my consciousness. I wanted to understand this experience of embodying the essence, this higher expression of love that neither increased nor decreased. The luminous power of God, which is offered in each moment, which fills everything and allows everything to ripen and bloom; this powerful, ever-present force, which continually arises from our innermost being and extends throughout the world; this infinity of God, this light, love and beauty beyond measure; this inextinguishable fire, which emanates universal wisdom from all awakened souls, which imparts spirit and transformative power with a brilliance beyond imagination, blessing all things: this radiation of love was where I wanted to immerse myself, to finally be swallowed up in the universal treasure of God's light.

In getting to know the people from this land, I realized that through this light-energy, souls awakened. Human beings were transformed and returned to their original purpose. Gaya had noticed that I was deeply absorbed and stood still. I had the clear sense of having directly penetrated something very powerful, the feeling that a divine spring had opened from deep within.

Gaya said nothing. She looked into my eyes for a short moment, and a soft smile broke over her face. Without my noticing it, we had arrived at the hut on the shore of the lake. The people living there interrupted their work to greet us. They knew immediately that we were coming from the monastery and invited us to tea. Three generations lived in that house. The youngest family member, a small girl, was only five weeks old. Although they had enough to eat, they were all razor-thin and had deeply carved features. Their bodies and faces seemed perfect mirrors of this rugged mountain region. But friendliness and joy shone in the eyes of everyone.

The grandfather, who sat in the corner, was a mere sack of skin and bones. He remained seated, no longer participating in social interactions, staring out the window. He had a constant cough, which stole much of his life energy.

Gaya was attentive to the old man and asked the oldest daughter how long he had been coughing and how he had come to be so weary and lethargic. After receiving a description of his illness, four of us went out to the garden and the surrounding fields, looking for specific herbs and leaves that Gaya had instructed us to gather. When we had found what we needed, Gaya set our collected treasures in a large clay bowl and soaked them in cold water. She then rubbed all the herbs and leaves together carefully, combining the separate organic elements into a powdery mixture. During this process, Gaya continued to sing different mantras that increased the healing power of the plants, infusing them with her wonderful life energy, a power that extended from her healing hands as well.

The resulting concoction was a greenish-brown broth, which was boiled briefly three times and then put out under the sun for an hour. Gaya sat next to the bowl the entire time, not speaking a word. The entire family had gathered in front of the house and watched Gaya with curiosity, admiration, and amazement.

No one dared to stand or speak. The atmosphere had become almost ceremonial. Even the small children had stopped running around and were sitting quietly next to their parents. Only the three brown pigs were active, grunting as they eagerly scavenged for waste from the kitchen. It seemed to me everyone had forgotten that Gaya was preparing medicine for the grandfather. They were simply taking time to enjoy something different, something they didn't see or experience often in their everyday lives.

After an hour or so, Gaya went outside and made a small fire. With graceful motions she then flung small quantities of rice and ghee to the flames, along with an assortment of herbs, as offerings of gratitude to the one original fire. This was again a clearly structured ritual, accompanied by corresponding mantras. I knew that Gaya had learned much from the Master, but she must have had another master who had specialized in medicinal science. She was obviously well versed in the ancient Vedic healing arts, though she had never said anything about it.

We waited patiently, watching quietly until the fire was gone completely. Then each person went by in procession and took a bit of cold ash and applied it to his or her forehead. Gaya put ash on my forehead as well as on her own. The oldest daughter of the family filled a small bowl with the remaining ash, and we went back inside.

Sunlight fell through an open window, allowing dust particles to dance in the rays. One of the small boys was intrigued and moved playfully within the shimmering fragments of light. The adults watched with amusement as the child tried repeatedly to seize the light between his small hands.

The persistent hacking of the old man's cough broke the silence. Then the daughter spread ash across his forehead, and Gaya carefully poured out the bitter liquid for him. He pulled his face away after his first deliberate attempts to swallow. His daughter had to encourage him continually, explaining that this was a medicine that would help him. The old man struggled, pleading to stop the treatment after each difficult sip.

But before long the medicine had been administered, and the old man fell asleep. Within a short time, his breathing became calmer and even, and the heavy coughing waned.

Soon we were all outside sitting down together, and Gaya was asked to speak about the root of life. "We should never forget that we are protected by the sacred environment that surrounds us," she said. "Every single thing in this natural world is divine, for in each creation of nature dwells the boundless power of the eternal spirit. Our original roots are embedded in goodness, in pure eternal love. Just as the ocean never sleeps, we have to be awake in order to know this infinite love.

"The gentle feeling of discovering the wondrous light of the spirit without striving: this is the meaning of our lives. The blood-filled body fades with time spent in this transient world, but the timeless spirit that resides deep inside is enduring and everlasting. The world of the heart is the world of the infinite, where one discovers the immeasurable beauty of things. The smile of the sun and the deep silence of night, along with all things, have their origin in the eternal One."

After Gaya had talked, she sat in stillness for a long time. It was as if what she said had penetrated through all worlds, and all of divine nature was listening. Her words were full of bliss, drops of pure light conveyed from the universe of the soul, beyond the limitations of the sensory world.

I was deeply moved by what was spoken. I could feel how the perfect pitch of her speech purified and healed, permeating all the layers of a person.

As we were preparing to leave, one of the small girls ran into the house and approached us with a small reddish stone. Glints of light sparkled from it as she presented it to Gaya. She told us proudly that she had found it herself.

We walked at a leisurely pace along the shore of the lake and glanced down at the ripples etched by the wind on the surface of the water. White clouds drifted in clusters over our heads, and the deep blue sky suspended above them was very bright. Within me, Gaya's words were shining like sunbeams through the foggy mist within my soul. As I looked out, I knew that I had never seen nature with these eyes before.

The words went still deeper, echoing within me. She had said that we have our roots in this divine natural environment. Everything here is divine. Everything in nature is an expression of the One who is the most divine of all. And at this moment I was sensing nature just as she had described it. It was a way of perceiving that was free of thought, time, and memory, an unrestricted flow that could not be expressed in words. All my efforts, all the worries and the many expectations to which I had subscribed during my time on the Earth, were now floating by like the white clouds high overhead. I didn't understand the things around me; I was those things myself! A tremendous joy expanded within.

Gaya whispered, "Having no joy is joy. Never let yourself be carried away with emotion. The eternal silence is silent." Her words penetrated again like intense light rays. I noticed how I had tried to settle in this timeless state and hold on to it as long as possible. In this way I was making it an object of worship. Once again I had succumbed to the temptation of trying to control the eternal within the restraints of time, and I had done this without being conscious of it.

On the brink of darkness we entered the monastery again. Bidding Gaya good-bye, I retired to my room.

THE GOLDEN EYE

After a long interval, my thoughts finally returned to what had motivated me to undertake this journey. I carefully opened my book of notes and skimmed through what I had written. It wasn't much. I would have to expand on the things I had noted and add many new ideas as well. But how could I bring to paper the intensity, variety, and intricacy of what I had encountered?

I sat next to a flickering lamp hovering over my notebook long into the night. I allowed the events and experiences of the previous months to float across my inner eye once more, so that I might recall the all the profound words and teachings concealed in my memory. I constantly inquired of myself whether I'd actually gotten a point right, or whether my mind had fabricated its own renderings. If the second was the case, perhaps it was possible to satisfy myself with a superficial and subjective explanation of everything.

I took note of several questions that I still felt unclear about. I intended to ask Gaya and the Master about them later. Oddly, I found that the questions sorted themselves out without me thinking much. It was obvious which question should be asked to which person. This renewed, concentrated attempt to clarify issues for myself helped me to discover new aspects of my inner life. Without effort on my part, answers rose up from that inner world I had been cultivating. Old ways of seeing and conceptual mental constructs dissolved, with no new ones arising. I recognized with greater clarity just how things are, and why they are the way they are, as I observed them in relation to the natural flow of energy originating in the infinite, inconceivable, inexpressible One.

The evening passed, as I sat before a closed window and gazed up into the night sky. At times the pale face of the moon poked from behind the clouds. In these brief moments the deep chasms between mountain peaks were visible.

Not a sound could be heard in the monastery. The monks slept. The peaceful atmosphere of this sanctified place expanded through the stillness. In my room, the oil lamp cast magical shadows that danced on the walls without pause. The peaceful atmosphere of this sanctified place expanded through the stillness.

"We have our roots in this divine natural environment. Everything here is divine. Everything in nature is an expression of the One who is the most divine of all."

These words touched me in a profound and powerful way. My heart longed to arrive on the distant boundless shore of the world of saints. My human existence was nothing more than a wink of an eye. How childish I had been prior to this trip, chasing after things of passing material value, captivated by my own self-interest!

In the light of my soul I felt I had a sense of how life would be when all the lower energies were overcome and only this blissful peace flowed through my heart.

I had just begun to doze when the gong rang to announce

the morning meditation. The vibrant tone penetrated even the farthest corners of the monastery. I stretched my body out like a cat, trying with juddering motions to shake the sleep out of my limbs. The monks were already shuffling through the corridor and into the meditation hall. Only the old monk walked at an easy even pace. I sought him out, and as I approached him, the glow of his smile lit up the symmetrical features of his face. He seldom visited the meditation hall, for he was meditation itself, through and through. He must have been there that morning for a reason I was not aware of.

Outside, it was dark and dreary. Inside, the hallways were barely lit, but the residents knew exactly where the stone steps dropped down. In the large hall, the windows stood wide open, though it was ice-cold. I breathed in deeply, tasting the sharp chill of the frosty morning air. There seemed to be an unusually large number of monks gathered in the hall. I assumed monks from nearby monasteries had arrived. The monk who had accompanied me up the mountain had said that sometimes monks came to the temple for a few days. He too had traveled to other monasteries, staying at each for several days. On the other side of the hall I noticed several women in long ocher robes with shaved heads, and Gaya sitting among them.

After everyone had taken their places the Abbot entered with the Master, who was shining like the sun. My heart leaped with joy and I wanted to run over to him right then and there, but the emotional response was quickly swallowed by the concentrated stillness of the hall.

The monks began to recite the sutras, their powerful voices producing a strong vibration inside the room. The intensity brought up strange feelings within me. After the chanting, we all became absorbed in a meditative silence. We were drawn backward into that natural flow from the boundless ocean of clear white light, which was imperceptible to the earthly senses.

As daylight drove the darkness from the hall, the morning meditation finished. I looked around for the Master, but he had already left. I was amazed that I hadn't suffered during the meditation, even though it was so cold. But I was happy not to be visiting there in the depths of winter, when many feet of snow would lie on the ground and the temperature would sink far below freezing.

Satiated with a deep inner peace, I went back to my room and waited for breakfast. Before long, there was a knock at the door. It was the Master, without a doubt! I could sense him through the wood. I enthusiastically opened the door and invited him in. We sat, and I expressed the joy I felt at seeing him again. But the Master was expressionless. He was the same as always, calm, composed, fresh as a cool summer breeze. A feeling of disappointment hoverd within me. I had expected the Master to express some sort of happiness at seeing me, just as I had expressed mine at seeing him. But he did not say a word. With each moment of silence, my ego crumbled.

"Has the time in the monastery been meaningful for you?" the Master asked me finally.

"Yes. It was a very beneficial experience," I answered. "Many things have become clear to me. By being with the community of monks, I've been exposed to a way of living that was completely foreign to me before. That was tremendously valuable."

"That is good," said the Master. "Tomorrow we will

leave. Some monks are headed in the same direction we are, and they will accompany us part of the way."

We sat for a long time together. I looked at him closely as he remained with his eyes closed. He seemed to have changed his appearance once again. He looked much younger than before and was now brighter than ever.

The questions I wanted to ask him were spinning around in my mind, yet I wasn't finding the right words. But the Master beat me to it; he didn't need words to know what was occupying me.

"The state of having no desire is, in fact, the state of liberation. And liberation is nothing but the liberation of the attachment to the ego. When you have freed yourself from the bonds of craving, you arrive at liberation. The whole construction of delusion vanishes like fog under the warmth of the sun, when the eternal seer, the witness, realizes that what he sees is solely and exclusively himself."

"What happens to knowledge then?" I asked.

"That disappears as well," he replied.

"What is this seer, this witness? Can you explain that to me?" I continued. "How does he see this world? I don't follow that. I'm wandering in the dark."

The Master seemed to be listening deeply within himself, as if looking for just the right words in order to give me an answer I could truly understand.

"You say you are wandering in the dark. When you find yourself in a dark room, where there is no light whatsoever, you come to the conclusion that it is dark. But it is impossible for the darkness itself to see the darkness. There is the seer, the witness. If he was not something that transcended the darkness, he could never discern that it is dark.

"Now look, there are two essential things here: the darkness, and the one that sees the darkness. How could you know that it's dark? Try to see that you are not the darkness you are looking at. You are the witness, the viewer of the darkness. When you close your eyes, you can experience exactly the same thing.

"Wisdom itself is the witness of the knower and his experiences. Don't let yourself be dragged down by the deceptions of a distorted, darkened world. Never forget: you are always the witness, the seer. You are not that which your senses see in the external world. Your thoughts are tied to what your senses experience: you interpret what you see, and then you model your life after what you experience and interpret in this way. But the one who sees is the sun; the things he sees are fog under the sun. Fog comes and goes. Never forget your true state of being for an instant. Don't forget yourself!"

He laughed and gave me a friendly pat on the shoulder. His laugh was loud and hearty, and so electric and infectious that I was actually shaking. It seemed that when the Master laughed, all of creation laughed with him.

The gong sounded, calling us to breakfast. The Master stood up, still laughing, and said, "Come. Let's go and eat those illusions!" Before I had a chance to think, he was up and standing in the hallway. I had to hurry to catch up with him.

The mood at breakfast was cheerful. Extra tables had been set up in the dining hall for the guests. Before the meal, a sutra was recited. The monks ate their food mindfully, something I noticed that morning for the first time.

After breakfast, the Abbot invited Gaya and me to follow him into the room where he welcomed guests. The

Master wanted to come later. The Abbot poured hot tea for us and introduced three young monks who, if the Master agreed, would accompany us. They nodded in a friendly manner. Two of them were very reserved and hardly spoke, while the youngest was animated and talkative. It wasn't long before the Abbot directed a question to him. "What are the greatest obstacles for those who are on the path of liberation?" he said to the young monk. "Can you tell me?"

I waited with anticipation for an answer, as this was a burning question in my mind as well. But the monk took his time, unhurriedly sipping on his tea.

Speaking from his deepest inner source he answered, "The past, the present, and the future."

"What is an obstacle of the past?" asked the Abbot, this time not allowing the monk to keep him waiting for an answer.

The monk spoke up quickly. "To bring the past into memory, to remember it and to let oneself be affected by it, that is the hindrance of the past." The monk continued without pause. "The obstacle of the present is more complex. More than anything it is giving meaning to superficial intellectual things, to cultivate these tedious thoughts, and to interpret and justify them. This is the obstacle of the present. The obstacle of the future is that you create worries, and you expect difficulties before they actually occur. This creates the obstacle of the future."

The Abbot nodded, satisfied with the monk's presentation. I already knew how well schooled the young novices were, but I was amazed at the grace and clarity with which this one answered the Abbot's questions.

Gaya, who had been sitting next to me and listening,

turned to the young monk and spoke. "You have spoken with great wisdom. If you don't mind I would like to add something." The young monk laughed his approval. "It is important, that we share our experiences and our insights with each other. It is also important that we control our senses and do not negate them. When the old forces of habit become weaker, the senses fall under the reign of the cleansed and purified spirit and are utilized by it. These faculties must be used for the purposes for which they are intended. Don't allow them to control you. Don't be deluded by the world of the senses. Control the senses, and they will function within clear guiding principles and fulfill their purpose in this way. Within these guidelines, one can observe what the heart pushes away, what causes it anxiety. Live in silence and let go of anxiety. The cause of all anxiety is the wrong application of the senses. Watch carefully over them, and you will see that they are there to help you uncover the secrets of life."

The eyes of the Abbot lit up like two great stars. "Well said!" The young monk put his palms together to express his gratitude. The other two had listened attentively. They sat motionless without adding anything to what had been said.

The Master entered the room and sat with us. The Abbot handed him a cup of tea and turned to us again. "I understand you will be leaving tomorrow, but please know that you always have a home here. When you desire and are able, you may always stay for as long as you wish."

The invitation was sincere and was meant to be taken seriously. Touched by the warmheartedness of the Abbot, I asked myself whether I shouldn't remain there. But after a few moments it was obvious to me that destiny had not brought me to the monastery as a final destination. Still, I could certainly imagine coming back for a longer stay.

Filled with gratitude, I gazed into the warm eyes of the Abbot. Suddenly, between his two eyebrows, a luminous golden eye appeared. At the moment I saw this, I felt a slight prickling between my eyebrows in exactly the same spot. I also felt a strange pulsation there. In the next instant I saw the illuminated aura that surrounded him, and the radiant energy extending from all objects around me. In this moment I understood the source-vibration where visible and invisible objects originate.

This vivid awareness did not last long, but it caused a fundamental shift in my attitude toward all things. The Abbot turned to me and elucidated. "Nothing is fixed. All bodies, yours included, are energetic dream-bodies and have no real substance. Truth is beyond dreams. Truth is now."

The Master laughed and said to me, "The 'I' has no body. The 'I' needs the rational mind with its intellect, and it needs the senses as devices in order to manage things so it can cultivate itself in the illusory material world. Its subjective movement takes place deep within human beings and is later put into action in the external world. This is how the subject creates his object, and how then the object has its effect on the subject again. This is the source of human perception, and process of interpreting an individual world. The 'I' is the platform on which the subjective worldview is built up. It then reflects itself outward.

"When the human uses his rational mind to analyze something in the external world, he is actually analyzing something within himself. Binding oneself to the rational mind kills the intuitive mind. So when we are looking deeply at things in this way, we should never forget that the 'I' has no body and will never have its own objective reality. It can only live, develop, and express itself within a time-conditioned relative dimension. Because it always changes, its development and external expression also change form constantly.

"What are we really, we who are sitting here right now in this room?" he asked, obviously prodding us.

The Abbot was so pleased with the Master's question that he burst out laughing. Smiling with delight from ear to ear, he turned to me and spoke. "The Heart Sutra, which we recite daily, expresses this very clearly. Listen carefully: 'Form does not differ from emptiness. Emptiness does not differ from form. That which is form is emptiness; that which is emptiness is form. The same is true of feelings, perceptions, impulses, and consciousness. There is never something born, nor something that dies. Nothing is tainted or pure, and nothing is increasing or decreasing. Therefore, in emptiness there are no feelings, no perceptions, no impulses, no consciousness, no eyes, no ears, no nose, no tongue, no body, no mind, no color, no world of mind, no consciousness, no ignorance, and no ending of ignorance, no old age, no death, and no ending of old age and death. No suffering, no origination, no stopping, no going, no coming, no path, and no achievement.'

"The completely awakened one knows no obstacles. He is no obstacle. He lives completely free, completely enlightened, in the state of Nirvana." The Abbot had closed his eyes. As he was speaking he had shifted into a deep state. Then, he suddenly opened his eyes and said, "That is all."

The Master stood, and we said our farewell. Although we weren't scheduled to leave until the next day, the Abbot was always busy in the morning, and he would have no time to spend with us.

I waited until everyone had left the room. The Abbot had intuited my wish to spend a moment alone with him and shut the door behind the young monk who was last to leave. "Come, sit down here next to me," he said.

I felt such a deep trust in his presence! It was as if I had known him forever. He spoke to me in a calm voice, "You have returned. That is good."

My heart began to beat loudly in anticipation as I posed my question. "Do we know each other from a previous life? I feel so much trust when I am around you."

"Whether we know each other from a previous life is something I don't know. It is also not important. What is important is that you have returned to your inner source. That is where we have indeed known each other forever. That is where we are deeply connected. That is where there is no difference, no separation between us. You have found your way to the Master, or he has found you. In any case, it shows clearly that you have been engaged for a long time in the work of completely transcending and liberating yourself from all limitations.

"I have noticed that your spirit is vital, that you understand complex teachings quickly, and what is most important, that you know to take what you have understood and apply it directly and correctly. That is the true way, to rid yourself of everything old and limited inside you. Continue to be alert. Never lose this vigilance! The dark forces in this world are powerful. Many are interested in keeping the world as it is, in its limited condition. You have to know this. Soon you will know for yourself what I mean. That is to say, even though you understand what I am saying, you are not fully conscious of it yet.

"As I explained before, there are two communities, two brotherhoods. One is universal and not from this world. One is from this world. The Brotherhood of Light, or the Lodge of the Transcendent, exists with no relationship whatever to the brotherhood of this world. You must guard yourself, because the brotherhood of this world also speaks of light and love, but its members follow the false light, the light of the dualistic world, which they control. Don't be blinded! Contemplate the words of Master Jesus: 'You will know them by their fruits.' The Brotherhood of Light has worked for the awakening of true cosmic consciousness that has been sleeping within all living things. Understand deeply that you are beyond this physical body. Understand deeply that you exist beyond birth and death. Understand deeply that the only true ones are those who find light, love, and wisdom that are not of this world. Understand deeply that true existence is neither in this world nor beyond this world. Both are dream-realms of the 'I.' Where material interests, power, and domination have value, be watchful. Dark forces are at work. The origin of the self-proclaiming 'I' in human beings is produced from these energies. Here, the 'I' can explain itself and justify itself.

"But do not understand this as simply black and white. However many states of consciousness vibrate in this transient world, that is the number of components the dark force has. This energy will surely be recognized as light, and it is light, the light of duality, a magnetic trap made up of two worlds, this one and the world beyond, the two realms of the dark force.

"I am not explaining these things to you to frighten you. I want to impress upon you the significance of completely transcending the 'I.'

"Here in the great vastness of the Himalayas there are also monasteries where the dark energies are cultivated and mastered. That you must also know. Not all that sparkles is made of gold. But it is also not true that we are the favored people and they are the bad people. They have chosen another path of experience, according to their state of consciousness, and apparently cannot act differently.

"The most important thing is that we do not judge or condemn anyone. With equanimity, we bring them respect, understanding, and unconditional love. As long as the 'I' is there, the dark energy is also there.

"Think about what I have said. It is important that you can perceive, recognize, and differentiate. Perhaps we will still see each other in the morning. I wish you much strength and all the best for your travels. May each step, each action, each feeling, and each thought fully liberate all beings."

Soon I was sitting in my room again trying to absorb what the Abbot had said and write it down. I understood that a truly free person needed nothing more from this world, including his body. The Master, the Abbot, and also Gaya were people of this sort. They helped all living creatures find the path to ultimate liberation.

I had observed how in the presence of the Master people were sometimes healed, sometimes brought to an awakening, or ultimately liberated according to their conscious state, their spiritual maturity. What I found most exceptional in the Master was his inconspicuous manner, the simplicity and humanity of his being. If I had met him somewhere without knowing who he was, I would have gone past him a hundred times without taking a second look. Other than the clear intensity of his eyes, which, though warm and gentle, pierced through to the root of everything, there were no external indications of his immensity. His true nature was an immensity which I could see only a minute part of, a vastness that was unfathomable, beyond imagination.

Only after listening to the Abbot was I aware of what incredible good fortune I had had that the higher powers of fate had brought me to the right place at the right time. I was free and fulfilled. I felt the need to thank God in silent prayer.

Sublime thoughts gently rose to the surface of my mind, and I wrote them down. I wanted to be able to remember those wonderful moments.

The words of the Abbot stayed with me for a long time. His instruction had been a complex communication intended specifically for me. There would have been no reason for him to mention those things to me had that not been the case. There were things I could not fully comprehend, and that left an unsettled feeling inside. But I was convinced that what remained obscure would one day reveal itself. The Abbot's penetrating and earnest words would serve as valuable tools for the rest of my life.

After awaking early the next morning, we were soon ready to leave. As we stood outside the main entrance to the monastery we learned that only two monks would accompany us. I had no idea what had happened to the third. No one else appeared, except the Abbot, who wanted to have one last moment with us. The others had already gone to work. Then the gaunt old monk appeared out of nowhere, standing under the doorway and waving to us. Gaya hurried over to him, thanking him for everything. He quickly withdrew and disappeared inside the building.

The Abbot addressed us. "We have never arrived, and we have never departed. That we are temporary guests on planet Earth is just a thought, an idea."

Encouraged with these words, we left the monastery behind. As I turned one last time to look at the large entry gate, I felt one eye crease into a smile, while the other began to well with tears. Gaya whispered in my ear, "Truly a wonderful place."

We trekked the entire day through raw mountain landscapes. The fertile valley was behind us now. At times we stopped for a break. Few words were spoken as we sat basking in the power and silence of the mountains. When we started walking again, the only noises to be heard were the crunching of earth underfoot and the forceful wind blowing along our trail. I felt protected, filled with a deep sense of security that increased with each step. I felt as if I was being carried, and I knew that this was a sign of the immeasurable love-energy that ceaselessly poured forth from the divine Self, streaming from the Master's body and blessing the entire region.

We traveled for a few days. We slept at night in caves or at the homes of mountain farmers. After many hours of not speaking, the young monk disrupted our tendency toward silence and asked me with childlike curiosity about my work, my lifestyle at home, and even my apartment. After he had heard enough to form his own image, he said, "I am very sorry for you. That is awful." He then continued along next to me, absorbed in thought. It was as if he had heard the most terrible story he could possibly imagine.

This reaction confused me. It hit me like a cold shower. I had tried to give the most unprejudiced description possible, portraying not only the disadvantages but also the benefits of life where I came from. His answer was perplexing. There were no criteria for me to analyze his response. The innocent young monk had unintentionally delivered a stunning blow. Of course I had always reflected on my life, but it was never so terrible that someone should pity me.

Yet the life I had lived previously was obviously in complete contrast to the life of the young monk. After a while I was able to let go of my emotional reaction to our exchange. Silence returned within. As I looked around, the words of Gaya emerged from my memory and echoed: "All nature is divine." The mysterious pulse that filled all of nature was vitally active in Gaya. It allowed her to feel that pulse, the heart in all things, and impart that pulse to those beings that needed it as well.

Powerful energies permeated this tough mountain world hidden from modern existence, but the restricted channels of my consciousness did not allow me to perceive them in their fullness. I could only recognize bits and pieces of this unending reality. I lived life with my consciousness harbored at a narrow inlet on the shore of an immense ocean. I experienced how the watchful soul inside me was waking, how it could discern hidden truths, penetrate into unfamiliar mysteries, and gaze into the indescribably radiant face of God. But my heart was too strongly bound by self-imposed barriers. The finite had not yet turned me loose. I felt as if I belonged to two worlds. Eternal truth seemed palpably near, but I had not yet become it myself. I was still constrained within the sphere of the rational mind, still caught in duality.

After we hiked down along a steep outcropping, we took some time at the bottom for a longer stop. I sat down close to Gaya and explained to her the dilemma that was plaguing me. She listened attentively, though I went on longer than I would have liked.

When I concluded my explanation, she breathed deeply and offered her thoughts to me. "This dilemma is known by everyone who is working for final liberation. That is why you have come here, and why you have met the Master. You have experienced the divine Self. You know that it is unlimited and functioning within you. It has the capability to channel eternal godly power, to transform it, and to use it when necessary. This is the energy that will guide you out of your dilemma. The 'I' cannot subordinate itself. With intense efforts, it can certainly approach the divine, but it cannot take the final steps on its own. That is why we need someone like the Master who gently takes away all our limits and restrictions and brings out the divine Self in us, so that we also learn to function within this pure energy. Let me pass on a little image, which a dear friend who has since left this world once offered me.

"The light of a candle cannot be compared to the light of the sun. The candlelight represents the limited rational mind. The light of the sun that shines above our heads cannot be compared to the light of the divine, because the sun above will also fade one day, just as the candle goes out. The ever-present Self cannot be extinguished. It is always the ever-present Self. But imagine that the candle would travel toward the sun. It would melt long before it arrived at its destination. The candle has limited capabilities when it comes to making such a journey.

"The divine spiritual warmth of the celestial sun flows through the Master. This warmth melts all ignorance. It cracks open the locks on spiritual power, but only insofar as humans can manage this energy, only to the point where people can live in harmony while they complete the processes of transformation."

I inhaled deeply, taking in the fresh air. I felt as if my body had been reloaded with energy. Meanwhile, the Master and the young monk, who had gone off earlier, were now standing directly in front of us reaching out with two hot cups of tea. But they had not made a fire, and there was no source of heat out here where we were trekking. So how did they manage to make the tea? I slurped down the hot drink with enjoyment, but that was the only noise I allowed myself to create. For once I was able to restrain my curiosity and not ask questions! Although the Master never confirmed it, I knew that he was closely observing every minute action and reaction of mine.

The following morning we arrived at a small town, where crowds of people filled the streets. The animated happenings there made me quite dizzy. It hade been a long time since I had been amid such a frenzy of human activity. I got a headache from all the noise and was hoping we would be leaving that place as soon as possible. The two monks said good-bye to us there. They were on their way to a monastery located outside the city. I was asking myself why we didn't do the same. But the Master made his way resolutely through the masses, and all alternative desires had to be forsaken.

The narrow main street pulsed with life. Children raced after dogs as merchants sang the merits of their wares. Buying, selling, and bartering were all happening simultaneously in various intensities of tone and volume, while the smell of roasting coffee tickled the inside of my nose. I turned longingly toward the small inn, where I saw several seated men conversing while nursing their cups of coffee.

Unfettered and imperturbable, unmoved by the stimulation of the sensory world, the Master continued on his way. Hardly any of the local people took notice of us. Here and there a few folks would glance over good-naturedly in my direction with an inquiring expression, their smiling eyes gazing out from rotund faces with features shaped by the harsh climate. Cows walked through the streets, placidly searching for something to chew on. A young woman sat on the edge of the road surrounded by sacks brimming with sweet-scented spices. She waved to us, making hand signs encouraging us to buy. Small sinewy horses with bells fastened near their throats and their heads sunk down to the ground trotted alongside us.

Things were calmer as we turned down a side street. Between the houses I could see wide-open fields far off in the distance. The green and yellow hues suggested that the harvest was not far off.

The Master came to a halt in front of an impressive house that was surrounded by a low wall. Chickens greeted us loudly as the Master went through the open wooden door and announced our arrival. It seemed no one was home, so we sat down on a roughly planed bench in front of the house and waited. The smell of hay quickly filled my nose, and I noticed that three cows were standing in a small stall nearby with their curious eyes set upon us.

Banks of clouds drew across the sky above us with great speed, heading east. Unburdened with thoughts, I let myself soak in the tranquillity at this spot. A strong intensity reverberated through me as words surfaced: "Silence is sacred."

Suddenly we heard excited voices calling out, "Master, Master!" An elderly couple appeared, followed by two women and a man whose pack was weighed down with groceries and other wares. The younger ones were apparently the children of the older pair. The old woman and her husband ran up to the Master and, demonstrating their reverence, bent down and touched his feet. The Master put his two hands gently on their heads in the gesture of a blessing. The greeting offered by the daughters and the son followed similarly. They also touched Gaya's feet and came toward me with the same intention. This was terribly embarrassing, but they didn't react to my discomfort or gestures, as I tried to indicate that they were mistaken in approaching me that way

The older woman went into the house and returned with water and sweets, which I later learned was the traditional manner of welcoming guests. "Will you visit the temple?" asked the old man. The Master confirmed that we would and then inquired about the well-being of the family and news of other relatives.

"It is a good time to visit the temple," said the Master at the end of his brief conversation. "At this time of year, shortly before the harvest, there are not so many people there." Our hosts nodded, and the Master suggested to them that they come along. They accepted the invitation gladly.

The evening was calm and peaceful. The living room was lit with several oil lamps. There was little talk. We could enjoy just being together quietly, often in complete silence. The man of the house asked me whether I had heard anything about the temple nearby. I said I hadn't. He explained that it had been visited by pilgrims for centuries. His wife added, "At the entryway of this temple, you will see that all worldly thoughts are as cold as the frost and carry no light. They must die."

Our host was eager to tell me more and proceeded to recount one story after another. As he spoke, I occasionally glanced over to the Master. Several times I noticed a slight smile on his lips. I must have been hearing stories that were often told when folks sat together at friendly gatherings such as this.

The house was bigger than I had imagined. We each had our own room. Moonlight broke through the deep blackness of night, while layers of fog hovered over the fields. I looked out on the vastness of the night sky, enjoying its magnificent arrangement and activity. Within this great expanse, Earth was moving, and in some tiny far-removed corner, I was sitting in a room, aware of my connection to everything.

I sat looking out into the silent evening for a long time. At some point I noticed the silhouette of someone moving away from the house. My eyes followed the figure as it stopped near four big trees and stood still. The more I concentrated my eyes, the more certain I was that the figure I saw was the Master. Initially I felt ashamed, my conscience heavy for spying on him like this. But I couldn't pull my eyes away.

Now it seemed he was conversing with someone, but there was no one else there that I could see. Perhaps he was speaking with the marvelous trees, I thought to myself. But then, out of nowhere a strong light appeared near him, a beam that continued to grow in intensity. Spellbound, I gaped as the heavens seemed to open, and from some imperceptible source an incredible illuminated being came into view, surrounded by radiance not from this world.

I pinched my arm to be sure I wasn't dreaming. Now the two forms were standing behind one of the massive trees, which obstructed my view. I guessed they were about five hundred feet away, but I could feel the powerful spiritual energy emanating from this illustrious being. I had never thought that something like this was possible.

From deep within me, the attraction to this pure being of light was almost overwhelming. Surges of ecstatic joy flowed through me. Tears welled up in my eyes. I had the sensation of merging with this unimaginable energy, melting into it, as if I was drowning in a sea of light. My feelings were detached from this world. The boundaries of the physical form had cleared away. This limitless majestic power was eternal love and wisdom itself.

A short flash lit the area below. The divine being had returned to the sphere of the eternal. I assumed the Master would return to the house now, but no, he went the other way. I followed him with my eyes as he walked across the fields and finally disappeared into the darkness.

Who was that? Who was this spiritual master who communicated with the divine universe in such an amazing and open way?

I was becoming more aware of my own limitless nature. I felt a new force circulating within, a power linked to a new multidimensional awareness. I had had frequent glimpses of this new energy, but each time the voice of flesh and blood had brought shadows that covered over the pure light.

Now I knew with certainty that I had had a breakthrough. I would not again fall back to where I was before. I directly perceived that this was where and how the voice of flesh and blood would finally be muted. I was amazed at how unspectacular the whole process of transformation was. I viewed the appearance of this supernatural being in a different way as well. Human consciousness, which attaches itself primarily to heavy, impermanent material things, becomes just as heavy and impermanent. Consequently, it has no way to access the infinite.

I had spent so many years full of hopes, full of countless imaginary desires, years spent on the concentrated search for an inconceivable truth, a search taken up by the "I," the "I" filled with desire to understand this truth, grasp it, and own it. What a crazy chase! I was the perfect warden of the prison where I was my own prisoner, serving a sentence longer than time itself.

I had to laugh. My behavior, all my actions up to this point, had been simply ridiculous. I had been a truly superficial being. But from the moment I met the Master that began to change. I took a deep sigh and lay down to rest. Images of those overwhelming moments I had just experienced played over and over again in my mind; the luminous being stepping out of nothingness…and the incredible light.

The Master had explained that we humans are vibrating, flowing states of consciousness that are mistakenly identified with the body and the material world. In this way, limits and boundaries are constructed and maintained. He pointed out that the diversity among the manifestations of divine energy relates exclusively to the level and quality of each vibration. The highest vibrations in the divine universe are so intense and so tremendously powerful that they deserve to be called "peaceful."

His comprehensive explanation had been laced with such strong energy that these teachings would arise from my unconscious in their entirety at just the right moment, allowing an immediate clarification of the higher significance of each situation.

The next morning I was awoken by the loud cry of a hen standing directly under my window. I didn't know how I should behave at my next meeting with the Master. Should I tell him what I had seen the night before, or should I remain silent?

For reasons that were not explained to me, the visit to the temple had been postponed for a day. After we all took breakfast together, we spent the entire day assisting the family with their work in the fields. Again I was impressed with the Master's clear-cut manner when he offered our help at breakfast. His warmth, simplicity, and uncomplicated manner modeled a truly genuine way of living that functioned clearly in each and every aspect. Seeing this was a continuously profound transforming experience.

When we took time that afternoon to rest after the day of work, I was sitting directly across from the Master and slightly apart from the others. He had not spoken the entire day and was now looking directly into my eyes. It was as if the scrutinizing gaze of the universe was cast upon me, and I knew the Master could see the specks of uncertainty floating in my eyes.

"Is everything going well?" he asked.

"Yes Master, but I have to tell you something that is very uncomfortable for me." Then, in a slightly trembling voice, I told him what I had seen the night before. He sat motionless and listened attentively, but I didn't notice the slightest reaction.

After disclosing my description of the previous night's events, I felt much lighter. He nodded slightly and said with a smile, "Let's make ourselves useful for our hosts and get on with the work." Then he was up and off with the others, who had already resumed their tasks.

Once again I stood there, not understanding the world anymore. I had expected the Master to explain who this divine mystically illuminated being was and to identify this light that had visited the night before. At least he should have said something about my observing him.

But whenever I thought I was coming to understand something about the Master, an event would occur which would completely wipe out this assumption. Only gradually did I come to accept the fact that I would never get to know the Master in the way I wanted. He would never allow himself to be put into such a role. He lived in the eternal ocean of God's power. He emerged for moments as a pure sparkling diamond, only to dissolve back into that boundless sea. He expressed his limitless being in each encounter and with each word.

All day we had gathered stones from the land and stacked them along the edges of the fields. Much preparatory work was necessary before the ground could be plowed and made ready for sowing. At the evening meal our hostess told me how the stones would be put to use. "Each of the stones when set down mindfully enhances the beauty of our gardens and helps them to be productive and healthy."

The Master added, "Each act done consciously is a cosmic act, which creates order both inside and outside."

THE SOUND OF THE UNIVERSE

Early the next morning, we were on our way. Our path led us to a very fertile area. The tree line was at almost ten thousand feet above sea level. We passed cascading waterfalls as we entered a small valley. A temple stood in the distance that we'd visit on the way to our final destination. We met many pilgrims who were on their way to or returning from the temple, and the Master always exchanged a word or two with them.

The valley was filled with a soft morning light. After three hours of walking, we arrived at the temple's entrance. I stood in wonder in front of the huge structure rising up before me. At first glance it had seemed much smaller. I could already feel the strong spiritual energy emanating from the place. At the same time, I noticed that the act of thinking was almost impossible. When the flow of thoughts was overcome, time ceased to exist.

We entered the temple and went through a colonnade. People were sitting everywhere on the stone floor, absorbed in meditation. We walked through a row of halls before arriving at the heart of the sanctuary.

A deeply concentrated, all-absorbing silence reigned here. A large black oval stone with its smoothly polished surface shimmering stood in the center of the room. It was a Shiva Lingam, the symbol of the direct presence of godly power. It was evident now that we were in a Hindu temple, but this one differed in many ways from those I had visited before. Obviously the people coming here had backgrounds in other spiritual traditions. It was, in fact, a temple of the impersonal God itself, in which all religions melt into one, where each tradition hands over its particular characteristics to the energy of a universal love.

In this room at the heart of the temple, we sat in a corner on the floor. The moment I shut my eyes, I ceased to exist as a personality. There was only spiritual force. I was rooted in the divine universe. Each cell of my body was filled with this divine power. I breathed this light-energy, this heavenly nectar, feeling in complete harmony with the universal order. I had never known this quality in the breath before. I was inhaling and exhaling the entire universe.

My breath became slower, finer, then more transparent and subtle. Finally, without my noticing it, the movement of air came to a complete stop.

A sad voice began to wail within me, a voice without words, a voice that expressed itself in the form of dark and obscure images. It was trying to hinder me from arriving at true original emptiness. Death was dancing in front of me, masking over the eternal with its sorrowful call. This heartrending voice tried its best to bind me to the world of suffering, to make me its servant. It endeavored to deny me access to the original light. The soft and alluring voice attempted to justify a deceptive, faulty reality and bestow that reality with a royal preference. It promised me answers and solutions. My search for the truth would find success there. I moved through dark gloomy spheres, then very bright chambers, abundant with high spirits.

The voice would not go away, continuing its promises, dazzling me with amazing perspectives and possibilities.

But a substantial transformation had occurred within me in the previous months. I had detached myself so thoroughly from the trappings and deceptions of this transient world that I wasn't taken in. Behind the alternating voices of sorrow and sweet-talking, I could clearly make out the sleazy scowl of death and the self-proclaiming "I."

I lived through countless lives at lightning speed, sometimes in pictures, other times in blackness, all happening simultaneously. All at once it was clear to me that life as I had known it was nurtured and guided exclusively by those innumerable energies, events, and experiences. I knew also that I was the source of those energies, that I was living a world of my own creation.

The cause of birth, life, death, and rebirth, the house of the corporeal, was crumbling. I died a thousand simultaneous deaths and recognized the reality of all things existing at the same moment in time. The inner ties that had been holding me so tightly within now dropped away. My consciousness submerged to endless depths, where "all-knowing" was "not-knowing" and where the infinite took the form of a boundless zero. This lack of content, this limitless space of eternity, had nullified all nothingness in me. I was happy without any cause for being happy. An indescribable splendor, a bright and shining essence of true being, embraced me. I had entered the realm of God.

From some remote region in space, an urgent voice reached my ear. "Come back, come back!" I heard. Gradually I became aware of my body again. As I opened my eyes, I saw the Master. He was bending over me, massaging my stiff limbs. I had been unconscious. My body had been carried out of the temple and set down on a blanket our hostess had brought along. But the Master and I were alone. I would have asked him where the others were, but speaking was unnecessary. "You were far away! The sound of silence carried you off." The Master's eyes glowed with understanding. He massaged my legs, and I felt the pulse of life slowly returning to my body.

Now I asked him, "Did I die?"

He nodded.

"And you brought me back?"

He nodded again and said, "Your time to leave this body once and for all has not yet come."

Soon I could sit up. The Master gave me some water and sweet cakes. I asked him, "Where are Gaya and the family?"

He explained that they were visiting another place not far away but would not be back for several hours. He added, "There is a small guesthouse for pilgrims not far from here. We will spend the night there. The walk back would be too strenuous for you. You will have to build up your strength a bit more."

I could feel that he was right, though in another half-hour I was able to stand. The Master spoke again. "Many sick people come here to pray for their healing and recovery from illness. Indeed, many people are healed from their suffering. Now come along. You have to get moving. We have to go farther up the mountain."

We climbed silently upward along a narrow path. My lifeless limbs worried me initially, but with each step my body became more responsive. Eventually my natural movement returned.

A powerful change had taken place in my psyche. An

inner boundary in relation to life and death had been completely erased. Fear of the unknown--the great insecurity of confronting the invisible door through which we all go when we leave our physical body--was gone. My experience had pulled a veil away from my inner eye. Death, the one inside who dies, did not exist anymore.

We passed by several caves along the way. According to the Master, many of them were inhabited. Living near the temple had great benefit for those doing spiritual practices, he told me, and I could well imagine that this was true.

"Can you tell me why this place is so deeply imbued with spiritual energy?" I asked.

We sat down, and the Master explained. "The planet Earth is a living, spiritually energized organism. Many energy lines pass through it, and at specific spots spiritual energy flows out with stronger intensity. This temple sits on an exceptionally strong energy point. Two large light meridians of the planets cross here. In the last few hundred years, many people have arrived at total liberation here."

We trekked on. We had to pause often, as my body required intermittent rest. "Come on," said the Master, as he led me along a very uninviting narrow path that took us up to a large cave. At the entrance sat a man, stark naked. His eyes were closed, and his entire body was covered with ash. His long matted hair hung down almost to the ground.

As I looked closer, a jolt of fear came over me. A snake was right next to him. The moment it perceived our arrival, it disappeared into the nearby bushes. The yogi sat motionless. I was almost certain that he was unaware of our coming.

The Master spoke softly. "This is an avaduta. He has completely renounced the world. It has been more than twenty years since I visited this place. He was already sitting here then. An old woman I met in the temple at that time told me that every week they bring him some milk and a small snack to eat. Her father did the same, as did his father. No one knows where the avaduta siddha comes from or how old he is."

We sat for a while near him, and the Master directed a few friendly words to the yogi, who sat without betraying the slightest movement. The Master's tone of voice conveyed his respect. He turned to me. "He is a siddha. He masters his body and the forces of nature, and yet his inner core merges with the absolute."

I wondered to myself, "What is he actually seeing and experiencing?"

After we had stood again and made our gestures of leaving, a voice became audible, a voice from within me. It spoke in a language I had never heard, but I could understand each word. I turned around. The yogi was sitting as before, completely detached from the world. Not knowing whose voice I was hearing, I opened myself to this gentle offering of words filled with enormous power.

"Those who believe that equilibrium of consciousness is liberation are mistaken. It is the 'I'-consciousness that sees the Earth, the stars, and the sky, and it is the 'I' that identifies with them. For those who are empty, detached, and without consciousness, there is no Earth, no stars, no sky, no world. The world of things, names, and forms is the world of consciousness, and when consciousness dies, the world dies with it. Only THAT remains."

I bowed my head slightly and expressed my gratitude

to the yogi internally. He had expressed in clear and simple terms what I had recently experienced in the temple.

The Master walked close beside me as we continued on our way. As I went along next to him, I imagined that he had no idea of the discourse I had received. My "I" had risen up from my heart and begun to go about its business again, creating muddy thought-filled stains within my mind. I was not yet internally mature enough to inhabit the body and live fully in the divine universe without this dark intruder arising and immediately constructing its double-jointed world. To be One, that was the truth. But at this point I made another discovery that filled me with anxiety. I saw a deeply implanted fear within me, the enormous fear of stepping over the threshold and through the door where the whole world with everything that belongs to it is wiped away forever. I dreaded this absolute resolution, although I knew I would certainly take this irrevocable step one day.

We arrived back at the temple the next day. Gaya and the family were already there. Inside I still felt very fragile, though my body was restored to its normal state of well-being.

We soon left the temple and moved toward our lodgings. The sun disappeared, a huge fiery ball vanishing over the horizon of the western sky, bathing the snowcaps of the hovering mountains in a glowing scarlet. Scattered clouds, suffused with purple and gold, lofted high over our heads. A thick fog slowly crept up through the valley and would soon spread a soft covering over the nature below. The vastness that surrounded us at this moment was expressing itself in an almost surreal beauty.

The darkness of night was upon us as we entered the

guesthouse. The smell of hay and animals tickled my nose. A few shaggy yaks standing next to the house fixed their eyes on me. The Master and the family went inside, but I stayed outside awhile, absorbing the ambience of the evening. My thoughts were still with the siddha. What did he want to do in this moment? What kind of person can completely renounce the world? I breathed in the cool night air. Now I was seeing, with a stark clarity that was frightening, how much I had distanced myself from my previous life, a life constrained by the regimented norms of society, and a life I would have to return to one day! This thought was truly terrifying. I wondered seriously if I was even capable of returning to that existence at all.

Soon the poisons of insecurity and doubt were eating away at me, and in the process stealing my sense of stability. Grieving at my fallen state, I went back into the house and sat down with my friends at the table. Many families with numerous children were occupying the chairs. All were cheerful and easygoing, and the room filled with laughter and animated conversation. I, on the other hand, was caught in an estranged frame of mind. I took everything in without engaging, feeling isolated and distant. I let my eyes wander out through the window. The pale light of the moon had settled on the looming mountains on the other side of the valley, creating a ghostly profile. And that is how I felt: pale, without my own inner fire-power, my own light. How strange. Although I had believed that I had cut through the inner veil of death, I could now observe how a clustering had formed, an invisible logjam that bound me to the world of the senses and emotions and was generating these heavy moods. Thought had constructed its own isolated world again, a world of suffering and dissatisfaction.

I lethargically raised the pieces of food I was offered to my mouth and stuck them in. Soon I had a young boy with playful eyes show me to a room where I could withdraw. Once inside, the youngster remained standing in the room, his face full of anticipation. As I handed him a color pen as a gift, his eyes sparkled like tiny crystals.

I had barely sat down on an aged, roughly fashioned stool when I heard a knock on the door. When I opened it, five children were standing in front of me, extending their expectant empty hands in my direction. The most adamant of them, standing in front, was the small boy to whom I had just given the pen.

None of them would go away until each child had received a small gift from me. I had to rummage through my belongings quite awhile before I could manage to satisfy them all. Finally they left, exiting my room with loud immodest laughter, the last one slamming the door. Exhausted, I lay down on the bed and pulled a dusty blanket up above my shoulders. I wasn't able to fall asleep. Wild images raced through my mind, my inner eye filled with the extraordinary impressions and experiences of this unusual day.

Once again I felt myself a citizen of two worlds, tugged back and forth by unseen forces. And on this immense invisible battlefield a hidden war was raging. Divine power and earthly forces were crashing against each other with tremendous force. Both assured me they were best, and though I had decided long ago that I would follow the way of the divine, other powers that had been hanging around for centuries simply would not go away.

I was aware that this was a fight no one else could undertake for me. I had underestimated the depth and breadth of the energies I was up against, the hostile forces that were the source of my limitations. I had never imagined that my narrowly confined thought-created world had so much power. My thinking mind was still chained to the realm of cause and effect. The "I" had anchored itself deeply within me, in my blood.

But destiny had brought me into contact with people who had already traversed this battlefield, people who now lived in peace, dwelling deeply within the Great Silence. Their presence and their way of life offered me confidence and the knowledge that it was in fact possible to win this fight. The magnificent reality of God had affected me profoundly and was now filling each moment of my life. I was convinced beyond all doubt that the divine light in me would gradually disperse all my ignorance and shadows.

The voice of a night bird broke the dark silence. I fell asleep at some point but was awoken by the howling of a formidable wind. I hoped that the small house could withstand the force and not be damaged. Only after the storm passed was I able to fall asleep again.

THE OTHER LIGHT

When I awoke the next morning from a dreamless sleep, I noticed that something deep within me had changed. I felt carried by a power that was not subject to coming and going. Thoughts floated up and vanished again, but as I watched each of them I was unmoved inside. I was the silent observer.

The experience of the Great Truth was living within me. I knew that which never changed, and knew that it was I. I recognized thoughts as small, multicolored bubbles of light dancing on the surface of my mind. I followed them as they made their way onto an invisible stage, only to be drawn off again.

I was filled with an abundant happiness that had no cause or motive. The power of light had taken hold of me.

Primal visions flashed in my mind, released from almost completely dissipated chambers of the soul. The space where these thoughts were active was a mere fleck in which fluttering dreams appeared and inevitably dissolved into nothingness. I had gone over the threshold of time. It felt as if I had stripped off an outer mold to reveal the ghosts that had been roaming inside. A subtle experience of delight, a feeling detached from any sense of time, surged through me. There was no more sense of the stagnant "I." Without passions and without words I was perched in the most profound regions of reality.

People were already expecting me in the small dining room. My meal was served just as I sat down. A young woman poured a steaming cup of hot tea for me and asked whether I had slept well. The youth to whom I had given the colored pen the night before was poking a stick into the open fireplace, adding patties of yak dung to the glowing fire until it was blazing hot.

The pungent smell of burning manure made me queasy. I pushed down the food as best I could. The other pilgrims had already set out. We would be the last to get moving. My fellow travelers sat at the table watching me eat, as they had finished their meal long before. No one attempted to hurry me, and I did not pressure myself either. These people were so kind and human, so natural. Gaya conversed with our hostess while the Master gazed silently into the dancing flames of the fire. I continued to nourish my body as best I could.

The previous night had offered a teaching. I was now fully conscious that this body is as vulnerable as a young blossom. One day it would weaken, wilt, break down, and dissolve again into the soil, or be consumed by fire and reduced to ashes. But my illuminated soul had identified the sentry blocking the entrance to God's realm. He could no longer stop me from bypassing him and returning to the original source of everlasting God.

We were soon on our way, moving through another rugged region. We trekked along a river and descended into a broad stone-filled valley. In the afternoon we returned to the house of our hosts. It felt as if a great awakening had taken place, a demystification of my attitude toward myself. How amazingly simple it was, this eternal truth.

In the evening, Gaya read aloud from old scriptures. Everyone listened attentively. Relatives from nearby had come to visit, and any place where it was at all possible for someone to sit down was taken. Later there were discussions on all sorts of topics. I remained seated and was quiet until the lids over my eyes began to droop. I finally turned in to get some sleep.

During this night I had a bizarre dream, the intensity of which left traces with me the following day.

In the dream, I stood in the middle of a large light-filled room within a house. I was in the company of a young woman, whose dark eyes glittered like luminous stars on her pleasant face. There was something about her I liked very much and trusted very deeply.

"Come," she said to me in a soft voice as she took my hand. We took three steps, and suddenly we were standing in another room, though we had not passed through any doorway or left through any other kind of opening.

A peculiar sensation was reverberating within my body. I looked over at my companion enquiringly. "What you have just experienced in the ethereal world with your light-body will be realized in the dense material world when your physical body has been thoroughly instilled with spiritual light. You are a moving, vibrating condition of being in this infinite world of God. Your earthly body is like a cold empty house. It fulfills its purpose only when it moves. When it is not permeated with the light of the awakened soul, it is unused, ugly, and lacking in grace. When the soul is not enlivened, enriched, and elevated with radiant divine spiritual energy, it cannot see into the source and cannot merge with it. The body, the soul, and the mind must all exist in complete harmony with each other for the highest cultivation of your being to be possible. As long as the flesh has not been transformed into pure fluid gold, you are living in a dead house! This sinuous gold is the pure light of God, which, like a shiny new robe, protects you and fills you with universal wisdom. Those who enter this flow of light enter into the highest and holiest of all spheres. Those who live without love and without wisdom are dull and heavy like stones. Those who have true love and respect for God receive God's love and respect, and he opens the gates to his treasure of light for them.

"Come," said the woman, her being shining like the sun itself. Once again we stood in another room. "Heart, body, and mind must be in harmony with the highest powers. Only then will the body serve as a house of light for those highest, unbounded forces. Only then can the body exist without limits. The realm of light is within you! You become this light, according to the extent to which you can recognize and bring expression to it."

The next moment I found myself lying in bed, my eyes open, wide-awake. I had no idea whether I had really slept, or if I had simply been dreaming, or if there was another explanation for what was happening. But my body was vibrating with such intensity that I could no longer distinguish whether I was sensing my physical body or a strong energy field. It seemed that the dense solidity of the flesh had been transformed into flowing light.

Gradually this intensified state began to settle, and I had the odd feeling that a vague object in some far-off location was coalescing and taking a distinctive form. I was witnessing the process of my body's amalgamation and found it extremely unsettling. I felt shaken to my core, and I knew I wasn't just imaging things. I now had another way of seeing, another perspective. I had cut through the blazing curtain of fire that separated the highest consciousness from the ordinary.

A gentle morning light began to fill the room. Still insecure due to my strange experience of the night before, I dared not risk shifting my body in the slightest way for a long time. When I did finally sit up, my awareness of the body was completely unlike my previous perception. I felt transparent and buoyant. My body trembled slightly and was saturated with light-energy that continually expanded and streamed out of me.

I left the house through a rear door and wandered awhile along the edge of the wheat fields. I needed to be alone. The sky was covered in grey-and-black rain clouds escorted north by the wind. I had the definitive sense that I had released the limited constructions of my inner being. I was now attuned to a new, deeper, and more sensitive way of perceiving. My soul, now vigilant, was ready to probe beyond the world of appearances and inquire into the unknown.

I had no idea how long I had been walking when, unexpectedly, the Master appeared, coming toward me from the other direction. He was returning to the house, and I decided to join him.

A broad grin filled his face. "Ah, hah! Sunlight is flowing out of you; that is very good. Now you can overcome all deceptive shallow energies. You have the right instrument for it. This radiating sunlight that flows from the well of God will help you wander unharmed through the astral chaos, with its demons and disruptive spirits, with its enchanting voices, its magical powers, and its deities. You will conquer them. You will extinguish them. The true seeker who strives for complete liberation wanders through this internal realm without a body, slashing through the darkness, overflowing with pure light. The heart of the awakened person is unmoved when the deadly eyes of darkness stare down on him. This radiant brightness dispels all phantoms of the lower world. At the same time it introduces an inconceivable process of transformation, which consumes the entire body. We have already talked about this. When the eternal light has swallowed up the world of time, the soul is adorned with boldness and power and steps outside the realm of death.

"The transitory world of appearances can only live and thrive where the tendency of identifying oneself in this lower world exists. This is where delusive fantasies arise. These fantasies are self-generated, and this delusive way of thinking produces the dream of creating something that will endure. One is infatuated with oneself, in love with one's own thoughts and actions, and stays involved with these dream-images. All of these fleeting fancies are a grand display of desire, the desire for satisfaction within the transient world. This energy sucks the mortal world in and chains it to your soul. But nothing on this level will ever completely satisfy you. It is all a seduction. Objects appear to manifest fully for an instant, but they never exist completely.

"As variable as the wind, you have incarnated many hundreds of times, and have gathered countless experiences. Now, be fully and completely clear that you are not the body. It is only a draping over infinite divine essence. That which the eye perceives in absolute wakefulness is not the body."

A fiery morning red seared through the horizon, a foretaste of the approaching day. I felt unspeakable gratitude to the Master for his words, always offered at just the right moment. Riding on waves of light, he had raised me gently, almost imperceptibly, up to the divine world of eternity. He made sure that each experience, each opening I was allowed to go through, was thorough and irreversible.

"I will be visiting my master. He has allowed me to bring you with me," he said in a calm definitive voice.

I stood speechless, overwhelmed by his proposal.

"Would you like to come?" He observed me from the side. I was so stunned that I could offer no answer at all. I was eventually able to give a little nod.

An aspiration had been ripening within me for a long time now, the wish to stay by the Master always, completely giving up my previous life. But the moment to speak with him about this had not yet come. I resolved to wait until I had met his master before talking with him about the possibility.

The sun gradually climbed above the horizon, offering life and luster to the waking world below. Never had I felt so close to someone. Never had I felt so much trust in anyone. I had to laugh as I recalled my first encounters with the Master. He had told me at the beginning, "You see, at first it doesn't go as you think it will. And from then on, it doesn't go as you think it will either."

We returned to the house just in time for breakfast. The weather had changed dramatically in a short time. It was a sparkling beautiful day.

At breakfast, our hosts invited us to stay there with them as long we wished. We would always be welcome to stay with them as guests. When Gaya arrived a bit later, they extended this invitation to her as well. We thanked them for their generosity, but I was actually hoping to depart as quickly as possible. I could hardly wait to meet the Master's master. This anticipation had ignited the flame of impatience. The Master told our guests that we would be very happy to stay a few more days and assist them with the work that needed accomplishing. He looked over at Gaya and me, and saw we were both in agreement with his suggestion.

The next day I found myself standing on the roof of our host's house with one of their sons, repairing several damaged sections. The son was married and lived in another valley. He had arrived for a short visit with his parents. I was able to learn much from him about the hardships of everyday life up here in the mountains. Many of his friends had moved to the flatlands, into the big cities, where they hoped to find a more advantageous life. He confided with obvious remorse that he too would have moved away. That was his dream, but circumstances had never allowed him to realize it.

I also noted that he didn't find much value in anything having to do with religion. The one thing that was important to him was improving his standard of living. After I had heard under what conditions he lived, and how difficult it was to gain mastery over his daily life, I could understand his attitude. And undoubtedly he was not the only one who had to battle for his livelihood up here in the mountains.

The next day I took upon myself a few small tasks that

I could accomplish on my own. I contemplated the words of the Master from our most recent conversation. It had become clear to me that the book of life written by each and every person stood wide open. With a bit of sensitivity, one could read it. Thanks to this new perception, I could recognize the two spheres within me distinctly: the sphere of thought, and the sphere of intuition.

Thoughts that arise from the material world are the creative currents of energy responsible for form, for embodiment, with all that is included in that process. But pure spirit is imperceptible to these streams of thought.

The energetic impulse of perfect wisdom originates in the purity of the divine spirit. This creative force reflects itself through the soul. As pure intuition it perceives the realm of God, the Self that was never born and will never die.

The outer person is a reflection of the inner abiding person who exists within the unlimited divine spheres of this impulse. I noticed how important it was that I observed my thoughts precisely, as well as the underlying energies they carried. I was aware of which possibilities were open to me when this sphere of thought was pure and well synchronized with the inner divine person.

I could see with great clarity where individual life ends and where universal life begins, where the dividing line between God and the limited human condition disappears. The intricate arrangement of life acquired a completely new meaning. This was the commencement of an illuminated journey of discovery through the depths of my true Self. Something that had been sleeping within me for hundreds of thousands of years was now intensely awake.

I stood on the border now, at a point where I would have to make a decision. Who did I want to serve: the immense light of God, which cut through, extinguished, and liberated; or the light of the world, where the individual's wants and needs were the measure of all things? The "I" from which we lived in the physical world had dressed itself in dramatic colors. It had accumulated knowledge and formulated strategies to raise itself up as the autonomous ruler of the world. It collected and recorded inexhaustible volumes of information and experiences in order to fill its own emptiness. And now the radiance of God had gotten through to me and had led me to this edge, an edge that the "I" could not cross over, the point at which it would have to surrender its authority completely. The processes of expanding awareness and cultivating former states of consciousness were confronted with an invincible barrier. The light of this higher truth was reflecting itself in me, bestowing unwavering strength. An entirely new vibration had been released and was surging through me now. I knew that there was nothing more for me to seek on this path toward ultimate liberation.

This inner clarity prompted a resolution that could not be mystical or intellectual. Its implementation would have to occur in my future actions, in my behavior from moment to moment.

My inner resolve had taken hold. I sat on a bench in front of the woodshed behind the house and prayed from my deepest heart to the all-pervasive God that he would ennoble my soul and open the gate, that I could finally enter his limitless realm. This flame blazing within me was not hope, nor was it an idealized state. No, it was an absolute sense of "I can't do anything else but this."

The steps I had completed in order to arrive at this eternal sphere had awakened an ability to discern clearly. I recognized the higher intuition that united me with this eternal light-realm. I recognized the mistaken modes of behavior and the instincts that I shared with the animal world and how an astral bond with them was created. Wherever I sent my thoughts, there I was!

Pure thinking was clear seeing and the clear expression of divine intelligence. Pure selfless thinking had the power to elevate the world, to transform it, to infuse it with spirit. Hence, God's vision could be realized, a vision imbued with absolute beauty and tenderness. In this way the external could unite with the internal, the temporary with the unchanging, and the mortal with the immortal. From the fundamental source of all things, insights streamed down upon me like golden drops of light.

Within this flow of thoughts rushing toward eternity, I had forgotten myself completely. Now the voice of our host was calling me back into the house. It was time to eat.

Our stay was continuing longer than I had assumed upon our arrival. We had already been there more than two weeks. We had completed an enormous amount of work in this relatively short time, tasks that would have been too strenuous for the old couple. But in the last days I had seen hints from the Master that our departure was not far off.

On one of those days I was working with Gaya on a small piece of land where eventually a garden would be planted. We spent the whole day digging out stones of all sizes and carrying them to a large pile behind the house.

In the late afternoon we sat down under a tall tree to have a conversation. Gaya said that she had something important to say. As we sat down and she began to speak, her face was very serious, almost sad.

"The Master has told me that you will be traveling on in two days. I will not be able to accompany you. The time has come for me to return. I am needed at home. The Abbot had suggested to me that I visit the monastery on my way and stay there for a while. This I will do. It will not be long before winter arrives, bringing the great snowfall. During this time it is almost impossible to travel."

Pain pierced through my heart like a flaming arrow. This separation was coming so suddenly and unexpectedly! "Will we see each other again?" I asked.

"True friendship is not bound by the physical body," responded Gaya. "Whether we will ever meet again on the physical level, I do not know. But you live on in my heart. I will not forget the time we have spent together.

"This is the way things go in the physical world. Visible bodies shift around like shadows on this level where the density of substance is quite thick. You breathe in while they appear, and breathe out while they disappear. We don't know how many breaths we have in this one life. But the time that is given to us should be used in order to find and return to our original wholesome condition. This is the only way we can be relieved of the many pains and sorrows we have carried for thousands of years in the world where things appear and disappear over and over again."

"I know you are right," I said. "But this pain isn't going away, not completely." Gaya nodded without saying a word. We continued to go about our work, and I kept my attention directed on the different states and emotions that wanted to swell and spread maliciously through my being. This time I didn't give in to them. I limited myself to this inner observing. What I experienced was like having dark storm clouds blow in, continue toward the horizon, and finally pass out of sight. It never rained. The clouds found no open space upon to unload their contents.

The forces of emotion were almost completely stripped of their power over me. I saw the mechanism of the thinking process more clearly than ever. I saw how certain thoughts and subjective feelings were condensed within the mind, thereby creating the conditions and values of my life, standards I then believed in and clung to. The words of the Abbot came to mind, when he talked to me about renunciation. "Having and losing are only imaginings in your mind, reflections that could never be the truth."

In the evening, Gaya again read from some sacred texts, which the Master explained afterward. Then he announced that we would be leaving in two days. Our hosts offered us a pair of small lean horses for our further travels. The Master expressed gratitude but refused their offer. Instead he showed them the hard skin on the soles of his feet and smiled, "These are my two horses!"

This upset me. I would have had no problem being carried on horseback to our next destination. As if the Master could read the thoughts and feelings inside me, he added, "And he over there has good shoes. Those are his horses!" I could only reply with a muffled voice, "Indeed."

I spent all of the next day with Gaya. We hardly spoke, but our silence was cheerful and relaxed, a mood that helped me refrain from pondering the fact that we would be going our separate ways the following day. I could well have imagined spending the rest of my life with her and the Master. At the threshold of death, there was indeed this unalterable fact of parting. This was a deep, fundamental lesson. And I had to learn it.

I knew now from my own inner experience that I was not the outer shell of spiritual essence. I was the essence itself. Centuries-old habits guided by nostalgic thinking and mechanical repetition made it possible for me to hold fast to the good times I had experienced on the physical level, and I had found myself continually trying to re-insert these moments in my life. These deluded images were like sticky molasses in my mind, hardly capable of movement. I could see that I was still not fully liberated from this transitory theater on the world stage. But I was equally clear in my attitude: this world drama, where mountains of pain rise up and valleys of tears flow down, must be relinquished once and for all.

We departed the next day. The farewells were short, but our hearts were full. Our hostess thanked us again for blessing their house with our presence. Gaya joined us for part of the way and then took her own path at a crossroads outside the city. At the moment of our parting, she folded her hands in front of her chest, just for an instant, and looked at us with a deep radiance glimmering from her soft dark eyes. Then she was off, not saying a word. I watched her for a long time as her feet gently moved along the surface of the rugged earth. It seemed a part of me was separating now as well.

In my veiled thoughts I had expected the Master to make a statement of some kind, but I was mistaken. He proceeded along our path evenly and serenely. I continued alongside him, absorbed in feelings. Soon mountains surrounded us again. In this world of massifs I was overtaken by an especially potent sense of loneliness. Again I felt lost.

We journeyed for many days and eventually left the towering snow-covered peaks behind. We then found ourselves on an extended high plateau. A broad river looped its way through the rocky and desolate terrain. As we reached a small rise, I was confronted with an astonishing sight. The entire wide expanse reaching to the far horizon consisted of innumerable small round hills.

We sat down on a large stone. The Master then pointed out two small hills in the distance. "Look there," he said, "that is the border. In a few hours we will cross it."

Clouds drifted lazily over our heads. They appeared to be so close we could reach out and take hold of them. Later in the afternoon we met two shepherds who were tending two groups of animals, a flock of sheep and a herd of horses. The Master spoke quite a while with the men and finally accepted their invitation to go with them to their tents, where we would spend the night. It seemed to me that the Master did not want to dishearten them by refusing. We followed them and later assisted in driving the animals back toward the tent area.

These people were nomads, four large families living together and sharing responsibility for their animals. They traveled from one grazing land to the next, moving on every few weeks, when the sparse vegetation offered from a meadow in this barren region was depleted.

Their tents were not far away. As we came nearer we were quickly surrounded by a large band of children.

They stared at us with innocent inquisitive faces as we moved toward the tiny settlement. Before we entered the tent area, the guard dog that had been baring its teeth at us had to be tied up.

We were received with incredible kindness. They were mystified at meeting foot travelers at this high elevation. Their perplexity persisted until the Master explained that we were on pilgrimage.

As the men bound the heads of the sheep together, the women began milking them. While they worked they told the Master about their breeding of the animals and described the pasture where they were soon headed. The Master showed interest, patiently listening to all that was said. I studied the tanned faces on which their rugged living conditions were depicted. The wrinkled complexions of the elders were perfectly sketched diagrams where one could read the toils and struggles of their way of life in entirety. Timid eyes followed us, amazed and curious. Inside one of the tents women cooked the evening meal in huge pots set upon large open fires. Men were sitting nearby sipping buttered tea. Gradually all the family members came inside, and the talking became lively, loud, and lengthy. I noticed right away that the women here often had the final say when decisions were necessary. But all issues were discussed calmly among everyone, and laughter could always be heard during their deliberations.

A small girl approached us. One of her legs remained stiff as she walked, using a wooden crutch to get along. She sat nearby and looked at me with huge beautiful eyes. I asked the mother whether the child was born with this handicap. It turned out that she had been injured when she was two years old. She had been playing near a steep overhang and fallen off. At that time she almost died, and since then the leg was stiff. It was sad, the mother explained, because she could not join the other children in most of their games.

The talking continued for a long time after the meal. Finally we went with one of the families to their tent to get some rest. Two yak pelts were set out for us to sleep on. It was a very odd experience for me to lie down in such close quarters with the entire family. Various thoughts and feelings shifted around within, keeping me awake for a long time. Meanwhile, the nomads had all fallen asleep within moments of setting their heads down.

I was awoken the next morning by a crying baby in a tent nearby. The Master was already sitting in front of our tent, joining our hosts in their morning tea.

A little later, a group of men and women said their farewells to us. They were going off to their daily work. We were almost the only ones remaining as we stood in front of the tent, and I had the feeling it was time for us to be moving on as well. But as the mother of the injured child went by at a distance, waving a friendly good-bye, the Master gestured her over to us. He invited her to bring her child and come inside the tent, which was now un-occupied. I stayed outside and conversed with two old ladies who were washing out the cooking pots.

After a while the Master came out of the tent and spoke to me. "So, we should be leaving now." I said my good-byes quickly, and soon we were off. As we left the nomad settlement behind, I turned around, for what rea-son I wasn't sure, glancing back at the cluster of tents. An electric shock ran through me. Under the canopy at the entrance of the tent, the little girl was jumping around her mother. Then she jubilantly threw her walking stick into the air. She appeared completely healed. A miracle had taken place! I could see the tears running down over the cheeks of her mother, a sight I will never forget. I was full of astonishment, at the same time full of gratitude, for this was something I could never explain in words. The little girl waved out to me, though she never stopped her jumping. I waved back, smiling. The two older ladies had not even noticed that this wondrous occurrence had taken place.

"Come, we have to keep moving." I knew that the Master didn't want to cause a stir or call attention to himself. He had waited until just the right moment, when he could be alone with the mother and child. I remembered how he had set the broken leg of an animal when I first met him. But what had just happened was something else, far beyond comparison.

The Master was always in complete equilibrium. In his eyes, nothing extraordinary had happened. He had simply applied the higher principle, just as he had explained to me before. But he knew I was still dumbstruck and said something to me about it. "Every person who really believes in God, in His infinite kindness and compassion, is capable of working in such a way, just as it happened here. Those who hesitate and doubt remain limited. You must be capable of accepting the entirety of God's creative intelligence. And then you must be capable of expressing this at the level where you now are living. This healing is not a miracle. It is an expression of the love of God.

"When you have let go of all the thoughts you limit yourself with, when all your ideas of being and nonbeing and individual personality have been wiped away, then it will be possible for you to raise the frequency of your vibration so far above the frequency of dense material that you can transcend physical death and all illnesses entirely. Then you are living within the pulse of the eternal reality of light. The entire molecular structure of the body is transformed, elevated, and instilled with completely new information, the wisdom of infinite being. In this way the body is a vessel, an instrument that you can use as you think appropriate and correct.

"For those who believe in the infinite God and his infinite capabilities, these things are as accessible and natural as anything else in the universe. Mortality, illness, and decay are the creations of human beings, the result of self-centeredness and misunderstanding. All limitations and boundaries have their roots there. We are not in this world to suffer. We are here to uncover the glory of God within us and to bring full expression to it."

We were walking through a desert-like region as the Master spoke. It seemed he then reflected on his own words, for he stopped walking and said, "Now pay attention. I will give you an example, an experience that will emphasize what I have just told you."

An instant later, he was hanging suspended in the air, about ten feet over my head. "A human being is light itself. Nothing holds it down. It has no limits." Then he was standing in front of me again. "Pay attention," he repeated, and again he disappeared from my field of vision. A moment later I heard him calling me. "Here I am again!" He was standing hundreds of feet away. He walked toward me casually; as he approached, he looked deeply into my eyes. The energy pouring out of him was almost too much for me. I was completely overwhelmed. I had the feeling I was dissolving.

Then the Master spoke to me in a serious voice that I had never heard him use before. "I have no interest in performing magic tricks or showing off an accomplished yoga practice. I think you have come to know the difference. I simply want to show the unlimited possibilities that exist for each person who lives completely with God. The true person of light is infinite and universal. Primal matter obeys the pure will of divine nature and has unlimited use of it. This will is intended exclusively for the liberation and transformation of the whole world.

"The entire substance of this work is something I will tell you about later, if it is important for you. That is, if without question you are to become a universal servant of God. It is an enormous work. A great responsibility goes along with it. God has led you to me, and you have stayed, and you are now prepared for deeper teachings. Instruction requires a pure heart and a wakeful spirit, one that possesses the capabilities of comprehending what is presented directly, to become it and function with it immediately."

The words of the Master sustained their power long after he had stopped talking. As I reflected, I recognized that the manner in which the Master had transported his body had not come across as something spectacular at all. It seemed normal, quite natural. Still, the demonstration of the Master had affected me deeply. It was my consciousness that had managed a quantum leap. That had been the very purpose of the demonstration. It had been a magical signpost directing me toward a world that was still unfamiliar.

We continued on our way. I observed the Master as he went along in the vibrant morning light. He was like a manifestation of the serene skies above, noble and graceful in his stride. Wisdom radiated from his glistening forehead. His countenance was like the oncoming day, permeated with light and filled with vital energy. The universal forces that constantly emanated from him with great power and majesty directly touched the living core of all sentient beings, blessing them, awakening them, rejuvenating them.

He had showed me that the inner treasure chamber of light in each being was readily available, not as symbol or allegory, but as the ever-present and immediate truth. Everything that has come into being arises from the unfathomable depths of this light; from here the path of life is revealed. That veil that hides this truth, that covers the soul with shadows through great misunderstandings and feeble thinking, is also nothing more than a passing image.

We walked for five days until our trail brought us to a massive gorge. Far below, a ferocious river surged past the large rock formations in its path. The air was filled with the powerful thrashing sounds of numerous waterfalls. A crisp wind was blowing in our faces. We climbed over wet rocks and huge boulders, moving slowly and carefully down the ravine. Stones constantly broke off under our feet, cascading to the depths below. Our path was hardly a safe one, but I had boundless faith in the Master and was convinced that no misfortune could befall us.

The gorge went on and on and on. It took us the entire day to reach its end. I was so tired that night that I fell asleep within moments of putting my head down to rest.

"It isn't far now," I heard the Master say as I opened my eyes the next morning. The journey in the cold damp air of the gorge had been brutal. My entire body was stiff and my limbs ached. I had often asked myself along the way if there wasn't an easier way to arrive at our destination. I got my answer as I took a clearer look at my surroundings. To the left and right of the gorge were towering mountains hoisted high up into the sky.

We climbed upward along a mountain ridge for the entire day. Our path was dotted with small bushes. Although I thought I had attuned myself well to the environment, the air was thinner at this altitude, and I had to stop often to catch my breath. Finally we came to level ground between two mountaintops. On the other side of the range we could see a plateau extending before us with a wide river flowing through it. The Master spoke, "My master lives in the small valley on the other side of the river."

I had to squint to see the direction he was indicating. My heart beat faster. I noted a certain anxiety arising. A part of me was deeply pleased to meet the Master's master. In another part, a strange fear emerged. Soon hostile energies were bubbling to the surface. Something in me was resisting this encounter, something didn't want to get any closer to this powerful light. Voices whispered in my ear, "Don't go. Everything in your life will be ruined."

I decided to express openly to the Master the fears plaguing me. He remained standing and looked at me with caring eyes. Finally he spoke. "There are antagonistic forces within people that are afraid of the liberating light. Earthly powers and their world have the soul tightly in their grip. They resist the light and instead lead human beings down disastrous back alleys where they are ambushed by the forces of death. Demonic voices whisper continually to all who enter their trap that they should feel at home in this world of appearances. In this way they are able to hold them hostage in the worlds of 'this side' and 'the beyond.'

"But the light of liberation tears away the mask of those energies. While they claim their authenticity, their identities are exposed to the soul, and as the universal light becomes visible, their insisting and resisting are futile. This light is the silhouette of God, none other than all-transcending true love. The darker egoistic energies already know that they have lost. They will continue their rebellion for a while until they are finally conquered, so do not worry. Do not fall into insecurity. Insecurity, doubt, and fear are their rightful faces. Look and see exactly what they are made of. See that they are hollow."

I nodded. That darkness had retreated back to the abyss from which it came. Again I was aware of the hypnotic energies the world contains. They had the soul and human consciousness under lock and key, trapped in the labyrinth of time. They were conceived from insensitive greed, which ceaselessly pushed the soul into the arms of lifeless objects. This darkness thrived because these binding forces were acknowledged as they manifested within the intellect. The intellect always searches within the world of the senses for its nourishment, looking hungrily for something new, something satisfying.

I could penetrate and see clearly the condition I was in. It was right in front of me. In the Master I could see a true example of someone who had overcome all these lower energies and was living in complete harmony, unified with God. This was possible for each person on Earth. The evidence for this stood next to me.

ENCOUNTER WITH THE UNIVERSAL MASTER

How ridiculous I had been, to think that I would come to these mountains for two or three weeks looking for a master and then be able to use his life to extract theoretical information. How incredibly grateful I was now that the Master had thrown me so quickly into the school of life, where the chaff could be peeled away from the wheat. Yes, I wanted only to stay with him. I wanted to follow the path of liberation in his presence.

We had now reached the river and walked alongside the flowing water. A subtle pulsation was enlivening my being, giving my body a vital power. I felt new strength with each step. I was experiencing something new that I couldn't understand.

The river and its banks ran through the land like a turquoise stripe painted on the earthen landscape. After we had walked upstream for a long while, the Master came to the spot where we could cross.

"Here is the place. Take off your shoes," he said to me. The water seemed fairly deep, but the Master insisted. "Come!" he directed me, and there he was, standing on the water.

I stuttered, "Master, I can't walk over the water." In seconds I was overrun with doubts and insecurity.

The Master laughed exuberantly. "I am not standing

on the water! There are stones out here. We can cross over them, but you must be careful. They are slippery."

His body seemed weightless as he lightly stepped across the rocks. Meanwhile, I gingerly hobbled from one stone to another. "Why do you have so little trust in your legs?" the Master called out to me, still laughing as I stalled apprehensively in the middle of the river. But finally I found myself on the other side. As I turned back and looked carefully, I could now see the stones that had assisted us on our crossing.

We immediately set off again. Patches of low brush dotted our path. We arrived at a narrow valley in the afternoon. A small stream ran through it that eventually surrendered its individuality and merged with the large river farther down. At places the basin was very broad, while other sections were walled off by steep rock faces to the left and right. After we had wound our way through the valley for a while, our surroundings shifted to a friendlier landscape filled with small round hills. Not far away I could see a few small dwellings pressed up close together, as if they were guarding each other. "We have arrived," said the Master. A narrow path led us up from the riverbank toward the houses.

I saw many deciduous and conifer trees growing from the rugged soil. Apparently most of them had been planted. Then I noticed a few men and women doing manual labor. Their tasks seemed identical to the daily chores of the villagers we had met everywhere in these mountains. This first impression was a bit disappointing. I had expected something more extraordinary. This place seemed like every other place we had been.

Three old men sat on a wooden bench in front of one of the houses. They were watching us, and as I approached I noticed I was slightly trembling. This inner pulsation increased and spread throughout my body.

As we came within a few steps of the old men, they stood up and greeted the Master warmly. They were obviously old acquaintances. After the Master said a few words concerning my presence, they offered me a friendly welcome as well. As they spoke, I perceived an extraordinary wave of kindheartedness break over me. A feeling of great suppleness and tenderness embraced my heart.

I continued to examine the three men. "Which of the three is the real master?" I asked myself. But I lacked the courage to divulge my thoughts. Two of the men sat down again as the third led us to a house. He showed us two rooms, which were large and nicely furnished. I felt a deep silence and peace returning to me.

It wasn't long before the Master arrived at my room. Right away the words spurted out, "Please tell me which of the three is your master!"

He laughed and explained that all three of them were students of his master. They had all been with him for more than a hundred years. No one knew the true age of their master. The Master also assured me that I would soon meet him. The man who had brought us to our rooms was now telling the Master's master of our arrival. "He will bring us to him right away. My teacher is not a man of many words, you know."

I was so excited that I could hardly keep still. My inner agitation was incomprehensible. Every minute went by like an hour. I tried to find sufficient words, to think of something to say that would be appropriate for the moment when I would meet this master face to face, but nothing that occurred to me made any sense.

Finally a knock came on the door. The old man and the Master stood in the doorway. "My master will receive us now. Come." His tone was serious, but I could also feel joy in his voice.

I followed the two men as if being carried by a cloud of light. All the people we met as we went along had a similar gentleness and kindness in their manner. We followed the old man to a house slightly apart from the others. Here he stopped and knocked once on the door.

We entered the room, and immediately uncontrollable tears began to stream down my cheeks. These were blissful tears. An energy of love flowed through me like a giant wave, and I felt as if my being had been completely consumed within it.

And then I saw him! It was not a vision. It was a revelation. The light that I saw was so powerful that I truly believed the sun itself had come into the room. This light was immeasurably beautiful, so tender and yet so intense that words of human beings could not describe it. The face of this master was crimson like the morning sun; it was peace itself. His entire being breathed transcendence. An extraordinary impression of saintliness radiated from him.

I couldn't look into his eyes for long. Their brilliance penetrated and exposed everything. I didn't know where to look. I stood mesmerized and could find no words to speak.

"Sit down," he said. His voice was full of warmth. Speaking directly to me, he chose his words with attention and care. "Brother, for this world, the fire of divine liberating energy is unbearable. The face that masks the words and wisdom of light cannot be seen by everyone. To enter the realm of God means to recognize the absolute emptiness of all causes and all effects, to recognize the absolute emptiness of consciousness and the absolute emptiness of everything that appears and that passes away. When your consciousness is no longer bound to doing and not doing, you will breathe in the sunlight of God. When your mind has learned not to seek any longer, then the seeker has died. In the eternal realm of light, there is nothing to find, nothing to gain, nothing to hold."

Every word, every breath of the saintly spirit that filled his body expressed transformation. His voice held such power that it gently carried me from one world to another, transporting me through unknown dimensions. Inner gateways opened. Old walls crumbled. As he spoke with my master, I observed him and was surprised to find myself sitting in front of a very young man. He could not have been more than thirty years old!

At some point the Master stood. I folded my hands in front of my chest and expressed my gratitude. The Master's teacher gave a short wave, and in a moment we were outside. Soon I was sitting alone in my room. My eyes were still filled with joyful tears. I had never thought that such a pure being was breathing here on the planet Earth.

Someone was knocking gently. I was sure it was the Master. Instead, I found a young man and woman at my door. "We want to give you a little something to eat," they said. "Surely you are hungry." They came in and spread food out on the table in the room. When they were finished they quickly left again.

I was taken aback by this sudden coming and going. The idea of eating had been wiped from my consciousness. But I gratefully accepted the simple meal and took a pleasurable drink of fresh water from a pitcher on the table.

Evening came to the valley. Stars oscillated in the breaks between the drifting clouds. I had hoped that the Master would come for me, but I remained alone. The people who lived here were all saturated with spiritual light. Everything here was that master, of that I was sure. What incredible grace had been bestowed upon me, to be brought to this place by my master! I could feel the concentrated silence and deep serenity in every cell of my body.

That night, I lay down in my bed and quickly fell asleep. But then something very peculiar happened. Though my body slept, I remained awake. I observed the images of my dreams just as I observed the thoughts and images that went through my mind in a waking state. In these moments I was light itself, pure perception, without the desire to hold on to or interpret what was happening. The inconceivable light-energy of this master extended through all worlds, leading me back to my original unborn condition where no body existed. At some point the dream-images were exhausted, and I was able to rest in "non-thinking" and "non-experiencing."

The next morning a strong impulse caused me to interrupt my sleep. Suddenly I was sitting up in bed wide awake. It was shortly before sunrise, and I felt inspired to step from the house, where I saw that all the inhabitants of the hamlet were walking toward the east. Without stopping to ponder, I followed them. Within moments the Master was standing next to me. He whispered, "You have heard the call." I didn't dare break the silence with a question.

I looked around for the Master's master, but he was not present. I hoped to see him again, perhaps later in the day. The broad path we were following was lined with trees and bristly bushes. I breathed in deeply, enjoying the fresh fragrances they provided. Soon we appeared to have arrived at our destination. We were on a hill that allowed us to look back down on the valley and the cluster of houses. We were standing on a huge horizontal saucer-shaped boulder. I was amazed at its symmetrical form, which led me to wonder if its structure was a wondrous whim of nature, or whether humans had somehow manipulated the landscape.

We made a large circle. In the middle stood a young woman, someone I had not seen before. The shadows of night were giving way to the coming day. It would not be long before the glowing face of the sun would rise over the darkened bare backsides of the mountain range in the eastern sky. There were no clouds to be seen, and the wind, which loved to race with vehemence through these valleys, was at rest. It seemed all of nature was content to be silent in anticipation of a special occasion.

Now the woman who was standing in the center of the circle raised her arms in blessing and acknowledged the heavenly directions. With a powerful voice, which initially I would not have thought her capable of, she began to speak.

"Eternal God, origin of all being, all the wonderful light-energy which overflows and blesses this divine Earth and all of creation comes from You.

"Source of universal love, life-giving spirit, Your brilliance and illumination awaken our hearts. In your splendid radiance, You reveal your magnificence.

"Lighter of the light, Your splendor penetrates and enlightens us. Give us deep insight, that we can fully comprehend and accept the energy of light you offer us, and that we rightly follow your principle in unity and harmony. This is how the river of wisdom is revealed to us, how it can enter and flow through us, how it can unfold in all its greatness. ONE in your divine light, ONE with your divine spirit. ONE in your divine presence. This is how you clarify for us, nourish us, and elevate us to your magnificence, where we breathe in your divine stream of light. This is how we discover our significance within You, ocean of light, ocean of love.

"May the space where the human heart emerges give itself completely to Your love, so that the doors of evil and misunderstanding in this world will be closed forever.

"Your love, Your glance, Your supreme light penetrate the world with immeasurable power and grace, illuminating everything, healing all, breathing spirit into all, all blessed in Your eternal realm of light.

"AUM,

"OM."

A colossal energy was being expressed through the group. Liberating rays of light penetrated throughout all of humanity and throughout all worlds. The entire assembly vibrated on a level of intensity, beauty, love, and power that surpassed everything I had ever experienced. The blessing emanating from this group extinguished all self-centeredness, ignorance, and death throughout the world. The realm where human souls reside was purified and awakened through the all-transforming energies of the divine, so that human beings could become aware once again of their true purpose.

The sun's light spilled out over the valley as we walked silently back to the hamlet. As we went along I looked into the faces of the people. They beamed like sunlight itself. Their extraordinary simplicity, their down-to-earth manner, their silence, all the qualities I had so esteemed in the Master, I found here in each and every person.

The Master accompanied me to my room. Much to my surprise, I found my breakfast waiting for me there on the table. The Master said he would come by later to get me, so I sat down. But it was odd. It seemed ridiculous to sit down and eat. I did it, even though I had the feeling I was offering food to something I no longer was. My true being was being nourished by something else, by the divine nectar that was now abundantly available to me.

I tried to recall some of the moments I had experienced that morning. Not without effort, I managed to retrieve the image of the elevated plateau, the huge plate of stone, and the assembly gathered under this master, with the hope of somehow experiencing what had happened one more time. Then, all of the sudden my body shuddered and my breath froze with dreadful fright. A loud and forceful voice called to me, saying, "Be still. Don't make so much noise. Be!"

No one was in the room. I had no idea whether the voice was inside or outside. I concluded it was better not to try to think about who was talking to me in this way. In any case, it seemed my thinking processes were impeded from every direction, all thoughts blockaded by the silence.

I was relieved to hear a knock on the door and the voice of the Master saying, "Are you ready? We want to make ourselves useful."

A new foundation for a house was being prepared. Several men and women from the community were busy with arrangements for the building site. We helped them in their work, and I concluded from looking at the formation on the ground that the building would contain three large rooms. The work was relaxed and not overly demanding. I thus had the chance to get to know these people a little better. We discussed different issues regarding the structure of the house, but there was plenty of joking and laughter as well. The easygoing atmosphere reflected the innocence these extraordinary people held in their hearts. These people lived fully in God.

One of the women, whose eyes shone like pearls, asked me, "Do you know whom you are building a house for?" The question surprised me. I had no idea.

The Master cleared his throat and told me, "The house is being built for me. My master has called me. My time at the cave has finished. The one reason I was there was you. I was waiting for you. The time has come for you to know this. You have been my student for many lifetimes. I have never let you out of my sight, not in the times you passed over the swells of death, and also not when you were moving in the astral ocean of the other world harvesting fruits from the seeds you had planted before. For you, the time has come that you can finally transcend the two worlds in which you were trapped. Only the unholy dwell in 'that side' and 'this side.' Divine souls, those who endure forever, do not stay there. The two spheres within the world of appearances are training grounds for the growth and ripening of the soul in God.

"All beings who live in this community have completely overcome the twofold world and live in the highest purest divine vibration. They are servants of God."

I now understood the deep loyalty and trust that I had always felt with the Master. But now I saw the immeasurable patience and love that were his essence. My heart laughed for joy. A thought flashed: was one of the three rooms of this house for me? Master must be waiting for the right time to share the surprise. I had no greater wish than to stay in that place forever.

Each morning we climbed up the slope to the elevated space. Each time we performed the powerful ceremony, offering blessings to humanity and the world. During the day we continued working on the construction of the house. Before long I knew all the people who lived there.

The Master often would take time to go with me on extended walks along the river and down through the valley. Abundant green grass grew along both sides of the water, and shades of intense green shone from the trees at our sides. The cool barren mountain faces behind them stood in deep contrast, their massive walls offering protection to this sacred area. This untainted beauty moved me deeply.

The Master spoke little. From the moment that powerful voice had obliged me to stay quiet, a shift had taken place. Words had taken on a new significance. I recognized that they were holy instruments that must be employed with discretion. I was able to take life as it presented itself from moment to moment without looking back or looking ahead. But I could not refrain from wondering to myself when the moment might come that I would see that amazing being of light once again, the one who was the teacher of all these masters. I felt an overwhelming need for another encounter, but I knew it was meaningless to inquire. I didn't even know if he was still here. And if he wanted to see me, he would let me know. It was out of my control. This period of waiting taught me something important, though I didn't notice it happening. I learned true humility. As the Master's house gradually took on a clearer form, I became calmer and more relaxed.

A woman approached me one morning and said, "Your Master's master would like to see you." My heart began to race. I felt wobbly. Just imagining myself sitting across from this being of light was totally flustering. I decided to ask the Master to accompany me. But he only shook his head, smiled, and said, "Just go. He wants to see you alone today."

The woman led me to the house where I had seen him the first day. She knocked on the door and then said to me, "Go inside." As I entered the room tears came again, streaming down from my eyes uncontrollably. Every cell of my body was filled with delight and the deepest sense of peace. Again it seemed as if the sun itself, shining with all its blazing power, was sharing the space of the room with me. The flow of love that radiated out from this being of light was pure grace.

"Come, sit next to me," I heard him say in a tender voice. I thanked him for receiving me. We sat alone together, and for a long time he was silent. I could feel how his elevated vibration lifted me into the realm of God. He then began to speak: "Many people in this world live within borders. Their souls are exhausted from countless experiences of death and rebirth. They are full of pain and suffering. They long for a return to the original pure life in God.

"Within the one who truly returns, a tree is growing. It is the mysterious inverted tree of pure light. It has its roots set in the eternal realm of God. The tree is nourished from here, not from the earth.

"The magnetic power, which is the breath of God, circulates in two ways on this tree. The branches of this divine tree reach down to the darkened plane of earth. They extend through the darkness in order to give souls that are sincerely searching the chance to climb up through this inverted tree and enter the halls of eternal light.

"Only the purified soul can understand the language of God. The sensitive heart is living light. God is light. Born from the divine fountain, liberating energies flow through all the worlds, never stopping, reviving and restoring all that exists. The power of God is transmitted down through those with pure souls who are awakened in God and live in God. In this way, God's power is expressed at a level where it can be acceptable and useful in this world. Each soul should be pure enough that it can reveal the realm of God.

"Your master, who loves you more than anything else, has brought you here. He will stay. This you already know. Soon he will share something very important with you. What he will say will also express my view. Peace be with you."

He stood up. I thanked him and left the house.

OTHER THAN EXPECTED

I went back to join the others working on the construction of the house. In a sudden flash, I understood that this outer work had yet another completely distinct inner meaning for me. Just at that moment I saw my master standing across from me. I looked into his lucid eyes, and he nodded in return.

The next morning we again walked together along the river. Two other members of the community joined us. Their presence was always pleasant, and they were extremely open for any topic of conversation. But on this day there was nothing to talk about. We sat down near the water where we were protected from the wind. After some time the Master had words for me. "You had a very complicated karma. It will, however, run its final course in this lifetime. Stay very aware and you can avoid getting caught in more karmic realms. Causes and their effects belong to the world of the ego and its awareness of the body. They are controlled by misguided thoughts, feelings, and actions. This you know by now. Raise yourself beyond the limited awareness of the body. In your innermost being you are in deep connection with divine energy. Thus, do not prize anything in this world, anything that has a transitory form. Be completely free of desires; let go of all things. Then God himself will guide your life. Desires create formidable shadows and chain you to the planes of anger and death.

"Offer your entire earthly life to the spiritual realm within you. Above all, trust God in all circumstances. He will be your master from now on, and he will lead you. The gradual mastery of all the aspects of the lower transitory world that have tried to cling to you will make you a master. But in truth there is no 'master.' There is only 'mastery,' a process each person can begin at any time.

"God is pure love. Other than God there is nothing. Without his presence no thought would have ever occurred to you, and no goodness could come of your deeds. Stay awake! See the self-seeking spotlight as it turns from God and tries to convince you that you are the powerful one. Recognize this Lord of Destiny and drive him out of your mind! Let your life be guided by God alone.

"This inner point of holding, the Lord of Cause and Effect, has been completely extinguished within the hearts of all the people living here. The fire of God's love washes away all darkness from the soul. It burns away all that is dead in human beings.

"Only the divine fire can burn through the karmic waste that clings within. Through the ceaseless elimination of the 'I' and its powers, the karmic storehouse is emptied once and for all.

"It is a great blessing to receive this human body. The experience of God that we are offered through it is beyond measure. The more you are immersed in the stream of God's radiance, the more your body becomes this pure light. God is this light. Progressively, all limitations and boundaries are removed. You become limitless. This is how the supreme power and wisdom of logos functions.

"In this way, through the grace of God, we are raised from darkness into light. Still, each individual has a personal fight to fight, according to the conditions of his or her karma. Do not worry: Where there is light, the shadows must draw back, or they simply become light themselves."

It was late afternoon before we returned to the house. Was that the message I was supposed to receive from the Master? I felt that the time had come to voice my request that I be allowed to remain with him. The following day I would take the first opportunity to do so.

At the large morning prayer the next day, I was surprised to discover that the Master was not in attendance. Later in the day, I joined a few folks to work on his house, but he was not there. No one could tell me where he was. Had he left me there alone?

Many of the things that happened in that place were puzzling. I knew that everyone there had spiritual gifts I could hardly fathom. But no one seemed to put these skills on display, or if they did, it was done discreetly in a graceful and unassuming manner corresponding to their lifestyle. But in all of the houses I entered, I never saw a kitchen. In fact, during my entire stay, I had seldom seen anyone eating. They had brought me my meals each day as if it was completely natural, and when I asked one of the folks carrying the trays to join me, they complied. But I couldn't help but feel they were taking food just to please me.

Gradually I had learned the words of the morning prayer by heart. Each line held such a potent blessing that I found myself repeating one of them quietly to myself for an entire day. The Master had encouraged me to do this, saying it was useful in the process of liberation.

The next morning the Master was present. In the meantime I had gained a greater ability to lay my noisy mind in God's hands, which put a stop to the formation of the unnecessary questions that habitually came into my head and too often rolled off my tongue. Curiosity, in all its various colors and shades, was finally coming to an end.

During the following days almost the entire community worked on the house. In a week it was just about finished, except for a few details. During this period I never managed to express my burning request to the Master, though several times I tried.

The house was finally finished. Two days later the Master invited me to accompany him on a walk. This time we were alone, and I knew that the right moment had arrived. We walked silently alongside the glistening stream until arriving at the place where we had stopped to sit the last time we had come this way.

A peculiar mood came over me. But just as I begun to express my desire to remain with him permanently, he spoke: "The time is right. You must now return to the country from which you came."

From the tone of his voice I knew he was sensitive to my feelings, but nevertheless I felt as if the world was collapsing on top of me.

"Tomorrow we will leave," he continued. "I will accompany you until we reach a larger village where you can take a bus. It will take you to the flatlands again."

He left no time whatsoever for me to respond with my heart's longing. The thought of returning to a world that had become so foreign to me, and of leaving the Master, whom I now loved more than anything, was unbearable. His heartbeat had become my heartbeat. This pain seemed to rip me right through the heart, tearing me to pieces.

The Master took my hand and spoke in a deep, compassionate voice. "It must be like this. You will offer the light of eternity to many people. God will send them to you. This will be your path to ultimate liberation. Don't be misled by shadows of sorrow. Soon you will see that everything is as it should be. Our friendship will never fade, for it is not tied to the passing material world."

"Master, I had no wish other than to be by your side forever!" I let out my feelings, unable to restrain any longer.

"I know," he responded softly. "But we have already discussed this. Desires are shadows, traps, ties that hold us back, and deep inside you know this well. God embraces you. Set your life in his hands. He knows what is best for you, and he will guide your steps. Don't forget this."

The next morning's prayer up on the elevated plain would be my last. Afterward, all the members of the community said their farewells. Without the need of words, they let me know I would always be a member of their community, that I was one of them. They also knew how difficult this departure was for me.

I asked the Master whether I could also meet his master one last time to say good-bye. "He has already said his farewell," he responded. "Otherwise, he would have called you. But you can be sure that he knows we are leaving now. You have his blessing."

We followed the river and went along the same path

that we had taken during our frequent walks. We then climbed up a steep incline from which I could take one last look back at the valley and the village where those extraordinary people lived. We wandered for many more hours that day through the uneven mountain terrain.

After several days we crossed back over the border. We had hardly spoken to one another. I had resigned myself to returning home, but I had no desire to contemplate what form my life would take afterward. From now on God was my life and my purpose, and whatever God had in store for me in this earthly existence was to be completely accepted and lived out. The inner-dwelling presence of God that I had experienced during the many months with the Master had become a living dynamic experience in the external world.

We trekked through dry prairie and numerous desert landscapes for eight days. Within these arid regions we crossed over two passes. On the ninth day we arrived at another high plateau. From there I could see the large village that was my next destination. The road that would take me there was visible as well.

The Master spoke softly. "This is where our ways part, my friend."

"Will we see each other again?" I asked.

He looked into my eyes for a long time. I felt his gentle love showering upon me. His last words engraved themselves forever in my memory. "You have never come here. You will never go anywhere. You are only a guest here on this earthly plane. Earthly consciousness, which holds to the body and the senses, is what reflects the appearances of coming and going. God is light! Light never comes or goes. There is only this eternal being."

He took my hand and held it tightly. Then he spoke one more time in the gentle voice I had come to know so well. "Live well, my friend. I am always with you in thought, and as God wills it, I will call you!"

He then took a few steps backward. A smile shone from his serene face, a smile that conveyed the love of the entire universe. The next moment his body dematerialized and disappeared right before my eyes through an imperceptible gate of light.

Flooded with deep feelings, I lingered at that spot a long while before finally descending to the village below.

For the next two days I sat in a bus, following a bumpy road, bouncing my way toward a country that had become completely foreign to me.

I continued to brood with such sentiments as I traveled back, feeling as if I was being forced to leave the sun-filled peak of a beautiful mountain and descend into the thickest fog below. To my surprise, I discovered the sun's rays still shining below the heavy layers of mist.

I have not seen the Master in his physical form since that time. But sometimes he appears in dreams, again showering me with love. I continue the morning prayer as I learned it with him and so remain internally connected to those amazing people he brought me to, to those who live completely within God.

The Master showed me how each person who trusts in God and purifies his heart can walk the path of divine mastery in simplicity, truth, and love. He or she will be continually refreshed with the grace of God's radiance.

And the Master demonstrated that words alone do not suffice. Behind each word there must be a genuine, clear liberating movement within.

We humans should recognize and accept the splendid opportunity that God is offering us on this earthly plane. If we truly do this, we will all encounter one another with pure hearts and fresh eyes in each moment, and each of our thoughts and actions will be filled with light, enriching the lives of all living beings. In this way, continually immersed in God's love and emanating its dynamic power, we ourselves will be a blessing for the whole of divine creation.

For more information on books and talks
from Mario Mantese/Master M
www.mariomantese.com

Other books in English
from Mario Mantese - Master M

„In Touch with a Universal Master"

This unusual biography portrays the life
and unbound spiritual work of this Master.

ISBN 978-3-7699-0626-4
www.drei-eichen.de

CPSIA information can be obtained at www.ICGtesting.com
Printed in the USA
LVOW10s1714130813

347707LV00034B/1443/P